JENNY
A NOVEL

By Sigrid Undset
TRANSLATED FROM THE NORWEGIAN
OF SIGRID UNDSET BY W. EMMÉ

PART ONE

1

AS Helge Gram turned the comer into Via Condotti in the dusk a military band came down the street playing "The Merry Widow" in such a crazy, whirling time that it sounded like wild bugle calls. The small, dark soldiers rushed past in the cold afternoon, more like a Roman cohort intent on attacking barbarian hosts than peaceful men returning to their barracks for supper. That was perhaps the cause of their haste, Helge thought, smiling to himself, for as he stood there watching them, his coat-collar turned up for the cold, a peculiar atmosphere of history had pervaded him — but suddenly he found himself humming the same tune, and continued his way in the direction where he knew the Corso lay.

He stopped at the corner and looked. So that was the Corso — an endless stream of carriages in a crowded street, and a surging throng of people on a narrow pavement.

He stood still, watching the stream run past him, and smiled at the thought that he could drift along this street every evening in the dusk among the crowds, until it became as familiar to him as the best-known thoroughfare of his own city — Christiania. He was suddenly seized with the wish to walk and walk — now and all night maybe — through all the streets of Rome, for he thought of the town as it had appeared to him a while ago when he was looking down on it from Pincio, while the sun was setting.

Clouds all over the western sky, close together like small pale grey lambkins, and as the sun sank behind him it painted their linings a glorious amber. Beneath the pale skies lay the city, and Helge understood that this was the real Rome — not the Rome of his imagination and his dreams, but Rome as she actually was. Everything else he had seen on his journey had disappointed him, for it was not what he had imagined at home when he had been longing to go abroad and see it all. One sight at last was far beyond his dreams, and that was Rome.

A plain of housetops lay beneath him in the valley, the roofs of houses new and old, of houses high and low — it looked as if they had been built anywhere and at any time, and of a size to suit the need of the moment. In a few places only a space could be seen between the mass of housetops, as of streets. All this world of reckless lines, crossing each other in a thousand hard angles, was lying inert and quiet under the pale skies, while the setting sun touched the borders of the clouds with a tinge of light. It was dreaming under a thin veil of white mist, which no busy pillar of smoke dared penetrate, for no factory chimney could be seen, and no smoke came from a single one of the funny little chimney pipes protruding from the houses. The round, old, rust-brown tiles were covered by greyish moss, grass and small plants with yellow blossoms grew in the gutters; along

2

the border of the terraces the aloes stood immovably still in their tubs, and creepers hung in dead cascades from the cornices. Here and there the upper part of a high house rose above its neighbour, its dark, hollow windows staring at one out of a grey or reddish-yellow wall, or sleeping behind closed shutters. Loggias stood out of the mist, looking like parts of an old watchtower, and small summer-houses of wood or corrugated iron were erected on the roofs. Above it all masses of church cupolas were floating — the huge, grey one, far on the other side of what Helge supposed to be the river, was that of St. Peter.

Beyond the valley, where the roofs covered the silent city — it well deserved the epithet "eternal" tonight — a low hill stretched its longish back toward the skies, carrying on the far-away ridge an avenue of pines, the foliage of which formed one large mass above the row of slender trunks. And behind the dome of St. Peter the eye was arrested by another hill with villas, built among pines and cypresses. Probably Monte Mario.

The dark leaves of the holly formed a roof over his head, and behind him a fountain made a curiously living sound as the water splashed against the stone border, before flowing into the basin beneath it.

Helge whispered to the city of his dreams, whose streets his feet had not yet touched, whose houses did not harbour one single soul he knew: "Rome — Rome — eternal Rome." He was suddenly struck by his own loneliness and startled at his emotion, though he knew that there was nobody to witness it, and, turning round, he hurried down the Spanish stairs.

And now when he stood at the corner of Condotti and Corso he experienced a quaint and yet pleasant anxiety at the thought of mixing with those hustling crowds and finding his way in the strange city — to wander through it as far as Piazza San Pietro.

As he was crossing the street two young girls passed him. They looked like Norwegians, he thought, with a slight thrill of pleasure. One of them was very fair and wore light-coloured furs.

It was a joy to him even to read the names of the streets carved in clear, Latin type on white marble slabs set in the corners of the houses.

The street he took ran into an open space near a bridge, on which two rows of lanterns burned with a sickly, greenish flame in the pale light pouring down from the restless sky. A low parapet of stone ran along the waterline, bordered by a row of trees with faded leaves and trunks, dropping their bark in big white flakes. On the opposite side of the river the street lamps were burning among the trees, and the houses stood out black against the sky, but on this side the twilight still flickered on the window-panes. The sky was almost clear now, and hung transparent and greenish blue over the hill with the pine avenue, with here and there a few reddish, threatening, slowly moving clouds.

He stopped on the bridge and looked down into the Tiber. How dull the water was! It flowed on rapidly, reflecting the colors of the evening skies, sweeping twigs and gravel and bits of wood on its way between the stone walls. A small staircase on the side of the bridge led down to the water's edge. Helge thought how easy it would be to walk down the steps one night, when one was tired of everything — had any ever done so? he wondered.

He asked a policeman the way to St. Peter's cathedral in German; the man answered him first in French and then Italian, and when Helge repeatedly shook his head, he spoke French again, pointing up the river. Helge turned in that direction.

A huge, dark stone erection stood out against the sky, a low, round tower with a jagged crest and the jet-black silhouette of an angel on top. He recognized the lines of the San Angelo fort, and went close up to it. It was still light enough for the statues by the bridge to show up yellow in the twilight, the red skies were still mirrored in the flowing waters of the Tiber, but the street lamps had gained power, and threw out paths of light across the river. Beyond the San Angelo bridge the electric tramcars with illuminated windows rolled over the new iron bridge, throwing white sparks from the connecting wires. Helge took off his hat to a man:

"San Pietro, favorisca?"

The man pointed with his finger and said something Helge did not understand. He turned into a dark and narrow street which, with a sensation of joy, he almost thought he recognized, for it was exactly like the Italian street of his imagination: shop after shop full of curios. He gazed into the poorly lit windows. Most of the things were rubbish — those dirty strips of coarse white lace hanging on a string were surely not Italian handiwork. There were bits of pottery exhibited in dusty box-lids and small bronze figures of a poisonous green, old and new brass candlesticks and brooches with heaps of stones that looked far from genuine. Yet he was seized by a senseless wish to go in and buy something — to inquire, to bargain, and to purchase. Almost before he knew it, he had entered a small, stuffy shop filled with all sorts of things. There were church-lamps hanging from the ceiling, bits of silk with gold flowers on red and green and white ground, and broken pieces of furniture.

Behind the counter a youth with a dark complexion and a bluish, unshaven chin was reading. He talked and asked questions while Helge pointed at various articles, "Quanto?" The only thing he understood was that the prices were excessive, but one ought not to buy until one knew the language well enough to bargain with them. Several pieces of china were standing on a shelf, rococo figures and vases with sprays of roses, which looked quite modern. Helge seized one at random and placed it on the counter: "Quanto?"

"Sette," said the youth, and spread out seven fingers.

"Quattro," said Helge, holding out four fingers in a new brown glove, and felt quite pleased with himself at this leap into the foreign language. He did not understand one word of the man's arguments, but each time he finished talking Helge raised his four fingers and repeated his quattro, adding with a superior air: "Non antica!"

But the shopkeeper protested, "Si, antica" "Quattro," said Helge again — the man had now only five fingers in the air — and turned towards the door. The man called him back, accepting, and Helge, feeling highly pleased with himself, went out with his purchase wrapped up in pink tissue paper.

He perceived the dark mass of the church at the bottom of the street outlined against the sky, and walked on. He hurried across the first part of the piazza with its lighted shop windows and passing trams towards the two semicircular arcades, which laid a pair of rounded arms, as it were, about one part of the place, drawing it into the quiet and darkness of the massive church, with its broad steps extending in a shell-like formation far out on the piazza.

The dome of the church and the row of saints along the roof of the arcades stood out black against the faint light of the sky; the trees and houses on the hill at the back seemed to be heaped one on top of the other in an irregular fashion. The street lamps were powerless here, the darkness streamed forth between the pillars, and spread over the steps from the open portico of the church. He went slowly up the steps close to the church and looked through the iron doors. Then he went back again to the obelisk in the middle of the piazza and stood there gazing at the dark building. He bent his head back, and followed with his eyes the slender needle of stone that pointed straight into the evening sky, where the last clouds had descended on the roofs of that part of the town whence he had come, and the first radiant sparks of the stars pierced the gathering darkness.

Again his ears caught the sound of water emptying into a stone cistern, and the soft ripple of the overflow from one receptacle into another into the basin. He approached one of the fountains and watched the thick, white jet, driven upwards as it were in angry defiance and looking black against the clear atmosphere, to break high in the air and sink back into the darkness, where the water gleamed white again. He kept staring at it until a gust of wind took hold of the jet and bent it towards him, raining icy drops on his face, but he remained where he was, listening and staring. Then he walked a few steps — stood still — and walked again, but very slowly, listening to an inner voice. It was true, then — really true — that he was here, far, far away from everything he had longed so intensely

5

to leave. And he walked still more slowly, furtively, like one who has escaped from prison.

At the comer of the street there was a restaurant. He made for it, and on his way found a tobacco shop, where he bought some cigarettes, picture cards and stamps. Waiting for his steak, he drank big gulps of claret, while he wrote to his parents; to his father: "I have been thinking of you very often today" — it was true enough — and to his mother: "I have already got a small present for you, the first thing I bought here in Rome." Poor mother — how was she? He had often been impatient with her these last years. He unpacked the thing and had a look at it — it was probably meant for a scent-bottle. He added a few words to his mother's card that he managed the language all right, and that to bargain in the shops was an easy matter.

The food was good, but dear. Never mind, once he was more at home here he would soon learn how to live cheaply. Satisfied and exhilarated by the wine, he started to walk in a new direction, past long, low, dilapidated houses, through an archway on to a bridge. A man in a barrier hut stopped him and made him understand that he had to pay a soldo. On the other side of the bridge was a large, dark church with a dome.

He got into a labyrinth of dark, narrow bits of streets — in the mysterious gloom he surmised the existence of old palaces with projecting cornices and lattice windows side by side with miserable hovels, and small church-fronts in between the rows of houses.

There were no pavements and he stepped into refuse that lay rotting in the gutter. Outside the narrow doors of the lighted taverns and under the few street lamps he had a vague glimpse of human forms.

He was half delighted, half afraid — boyishly excited, and wondering at the same time how he was to get out of this maze and find the way to his hotel at the ends of the earth — take a cab, he supposed.

He passed down another narrow, almost empty street. A small strip of clear, blue sky was visible between the high houses with their frameless windows, looking like black holes cut in the wall. On the uneven stone bridge dust and straw and bits of paper were tossed about by a light gust of wind.

Two women, walking behind him, passed him close under a lamp. He gave a start: they were the ones he had noticed that afternoon in the Corso and believed to be Norwegian. He recognized the light furs of the taller one.

Suddenly he felt an impulse to try an adventure — to ask them the way, so as to hear if they were Norwegian — or Scandinavian at any rate, for they were certainly foreigners. With slightly beating heart he started to walk after them.

The two young girls stopped outside a shop, which was closed, and then walked on. Helge wondered if he should say "Please" or "Bitte" or "Scusi" — or if he should blurt out at once "Undskyld" — it would be funny if they were Norwegians.

The girls turned a corner; Helge was close upon them, screwing up courage to address them. The smaller one turned round angrily and said something in Italian in a low voice. He felt disappointed and was going to vanish after an apology, when the tall one said in Norwegian: "You should not speak to them, Cesca — it is much better to pretend not to notice."

"I cannot bear that cursed Italian rabble; they never will leave a woman alone," said the other.

"I beg your pardon," said Helge, and the two girls stopped, turning round quickly.

"I hope you will excuse me," he muttered, coloring, and, angrily conscious of it, blushed still deeper. "I only arrived from Florence today, and have lost my way in these winding streets. I thought you were Norwegian, or at any rate Scandinavian, and I cannot manage the Italian language. Would you be kind enough to tell me where to find a car? My name is Gram," he added, raising his hat again.

"Where do you live?" asked the taller girl.

"At a place called the Albergo Torino, close to the station," he explained.

"He should take the Trastevere tram at San Carlo ai Catenari," said the other. "No; better take a No. 1 at the new Corso."

"But those cars don't go to the Termini," answered the little one.

"Yes, they do. Those that have San Pietro, stazione Termini, written on them," she explained to Helge.

"Oh, that one! It runs past Capo le Case and Ludovisi and an awful long way about first — it will take an hour at least to the station with that one." "No, dear; it goes direct — straight along Via Nazionale."

"It does not," insisted the other; "it goes to the Lateran first."

The taller girl turned to Helge: "The first turning right will take you into a sort of market. From there you go along the Cancellaria on your left to the new Corso. If I remember rightly, the tram stops at the Cancellaria — somewhere near it anyway — you will see the sign. But be sure to take the tram marked San Pietro, stazione Termini, No. 1."

7

Helge stood somewhat crestfallen, listening to the foreign names which the girls used with such easy familiarity, and, shaking his head, said: "I am afraid I shall never be able

to find it — perhaps I had better walk till I find a cab." "We might go with you to the stop," said the tall one.
The little one whispered peevishly something in Italian, but the other answered her decisively. Helge felt still more confused at these asides, which he did not understand.

"Thank you, but please do not trouble. I am sure to find my way home somehow or other."

"It is no trouble," said the tall one, starting to walk; "it is on our way."

"It is very kind of you; I suppose it is rather difficult to find one's way about in Rome, is it not?" he said, by way of conversation — "especially when it is dark."

"Oh no, you will soon get into it."

"I only arrived here to-day. I came from Florence this morning by train." The smaller one said something in an undertone in Italian. The tall one asked: "Was it very cold in Florence?"

"Yes, bitterly cold. It is milder here, is it not? I wrote my mother anyway yesterday to send my winter coat."

"Well, it is cold enough here too sometimes. Did you like Florence? How long were you there?"

"A fortnight. I think I shall like Rome better than Florence."

The other young girl smiled — she had been muttering to herself in Italian all the time — but the tall one went on in her pleasant, quiet voice:

"I don't believe there is any town one could love as much as Rome." "Is your friend Italian?" asked Helge.
"No; Miss Jahrman is Norwegian. We speak Italian because I want to learn, and she is very good at it. My name is Winge," she added. "That is the Cancellaria." She pointed towards a big, dark palace.

"Is the courtyard as fine as it is reported to be?"

"Yes; it is very fine. I wall show you which car." While they stood waiting two men came across the street.

"Hullo, you here!" exclaimed one of them.

"Good evening," said the other. "What luck! We can go together. Have you been to look at the corals?"

"It was closed," said Miss Jahrman sulkily.

"We have met a fellow-countryman, and promised to show him the right tram," Miss Winge explained, introducing: "Mr. Gram — Mr. Heggen, artist, and Mr. Ahlin, sculptor."

"I don't know if you remember me, Mr. Heggen — my name is Gram; we met three years ago on the Mysusaeter."

"Oh yes — certainly. And so you are in Rome?"

Ahlin and Miss Jahrman had stood talking to one another in whispers. The girl came up to her friend and said: "I am going home, Jenny. I am not in the mood for Frascati tonight."

"But, my dear, you suggested it yourself."

"Well, not Frascati anyway — ugh! sit there and mope with thirty old Danish ladies of every possible age and sex."

"We can go somewhere else. But there is your tram coming, Mr. Gram."

"A thousand thanks for your help. Shall I see you again — at the Scandinavian club, perhaps?"

The tram stopped in front of them. Miss Winge said: "I don't know — perhaps you would like to come with us now; we were going to have a glass of wine somewhere, and hear some music."

"Thank you." Helge hesitated, looking round at the others a little embarrassed. "I should be very pleased, but" — and, turning with confidence to Miss Winge of the fair face and the kind voice, he said, with an awkward smile, "you all know one another — perhaps you would rather not have a stranger with you?"

9

"Indeed no," she said, smiling — "it would be very nice — and there — your tram's gone now. You know Heggen already, and now you know us. We'll see you get home all right, so if you are not tired, let us go."

"Tired, not a bit. I should love to come," said Helge eagerly.

The other three began to propose different cafes. Helge knew none of the names; his father had not mentioned them. Miss Jahrman rejected them all.

"Very well, then, let us go down to St. Agostino; you know the one, Gunnar, where they give you that first-rate claret," and Jenny began to walk on, accompanied by Heggen.

"There is no music," retorted Miss Jahrman.

"Oh yes, the man with a squint and the other fellow are there almost every night. Don't let us waste time."

Helge followed with Miss Jahrman and the Swedish sculptor. "Have you been long in Rome, Mr. Gram?"
"No, I came this morning from Florence."

Miss Jahrman laughed. Helge felt rather snubbed. He ought perhaps to have said he was tired, and gone home. On their way down through dark, narrow streets Miss Jahrman talked all the time to the sculptor, and scarcely answered when he tried to speak to her. But before he had made up his mind he saw the other couple vanish through a narrow door down the street.

WHAT'S wrong with Cesca again tonight? We are getting too much of her tempers lately. Take off your coat, Jenny, or you'll be cold when you go out." Heggen hung his coat and hat on a peg and sat down on a rush chair.

"She is not well, poor girl, and that man Gram, you see, followed us a while before he dared to speak to us; and anything of that kind always puts her out of temper; she has a weak heart, you know."

"Sorry for her. The cheek of the man."

"Poor thing, he was wandering listlessly about and could not find his way home. He doesn't seem used to traveling. Did you know him before?"

"Haven't the slightest recollection of it. I may have met him somewhere. Here they are." Ahlin took Miss Jahrman's coat.

"By Jove!" said Heggen. "How smart you are tonight, Cesca. Pretty as paint."

She smiled, evidently pleased, and smoothed her hips; then, taking Heggen by the shoulders: "Move out, please, I want to sit by Jenny."

How pretty she is, thought Helge. Her dress was a brilliant green, the skirt so high-waisted that the rounded breasts rose as out of a cup. There was a golden sheen in the folds of the velvet, and the bodice was cut low round the pale, full throat. She was very dark; small, jet-black curls fell from under the brown bell-shaped hat about her soft, rosy cheeks. The face was that of a little girl, with full, round lids over deep, brown eyes, and charming dimples about the small, red mouth.

Miss Winge too was good-looking, but could not compete with her friend. She was as fair as the other was dark; her blonde hair brushed back from a high, white forehead had tints of flaming gold in it; her skin was a delicate pink and white. Even the brows and lashes round her steel-grey eyes were a fair, golden brown. The mouth was too big for her face, with its short, straight nose and blue-veined temples, and the lips were pale, but when she smiled, she showed even, pearly teeth. Her figure was slender: the long, slim neck, the arms covered with a fair, silken down, and the long, thin hands. She was tall, and so slim that she was almost like an overgrown boy. She seemed very young. She had a narrow, white turned-down collar round the V-shaped neck of her dress and revers of the same kind round her short sleeves. Her dress of soft, pale grey silk was gathered round the waist and on the shoulders — obviously to make her look less thin. She wore a row of pink beads round her neck, which were reflected in rosy spots on her skin.

Helge Gram sat down quietly at the end of the table and listened to the others talking about a friend of theirs who had been ill. An old Italian, with a dirty white apron covering his broad waistcoat, came up to ask what they required.

"Red or white, sweet or dry, what do you like, Gram?" said Heggen, turning to him. "Mr. Gram must have half a liter of my claret," said Jenny Winge. "It is one of the best things you can have in Rome, and that is no small praise, you know."

The sculptor pushed his cigarette-case over to the ladies. Miss Jahrman took one and lighted it. "No, Cesca — don't!" begged Miss Winge.

"Yes," said Miss Jahrman. "I shan't be any better if I don't smoke, and I am cross tonight."

"Why are you cross?" asked Ahlin. "Because I did not get those corals."

"Were you going to wear them tonight?" asked Heggen. "No, but I had made up my mind to have them."

"I see," said Heggen, laughing, "and tomorrow you null decide to have the malachite necklace."

"No, I won't, but it is awfully annoying. Jenny and I rushed down on purpose because of those wretched corals."

"But you had the good luck to meet us, otherwise you would have been obliged to go to Frascati, to which you seem to have taken a sudden dislike."

"I would not have gone to Frascati, you may be sure of that, Gunnar, and it would have been much better for me, because now that you have made me come I want to smoke and drink and be out the whole night."

"I was under the impression that you had suggested it yourself.

"I think the malachite necklace was very fine," said Ahlin, by way of interrupting — "and very cheap."

"Yes, but in Florence malachite is much cheaper still. This thing cost forty-seven lire. In Florence, where Jenny bought her crist alio rosso, I could have got one for thirty-five. Jenny gave only eighteen for hers. But I will make him give me the corals for ninety lire."

"I don't quite understand your economy," said Heggen.

"I don't want to talk about it any more," said Miss Jahrman. "I am sick of all this talk — and tomorrow I am going to buy the corals."

"But isn't ninety lire an awful price for corals?" Heggen risked the question.

"They are not ordinary corals, you know," Miss Jahrman deigned to answer. "They are contadina corals, a fat chain with a gold clasp and heavy drops — like that."

"Contadina — is that a special kind of coral?" asked Helge. "No. It is what the contadinas wear."

"But I don't know what a contadina is, you see."

"A peasant girl. Have you not seen those big, dark red, polished corals they wear? Mine are exactly the color of raw beef, and the bead in the middle is as big as that" — and she formed a ring with her thumb and forefinger the size of an egg.

"How beautiful they must be," said Helge, pleased to get hold of the thread of conversation. "I don't know what malachite is, or cristallo rossa, but I am sure that corals like those would suit you better than anything."

"Do you hear, Ahlin? And you wanted me to have the malachite necklace. Heggen's scarf-pin is malachite — take it off, Gunnar — and Jenny's beads are cristallo rosso, not rossa — red rock crystals, you know."

She handed him the scarf-pin and the necklace. The beads were warm from contact with the young girl's neck. He looked at them a while; in every bead there were small flaws, as it were, which absorbed the light.

"You ought really to wear corals, Miss Jahrman. You would look exactly like a Roman contadina yourself."

"You don't say so!" She smiled, pleased. "Do you hear, you others?" "You have an Italian name, too," said Helge eagerly.

"No. I was named after my grandmother, but the Italian family I lived with last year could not pronounce my ugly name, and since then I have stuck to the Italian version of it."

"Francesca," said Ahlin, in a whisper.

"I shall always think of you as Francesca — signorina Francesca."

"Why not Miss Jahrman? Unfortunately we cannot speak Italian together, since you don't know the language." She turned to the others. "Jenny, Gunnar — I am going to buy the corals tomorrow."

"Yes; I think I heard you say so," said Heggen. "And I will not pay more than ninety."

"You always have to bargain here," said Helge, as one who knows. "I went into a shop this afternoon near St. Pietro and bought this thing for my mother. They asked seven lire, but I got it for four. Don't you think it was cheap?" He put the thing on the table.

Francesca looked at it with contempt. "It costs two fifty in the market. I took a pair of them to each of the maids at home last year."

"The man said it was old," retorted Helge.

"They always do, when they see that people don't understand, and don't know the language."

"You don't think it is pretty?" said Helge, downcast, and wrapped the pink tissue paper round his treasure. "Don't you think I can give it to my mother?"

"I think it is hideous," said Francesca, "but, of course, I don't know your mother's taste."
"What on earth shall I do with it, then?" sighed Helge.

"Give it to your mother," said Jenny. "She will be pleased that you have remembered her. Besides, people at home like those things. We who live out here see so much that we become more critical."

Francesca reached her hand for Ahlin's cigarette-case, but he did not want to let her have it; they whispered together eagerly, then she flung it away, calling: "Giuseppe!"

Helge understood that she ordered the man to bring her some cigarettes. Ahlin got up suddenly: "My dear Miss Jahrman— -I meant only to . . . you know it is not good for you to smoke so much."

Francesca rose. She had tears in her eyes. "Never mind. I want to go home."
"Miss Jahrman — Cesca." Ahlin stood holding her cloak and begged her quietly not to go. She pressed her handkerchief to her eyes.

"Yes; I want to go home — you can see for yourself that I am quite impossible tonight. I want to go home alone. No, Jenny, you must not come with me." Heggen rose too. Helge remained alone at the- table.

"You don't imagine that we would let you go alone this time of night?" said Heggen. "You mean to forbid me, perhaps?"

"I do absolutely."

"Don't, Gunnar," said Jenny Winge. She sent the men away and they sat down at the table in silence, while Jenny, with her arms round Francesca, drew her aside and talked to her soothingly. After a while they came back to the table.

But the company was somewhat out of sorts. Miss Jahrman sat close to Jenny; she had got her cigarettes and was smoking now, shaking her head at Ahlin, who insisted that his were better. Jenny, who had ordered some fruit, was eating tangerines, and now and again she put a slice in Francesca's mouth. How perfectly lovely she looked as she lay with her sad, childish face on Jenny's shoulder, letting herself be fed by her friend. Ahlin sat and stared at her and Heggen played absent-mindedly with the match-ends.

"Have you been in town long, Mr. Gram?" he asked.

"I have taken to saying that I came from Florence this morning by train." Jenny gave a polite little laugh, and Francesca smiled faintly.

At this moment a bare-headed, dark-haired woman with a bold, yellow, greasy face entered the room with a mandolin. She was accompanied by a small man in the threadbare finery of a waiter, and carrying a guitar.

"I was right, you see, Cesca," said Jenny, speaking as to a child. "There is Emilia; now we are going to have some music."

"That's jolly," said Helge. "Do the ballad singers really still go about here in Rome singing in the taverns?"
The singers tuned up "The Merry Widow." The woman had a high, clear, metallic voice. "Oh, how horrid," cried Francesca, awakening; "we don't want that, we want something Italian — la luna con palido canto, or what do you think?"

She went up to the singers and greeted them like old friends — laughed and gesticulated, seizing the guitar, and played, humming a few bars of one or two songs.

The Italian woman sang. The melody floated sweet and insinuating to the accompaniment of twanging metal strings, and Helge's four new friends joined in the refrain. It was about amove and bacciare.

"It is a love song, is it not?"

"A nice love song," laughed Miss Jahrman. "Don't ask me to translate it, but in Italian it sounds very pretty."

"This one is not so bad," said Jenny. She turned to Helge with her sweet smile: "What do you think of this place?

Is it not a good wine?"

"Excellent, and a characteristic old place."

But all his interest was gone. Miss Winge and Heggen spoke to him now and again, but as he made no effort to keep up a conversation, they began to talk art together. The weedish sculptor sat gazing at Miss Jahrman. The strange melodies from the strings floated past him — he felt that others understood. The room was typical, with a red stone floor, the walls and the ceiling, which was arched and rested on a thick pillar in the middle of the room, being distempered. The tables were bare, the chairs had green rush bottoms, and the air was heavy with the sourish smell of the wine barrels behind the counter.

This was artist life in Rome. It was almost like looking at a picture or reading a description in a book, but he was not in it — on the contrary, he was hopelessly out of it. As long as it was a question only of books and pictures, he could dream that he was a part of it, but he was convinced that he would never get in with these people.

Confound it — well, never mind. He was no good at associating with people anyway, least of all with people like these. Look at Jenny Winge now, how unconcernedly she holds the smeared glass of dark red wine. It was a revelation to him. His father had drawn his attention to the glass, which the girl in Barstrand's picture from Rome in the Copenhagen museum holds in her hand. Miss Winge would probably think it a poor picture. These young girls had probably never read about Bramante's courtyard in the Cancellaria — "this pearl of renaissance architecture." They might have discovered it one day by chance, when they went out to buy beads and finer}', and had perhaps taken their friends to see this new delight, of which they had not dreamt for years. They had not read in books about every stone and every place, until their eyes could not see the beauty in anything, unless it exactly corresponded to the picture already in mind. They could probably look at some white pillars standing against the dark blue sky and enjoy the sight

16

without any pedantic curiosity as to what temple they were part of and for what unknown god it had been built.

He had read and he had dreamed, and he understood now that nothing in reality was what he had expected it to be. In the clear daylight everything seemed grey and hard, the dream had enveloped the pictures of his fancy in a soft chiaroscuro, had given them a harmonious finish, and covered the ruins with a delicate green. He would now only go round and make sure that everything he had read about was really there, and then he would be able to lecture on it to the young ladies at the Academy, and say that he had seen it. Not a single thing would he have to tell them that he had discovered for himself; he would learn nothing that he did not already know. And when he met living beings he conjured up in his mind the dead forms of poetry that he knew, to see if one of them were represented, for he knew nothing of the living, he who had never lived. Heggen with the full, red mouth would hardly — he supposed — dream of romantic adventure, like those one reads of in the popular novelettes, if he fell in with a girl one evening in the streets of Rome.

He began to feel conscious of having drunk wine.

"You will have a headache tomorrow if you go home now," said Miss Winge to him, when they stood outside in the street. The other three walked ahead; he followed with her.

"I am sure you think me an awful bore to take out of an evening."

"Not at all, but you do not know us well enough yet, and we don't know you."

"I am slow at making acquaintances — in fact, I never really get to know people. I ought not to have come tonight, when you were kind enough to ask me. Perhaps one needs training to enjoy oneself too," he said, with a short laugh.

"Of course one does." He could hear from her voice that she was smiling.

"I was twenty- five when I started and, you can take it from me, I had no easy time at first."

"You? I thought that you artists always. . . . For that matter, I did not think you were twenty-five or near it."

"I am, thank goodness, and considerably more."

"Do you thank Heaven for that? And I, a man, for every year that drops from me as it were into eternity, without having brought me anything but the humiliation of finding that nobody has any use for me — I" He stopped suddenly, terrified. He heard that his voice trembled, and he concluded that the wine had gone to his head, since he could speak like that to a woman he did not even know. But in spite of his shyness he went on: "It seems quite hopeless. My father has told me about the young men of his time, about their eager discussions and their great illusions. I have never had a single illusion to talk about all these years, that now are gone, lost, never to return."

"You have no right to say that, Mr. Gram. Not one year of one's life is wasted, as long as you have not reached a point where suicide is the only way out. I don't believe that the old generation, those from the time of the great illusions, were better off than we. The dreams of their youth stripped life bare for them. We young people, most of the ones I know, have started life without illusions. We were thrown into the struggle for existence almost before we were grown up, and from the first we have looked at life with open eyes, expecting the worst. And then one day we understood that we could manage to get something good out of it ourselves. Something happens, perhaps, that makes you think: if you can stand this, you can stand anything. Once you have got self-reliance in that way, there are no illusions that any one or anything can rob you of."

"But circumstances and opportunities may be such that one's self-reliance is not much use when they are stronger than oneself."

"True," she said. "When a ship sets sail, circumstances may cause it to be wrecked — a collision or a mistake in the construction of a wheel — but it does not start with that presumption. Besides, one must try and conquer circumstances; there is nearly always a way out of them."

"You are very optimistic, Miss Winge."

"I am," she said, and after a while: "I have become an optimist since I have seen how much people really can stand without losing courage to struggle on, and without being degraded."

"That is exactly what I think they are — reduced in value, anyway."

"Not all. And even to find one who does not allow life to abase or reduce him is enough to make you optimistic. We are going in here."

"This looks more like a Montmartre café, don't you think?" said Helge, looking around. Along the walls of the small room were plush-covered forms; small iron tables with marble tops stood in front of them, and the steam rose from two nickel boilers on the counter.

"These places are the same everywhere. Do you know Paris?"

"No, but I thought. . . ." He felt suddenly irritated with this young girl artist who went about the world as she pleased — and God knows where she got the money from. It seemed to her quite as natural for him to have been in Paris as in a restaurant in Christiania. It was easy for people like her to speak of self-reliance. An unhappy love affair in Paris, which she forgot in Rome, was probably the greatest of her trials, and made her feel so confident and brave and able to solve the questions of life.

Her shape was almost scraggy, but the face was healthy and the coloring beautiful. He wished he could speak to Miss Jahrman, who was wide awake now, but she was engaged by Ahlin and Heggen. Miss Winge was eating a poached egg and bread and drinking hot milk.

"The customers of this place look rather mysterious," he said, turning to her. "Perfect criminal types, it seems to me."

"Possibly — we have a little of everything here, but you must remember that Rome is a modem metropolis and that many people have night work. This is one of the few places open this time of night. But aren't you hungry? I am going to have some black coffee."

"Do you always stay out so late?" Helge looked at his watch; it was four o'clock.

"Oh no," she laughed. "Only now and then. We watch the sun rise and then go and have breakfast. Miss Jahrman does not want to go home tonight."

Helge scarcely knew why he stayed on. They had some green liqueur and he felt drowsy after it, but the others laughed and chatted, mentioning people and places unfamiliar to him.

"Don't talk to me about Douglas — with his preaching — I have done with him. One day last June, when he and the Finn — you remember him, Lindberg? — and I were alone in the life class, the Firm and I went out to have some coffee.

When we came back Douglas was sitting with the girl on his knee. We pretended not to see, but he never asked me to tea after that."

"Dear me," said Jenny. "Was there any harm in that?"

"In spring-time and in Paris," said Heggen, with a smile. "Norman Douglas, I tell you, Cesca, was a splendid chap — you cannot deny that — and clever too. He showed me some beautiful things from the fortifications."

"Yes, and do you remember that one from Pére Lachaise, with the purple rosaries to the left?" said Jenny.

"Father! It was a gem; and the one with the little girl at the piano?"
"Yes, but think of the dreadful model," said Miss Jahrman — "that fat, middle-aged, fair one, you know. And he always pretended to be so virtuous."

"He was," said Heggen.

"Pugh! And I was on the verge of falling in love with him just because of that." "Oh! That of course puts it in another light."

"He proposed to me lots of times," said Francesca pensively, and I had decided to say yes, but fortunately I had not done it yet."

"If you had," said Heggen, "you would never have seen him with that model on his knee."

The expression on Francesca's face changed completely; for a second a shadow of melancholy passed over her soft features.

"Nonsense! You are all alike. I don't believe one of you. Per Bacco!"

"You must not think that, Francesca," said Ahlin, lifting his head for a moment from his hand.

She smiled again. "Give me some more liqueur."

Toward dawn Helge walked beside Jenny Winge through dark, deserted streets. The three in front of them stopped; two half-grown boys were sitting on the stone steps of a house. Francesca and Jenny talked to them and gave them money.

"Beggars?" asked Helge.

"I don't know — the big one said he was a paper-boy."

"I suppose the beggars in this country are merely humbugs?"

"Most of them, but many have to sleep in the street even in winter. And many are cripples."

20

"I noticed that in Florence. Don't you think it is a shame that people with nasty wounds or terribly deformed should be allowed to go about begging? The authorities ought to take care of those unfortunate people."

"I don't know. It is the way out here. Foreigners can hardly judge. I suppose they prefer to beg; they earn more that way."

"On the Piazza Michelangelo there was a beggar without arms; his hands came out straight from the shoulders. A German doctor I was living with said the man owned a villa at Fiesole."

"All the better for him!"

"With us the cripples are taught to work so that they can earn their living in a respectable way."

"Hardly enough anyhow to buy a villa," said Jenny, laughing.

"Can you imagine anything more demoralizing than to make one's living by exposing one's deformity?"

"It is always demoralizing to know that one is a cripple in one way or another." "But to live by invoking people's compassion."

"A cripple knows that he will be pitied in any case, and has to accept help from men — or God."

Jenny mounted some steps and lifted 'the corner of a curtain that looked like a thin mattress. They entered a small church.

Candles were burning on the altar. The light was reflected manifold on the halo of the tabernacle, fluttered on candlesticks and brass ornaments and made the paper roses in the altar vases look red and yellow. A priest stood with his back turned to them, reading silently from a book; a pair of acolytes moved to and fro, bowed, made the sign of the cross and various other movements which seemed meaningless to Helge.

The little church was dark; in the two side chapels tiny nightlight flames flickered, hanging from brass chains in front of images blacker than the darkness itself.

Jenny Winge knelt on a rush stood. Her folded hands rested on the prie-Dieu, and her head was raised, showing her profile clearly outlined against the soft candlelight, which trembled in the fair waves of her hair and stole down the delicate bend of her bare neck.

21

Heggen and Ahlin took two chairs quietly from the pile against one of the pillars.

This quiet service before dawn was quaint and impressive; Gram followed attentively every movement of the priest. The acolytes hung a white garment, with a golden cross on it, over his shoulders. He took the Host, turned round and held it up to the light. The boys swung the incense, and the sharp, sweet smell of it floated to where Helge stood, but he waited in vain for music or singing.

Miss Winge apparently made some pretence of being a Catholic, since she was kneeling like that. Heggen sat looking straight in front of him towards the altar. He had laid one arm about the shoulders of Francesca, who had fallen asleep leaning against him. Ahlin sat behind a pillar, probably asleep too — he could not see him.

It was extraordinary to sit here with utter strangers; he felt lonely, but no longer depressed. The happy feeling of freedom from the previous night returned. He looked at the others, at the two young girls, Jenny and Francesca. He knew their names now, but little more. And none of them knew what it meant to him to sit there, what he had left behind by coming, the painful struggles, the conquering of obstacles and the breaking of bonds that had held him. He felt strangely happy, almost proud of it, and he looked at the two women with a mild pity. Such a little thing as Cesca — and Jenny — young and high-spirited, with ready, confident opinions behind their white, small foreheads. Two young girls treading an even path of life, with here and there a small stone perhaps to move away, but who knew nothing about a road like his. What would they do, poor girls, if they had to try it? He started -when Heggen touched his shoulder, and blushed, for he had been dozing.

"You have had a nap, too, I see," said Heggen.

Out in the street the high, quiet houses slept with closed shutters. A tram drove up in a side street, a cab rattled over the bridge, and one or two cold and sleepy stragglers walked on the pavement.

They turned into a street from where they could see the obelisk in front of Trinita-dei-Monti — it stood white against the dark hollies of Pincio. No living being was to be seen and no sound heard but their own steps on the iron bridge and the ripple of a fountain in a yard. Far away the murmur of the waters on Monte Pinco came through the stillness. Helge recognized it, and as he walked towards it, a growing feeling of joy filled him, as if his pleasure from the previous evening were waiting for him up there by the fountain under the hollies.

He turned to Jenny Winge, not realizing that his eyes and his voice betrayed his feeling. "I stood here last night and saw the sun set; it seemed so strange to be here. I have been working for years to get here. I had to come because of my studies. I wanted to be an archaeologist, but I have been obliged to teach from the time I got my degree. I have been waiting for the day when I could come out here — sort of prepared myself for it. Yet, when I stood here yesterday so suddenly, I was almost taken unawares." "I quite understand," said Jenny.

"The moment I stepped out of the train yesterday and saw the ruins of the Thermes opposite, surrounded by modern buildings with cafés and cinemas, with the sun shining on the mighty, yellow ruins, I loved it. The trams in the piazza, the plantations, the gorgeous fountains with such quantities of water. I thought the old walls looked so pretty in the midst of the modern quarters with the busy traffic."

She nodded pleasantly. "Yes," she said; "I love it too."

"Then I went down to the town; it was delightful. Modern buildings among the old ones, and fountains flowing and plashing everywhere. I walked right out to San Pietro; it was dark when I got there, but I stood a while and looked at the water. Do they play all night in this city?"

"Yes, all night. You see and hear fountains almost everywhere. The streets are very quiet at night. Where we live, Miss Jahrman and I, there is one in the courtyard, and when the weather is mild we sit on our balcony late at night and listen to it."

She had sat down on the stone parapet. Helge stood in the same spot as the evening before and gazed again at the town, with its background of hills under a sky as clear as the one over the mountain-tops at home. He filled his lungs with the pure, cold air.

"Nowhere in the world, are there such mornings as in Rome," said Jenny. "I mean when the whole town is sunk in a sleep that grows lighter and lighter, and then suddenly awakes rested and fit. Heggen says it is because of the shutters; no window- panes to catch the morning light and throw it on to your face." They sat with their backs to the breaking dawn and the golden sky, where the pines in the Medici garden and the small church towers, with pavilions on top, appeared in hard and sharp outlines. The sun would not rise yet for some time, but the grey mass of houses began slowly to radiate color. It looked as if the light came from within through transparent walls; some houses seemed red, others turned yellow or white. The villas in Monte Mario rose distinctly from a background of brown grassbanks and black cypresses.

All at once there was a sparkling as of a star somewhere on the hills behind the town — a window-pane had caught the first sunray after all — and the foliage turned a golden live.

A small bell began to peal down in the city.

Miss Jahrman came close to her friend and leaned sleepily against her: "Il levar del sole."

Helge looked up against the limpid blue sky; a sunray brushed the top of the spray and made the waterdrops scintillate in gold and azure.

"Bless you all, I am desperately sleepy," said Francesca, yawning carelessly. "Ugh! it is freezing! I cannot under- stand how you can sit on that cold stone, Jenny. I want to go to bed at once — subito!"

"I am sleepy too." Heggen yawned. "We must go home, but I am going to have a cup of hot milk at my dairy first. Are you coming?"

They went down the Spanish stairs. Helge looked at all the little green leaves that peeped out between the stone steps.

"Fancy anything growing where so many people walk up and down."

"Everywhere, where there is some earth between the stones, something grows. You should have seen the roof below our house last spring. There is even a little fig-tree growing between the tiles, and Cesca is very concerned about it lest it should not stand the winter, and wonders where it will get nourishment when it grows bigger. She has made a sketch of it."

"Your friend is a painter, too, I understand?" "Yes — she is very talented."

"I remember seeing a picture of yours at the autumn exhibition at home," said Helge. "Roses in a copper bowl."

"I painted it here last spring, but I am not altogether pleased with it now. I was in Paris for two months in the summer, and I think I learned a lot in that time. But I sold it for three hundred kroner — the price I had marked it for. There are some things in it that are good."

"You are a modem painter — I suppose you all are?" Jenny smiled slightly, but did not answer.
The others waited at the bottom of the stairs. Jenny shook hands with the men and said good morning.

"What do you mean by that?" said Heggen. "You are not really going off to work now?"
"Yes; that is what I mean."
"You are marvelous!"

"Oh, don't, Jenny, come home!" Francesca shivered.

"Why shouldn't I work? I am not a bit tired. Mr. Gram, hadn't you better take a cab home from here?"

"I suppose so. Is the post office open now? I know it is not far from the Piazza di Spagna."

"I am going past it — you can come with me." She nodded a last time to the others, who began to walk homeward. Francesca hung limp on Ahlin's arm, overcome with sleep.

WELL, did you get a letter?" said Jenny Winge when he returned to the entrance hall of the post office, where she had been waiting for him. "Now I will show you which tram to take."

"Thank you, it is very kind of you."

The piazza lay white in the sunshine; the morning air was crisp and clear. Carts and people from the side streets were hurrying past.

"You know, Miss Winge, I don't think I will go home. I am as wide awake as I can be, and I should like to go for a walk. Would you think me intruding if I asked to be allowed to accompany you a little bit of the way?"

"Dear me, no. But will you be able to find the way to your hotel?" "Oh, I think I can manage it in broad daylight."
"You will find cabs now everywhere."

They came out into the Corso, and she told him the names of the palaces. She was always a step or two ahead of him, for she moved with ease between the many people who had already come out on the pavements.

"Do you like vermouth?" she asked. "I am going in here to have one."

She drank it all in one gulp, standing at the marble counter of the bar. He did not like the bitter-sweet drink, which was new to him, but he thought it fun to look in at a bar on their way.

Jenny turned into narrow streets where the air was raw and damp, the sun reaching only the top part of the houses. Helge noticed everything with great interest: the blue carts behind mules with brass-studded harness and red tassels, the bareheaded women and dark-hued children, the small, cheap shops and the display of vegetables in the porches. In one place a man was making doughnuts on a stove. Jenny bought some and offered him, but he refused politely. What a queer girl, he thought. She ate and seemed to enjoy them, while he felt sick at the mere thought of those greasy balls between his teeth on top of the various drinks in the night, and the taste of vermouth still in his mouth. Besides, the old man was very dirty.

Side by side with poor, decrepit houses, where greyish wash hung out to dry between the broken ribs of the Venetian blinds, stood massive stone palaces with lattice windows and protruding cornices. Once Jenny had to take him by the arm — a scarlet automobile came hooting out of a gate in baroque style, turned with difficulty, and came speeding up the narrow street, where the gutters were full of cabbage leaves and other refuse.

He enjoyed it all — it was so strange and southern. Year after year his fantastic dreams had been destroyed by everyday petty reality, till at last he had tried to sneer at himself and correct his fancies in self-defence. And so now he tried to convince himself that in these romantic quarters lived the same kind of people as in every other big city — shopgirls and factory workers, typographers and telegraph operators, people who worked in offices and at machines, the same as in every part of the world. But it gave him pleasure to think that the houses and the streets, which were the image of his dreams, were obviously real as well.

After walking through small, damp and smelly streets they came into an open space in the sunlight. The ground was raked up at random; heaps of offal and rubbish lay between mounds of gravel; dilapidated old houses, some of them partly pulled down, with rooms showing, stood between classical ruins.

Passing some detached houses, which looked as if they had been forgotten in the general destruction, they reached the piazza by the Vesta temple. Behind the big, new steam-mill and the lovely little church with the pillared portico and the slender tower, the Aventino rose distinct against the sunny sky, with the monasteries on the hill, and dust-grey, nameless ruins among the gardens on the slope.

The thing that always gave him a shock — in Germany and in Florence — was that the ruins he had read about and imagined standing in a romantic frame of green leaves with flowers in the crevices, as you see them in old etchings or on tire scenery in a theatre, were in reality dirty and shabby, with bits of paper, dented, empty tins and rubbish lying about; and the vegetation of the south was represented by greyish black evergreen, naked, prickly shrubs, and yellow, faded rushes.

On this sunny morning he understood suddenly that even such a sight holds beauty for those who can see.

Jenny Winge took the road between garden walls at the back of the church. The walls were covered with ivy, and pines rose behind them. She stopped to light a cigarette.

"I am a pronounced smoker, you see," she said, "but I have to refrain when I am with Cesca, for her heart does not stand it; out here I smoke like a steam-engine. Here we are."

A small, yellow house stood inside a fence; in the garden were tables and forms under big, bare elms, and a summer-house made of rush stalks. Jenny greeted the old woman who came out on the doorstep.

"Well, Mr. Gram, what do you say to breakfast?"

"Not a bad idea. A cup of strong coffee and a roll and butter."

"Coffee! and butter! Listen to him! No, eggs and bread and wine, lettuce and perhaps some cheese. Yes, she says she has cheese. How many eggs do you want?"

While the woman laid the table Miss Winge carried her easel and painting accessories into the garden, and changed her long, blue evening wrap for a short coat, which was soiled with paint.

"May I have a look at your picture?" asked Helge.

"Yes _ — I am going to tone down that green — - it is rather hard. There is really no light in it yet, but the background is good, I think."

Helge looked at the painting; the trees looked like big grease splashes. He could see nothing in it.

"Here's breakfast coming. We'll throw the eggs at her if they are hard. Hurrah, they aren't!"

Helge was not hungry. The sour white wine gave him heartburn, and he could scarcely swallow the dry, unsalted bread, but Jenny bit off great chunks with her white teeth, put small pieces of Parmesan in her mouth, and drank wine. The three eggs were already done with.

"How can you eat that nasty bread without butter?" said Helge.

"I like it. I have not tasted butter since I left Christiania. Cesca and I buy it only when we are having a party. We have to live very economically, you see."

He laughed, saying: "What do you call economy — beads and corals?"

"No; it is luxury, but I think it is very essential — a little of it. We live cheaply and we eat cheaply, tea and dry bread and radishes twice or three times a week for supper — and we buy silk scarves."

She had finished eating, lit a cigarette, and sat looking in front of her, with her chin resting on her hand:

"To starve, you see, Mr. Gram — of course I have not tried it yet, but I may have to. Heggen has, and he thinks as I do — to starve or to have too little of the necessary is better than never to have any of the superfluous. The superfluous is the very thing we work and long for. At home, with my mother, we always had the strictly necessary, but everything beyond it was not to be thought of. It had to be — the children had to be fed before anything else."

"I cannot think of you as ever having been troubled about money." "Why not?" "Because you are so courageous and independent, and you have such decided opinions about everything. When you grow up in circumstances where it is a constant struggle to make ends meet, and you are always reminded of it, you sort of dare not form any opinions — in a general way — it is so tantalizing to know that the coins decide what you can afford to wish or to want."

Jenny nodded pensively. "Yes, but one must not feel like that when one has health and youth and knowledge."

"Well, take my case, for instance. I have always believed that I have some aptitude for scientific work, and it is the only thing I would like to do. I have written a few books — popular ones, you know — and I am now working at an essay on the Bronze Age in South Europe. But I am a teacher, and have a fairly good position — that of a superintendent of a private school."

"You have come out here to work, to study — I remember you said so this morning." He did not answer, but continued: "It was the same thing with my father. He wanted to be an artist — wanted it more than anything else, and he came out here for a year. Then he married, and is now the owner of a lithographic press, which he has kept going for twenty-six years under great difficulties. I don't believe my father thinks he has got much out of life."

Jenny Winge sat as before, looking thoughtfully in front of her. In the orchard below grew rows of vegetables, small innocent tufts of green on the grey soil, and on the far side of the meadow one could see the yellow masses of ruins on the Palatine against the dark foliage. The day promised to be warm. The Alban mountains in the distance, beyond the pines of the villa gardens, looked misty against the soft blue of the sky.

Jenny drank some wine, still looking straight ahead. Helge followed with his eyes the smoke of her cigarette — a faint morning breeze carried it out in the sunshine. She sat with her legs crossed. She had small ankles, and her feet were clad in thin purple stockings and bead-embroidered evening shoes. The jacket was open over the gathered silver-grey dress with the white collar and the beads, which threw pink spots on her milky-white neck. The fur cap had slid back from her fair, fluffy hair.

"I suppose you have the support of your father, though, Mr. Gram — I mean, he understands you, doesn't he? Surely he sees that you can't get ahead so quickly at that school, when you have quite different work at heart?"

"I don't know. He was very pleased that I could go abroad, of course, but" — after some hesitation — "I have never been very intimate with my father. And then there is mother. She was anxious lest I should work too hard, or be short of money — or risk my future. Father and mother are so different — she has never quite understood him, and kept more to us children. She was a great deal to me when I was a boy, but she was jealous of father even — that he should have greater influence over me than she had. She was jealous of my work too, when I locked myself up in a room of an evening to read, and always anxious about my health and afraid I should give up my post."

Jenny nodded several times thoughtfully.

"The letter I fetched at the post office was from them." He took it out of his pocket and looked at it, but he did not open it. "It is my birthday today," he said, trying to smile. "I am twenty-six."

"Many happy returns." Miss Winge shook hands with him. She looked at him almost in the same way as she looked at Miss Jahrman when she nestled in her arms.

She had not noticed before what he looked like, though she was under the impression that he was tall and thin and dark. He had good, regular features on the whole, a high, somewhat narrow forehead, light brown eyes with a peculiar amber-like transparency, and a small, weak mouth with a tired and sad expression under the moustache.

"I understand you so well," she said suddenly. "I know all that. I was a teacher myself until Christmas last year. I started as a governess and went on till I was old enough to enter the seminary." She smiled a little shyly. "I gave up my post in the school when I was left a small amount of money by an aunt, and went abroad. It will last me about three years, I think — perhaps a little longer. Lately I have sent some articles to the papers, and I may sell some pictures. My mother did not approve of my using up all the money, and did not like my giving up my post when I had got it at last after all those years of private teaching and odd lessons here and there at schools. I suppose mothers always think a fixed salary. . . ."

"I don't think I would have risked it in your place — burning all your bridges like that. It is the influence of my home, I know, but I could not help being anxious about the time when the money would be spent."

"Never mind," said Jenny Winge. "I am well and strong and know a lot; I can sew and cook and wash and iron. And I know languages. I can always find something to do in

England or America. Francesca," she said, laughing, "wants me to go to South Africa with her and be a dairy-maid, for that is a thing she is good at, she says. And we shall draw the Zulus; they are said to be such splendid models."

"That is no small job either — and the distance does not seem to trouble you."

"Not a bit — I am talking nonsense, of course. All those years I thought it impossible to get away, even as far as Copenhagen, to stay there some time to paint and learn. When at last I made up my mind to give up everything and go, I had many a bad moment, I can assure you. My people thought it madness, and I noticed that it made an impression on me, but that made me more determined still. To paint has always been my most ardent wish, and I knew I could never work at home as hard as I ought to; there were too many things to distract me. But mother could not see that I was so old that if I wanted to learn something I must start at once. She is only nineteen years older than I; when I was eleven she married again, and that made her younger still.

"The curious thing when you leave home is that the influence of the people with whom you accidentally have lived is broken. You learn to see with your own eyes and to think for yourself, and you understand that it rests with yourself to get something good out of your journey: what you mean to see and to learn, how you mean to arrange your life and what influence you choose to submit to. You learn to understand that what you will get out of life as a whole depends on yourself. Circumstances count for something, of course, as you said, but you learn how to avoid obstacles or surmount them in the way that comes easiest to your individuality, and most of the disagreeable things that happen to you are of your own doing. You are never alone in your home, don't you think?

The greatest advantage of traveling seems to me that you are alone, without any one to help or advise you. You cannot appreciate all you owe to your home, or be grateful for it, until you are away from it, and you know that you will never be dependent on it any more, since you are your own master. You cannot really love it till then — for how could you love anything that you are dependent on?"

"I don't know. Are we not always dependent on what we love? — you and your work, for instance. And when once you get really fond of people," he said quietly, "you make yourself dependent on them for good and all."

"Ye — s" — she reflected a moment, then said suddenly, "but it is your own choice. You are not a slave; you serve willingly something or somebody that you prize higher than yourself. Are you not glad you can begin the new year alone, entirely free, and only do the work you like?"

Helge remembered the previous evening in the piazza San Pietro; he looked at the city, the soft veiled colorings of it in the sun, and he looked at the fair young girl beside him.

"Yes," he said.

"Well" — she rose, buttoned her jacket, and opened the paint-box — "I must work now."

"And I suppose you would like to get rid of me?" Jenny smiled. "I daresay you are tired too."

"Not very — I must pay the bill."

She called the woman and helped him, squeezing out colors on to her palette meanwhile.

"Do you think you can find your way back to town?"

"Yes; I remember exactly how we came, and I shall soon find a cab, I suppose. Do you ever go to the club?"

"Yes, sometimes."
"I should like very much to meet you again."

"I daresay you will" — and after a moment's hesitation:

"Come and see us one day, if you care, and have tea. Via Vantaggio!. Cesca and I are generally at home in the afternoon."

"Thanks, I should like to very much. Good-bye, then, and thanks so much." She gave him her hand: "The same to you."

At the gate he looked back; she was scraping her canvas with a palette knife and humming the song they had heard in the café. He remembered the tune, and began to hum it himself as he walked away.

IV

JENNY brought her arms out from under the blanket and put them behind her neck. It was icy cold in the room, and dark. No ray of light came through the shutters. She struck a match and looked at her watch — it was nearly seven. She could doze a little longer, and she crept down under the blankets again, with her head deep in the pillow.

"Jenny, are you asleep?" Francesca opened the door without knocking, and came close to the bed. She felt for her friend's face in the dark and stroked it. "Tired?"

"No. I am going to get up now." "When did you come home?"

"About three o'clock. I went to Prati for a bath before lunch and ate at the Ripetta, you know, and when I came home I went to bed at once. I am thoroughly rested. I'll get up now."

"Wait a moment. It's very cold; let me light the fire." Francesca lighted the lamp on the table.

"Why not call the signora? Oh, Cesca, come here, let me look at you." Jenny sat up in bed.

Francesca placed the lamp on the table by the bed and turned slowly round in the light of it. She had put on a white blouse with her green skirt and thrown a striped scarf about her shoulders. Round her neck she wore a double row of deep red corals, and long, polished drops hung from her ears. She pulled her hair laughingly from her ears to show that the drops were tied to them by means of darning wool.

"Fancy, I got them for sixty-eight lire — a bargain, wasn't it? Do you think they suit me?" "Capitally! With that costume, too. I should like to paint you as you are now."

"Yes, do. I can sit to you if you like — I'm too restless nowadays to work. Oh dear!" She sighed and sat down on the bed. "I had better go and bring the coal."

She came back carrying an earthenware pot of burning charcoal, and stooped down over the little stove. "Stay in bed, dear, till it gets a little warmer in here. I will make the tea and lay the table. I see you have brought your drawing home. Let me have a look at it." She placed the board against a chair and held the lamp to it.

"I say! I say!"

"It is not too bad — what do you think? I am going to make a few more sketches out there. I am planning a big picture, you see — don't you think it is a good subject, with all the working people and the mule-carts in the excavation field?"

"Very good. I am sure you can make something of it. I should like to show it to Gunnar and Ahlin. Oh, you are up! Let me do your hair. What a mass of it you have, child. May I do it in the new fashion? — with curls, you know." Francesca pulled her fingers through her friend's long, fair hair.

"Sit quite still. There was a letter for you this morning. I brought it up. Did you find it? It was from your little brother, was it not?"

"Yes," said Jenny.

"Was it nice? — were you pleased?"

"Yes, very nice. You know, Cesca, sometimes — only on a Sunday morning once in a while — I wish I could fly home and go for a stroll in Nordmarken with Kalfatrus. He is such a brick, that boy."

Francesca looked at Jenny's smiling face in the glass. She took down her hair and began to brush it again.

"No, Cesca; there is no time for it."

"Oh yes. If they come too early they can go into my room. It is in a terrible state — a regular pigsty — but never mind.

They won't come so early — not Gunnar, and I don't mind him if he does, and not Ahlin either for that matter. He has already been to see me this morning; I was in bed, and he sat and talked. I sent him out on to the balcony while I dressed, and then we went out and had a good meal at Tre Re. We have been together the whole afternoon."

Jenny said nothing.

"We saw Gram at Nazionale. Isn't he awful? Have you ever seen anything like it?"

"I don't think he is bad at all. He is awkward, poor boy, exactly as I was at first. He is one of those people who would like to enjoy themselves, but don't know how to."

"I came from Florence this morning," said Francesca, imitating him, and laughed. "Ugh! If he had come by aeroplane at least."

"You were exceedingly rude to him, my dear. It won't do. I should have liked to ask him here tonight, but I dared not because of you. I could not take the risk of your being discourteous to him when he was our guest."

"No fear of that. You know that quite well." Francesca was hurt.

"Do you remember that time when Douglas came home with me to tea?" "Yes, after that model business, but that was quite a different matter." "Nonsense. It was no concern of yours."

"Wasn't it? When he had proposed to me and I had very nearly accepted him." "How could he know?" said Jenny.
"Anyway, I had not quite said no, and the day before I had been with him to Versailles. He kissed me there several times and lay with his head in my lap, and when I told him I didn't care for him he didn't believe me."

"It is not right, Cesca." Jenny caught her eye in the mirror.

"You are the dearest little girl in the world when you use your brains, but sometimes it seems as if you had no idea you are dealing with living beings, with people who have feelings that you must respect. You 'would respect them if you were not so thoughtless, for I know you only want to be good and kind."

"Per Bacco. Don't be too sure of that. But I must show you some roses. Ahlin bought me quite a load this afternoon at a Spanish stairs." Cesca smiled defiantly.

"You ought to stop that kind of thing, I think — if only because you know he cannot afford it."

"I don't care. If he is in love with me, I suppose he likes it." "I won't talk of reputation after all these doings of yours."
"No, better not speak about my reputation. You are quite right there. At home, in Christiania, I have spoilt my reputation past mending, once and for all." She laughed hysterically. "Damn it all! I don't care."

"I don't understand you, Cesca darling. You don't care for any of those men. Why do you want. . . . And as to Ahlin, can't you see he is in earnest? Norman Douglas, too, was in earnest. You don't know what you are doing. I really do believe, child, that you've no instincts at all."

Francesca put away brush and comb and looked at Jenny's hairdressing in the glass. She tried to retain her defiant little smile, but it faded away and her eyes filled with tears.

"I had a letter this morning, too." Her voice trembled. "From Berlin, from Borghild." Jenny rose from the dressing- table. "Yes, perhaps you had better get ready. Will you put the kettle on, or do you think we'd better cook the artichokes first?" She began to make the bed. "We might call Marietta — but don't you think we had better do it ourselves?" "Borghild writes that Hans Hermann was married last week. His wife is already expecting a child."

Jenny put the matchbox on the table. She glanced at Francesca's miserable little face and then went quietly up to her.

"It is that singer, Berit Eck, you know, he was engaged to." Francesca spoke in a faint voice, leaning for an instant against her friend, and then began to arrange the sheets with trembling hands.

"But you knew they were engaged — more than a year ago."

"Yes — let me do that, Jenny; you lay the table. I know, of course, that you knew all about it."

Jenny laid the table for four. Francesca put the counterpane on the bed and brought the roses. She stood fumbling with her blouse, then pulled out a letter from inside it and twisted it between her fingers.

"She met them at the Thiergarten — she writes. She says — oh, she can be brutal sometimes, Borghild." Francesca went quickly across the room, pulled open the door of the stove, and threw the letter in. Then she sank down in an arm-chair and burst into tears.

Jenny went to her and put one arm round her neck. "Cesca, dearest little Cesca!"

Francesca pressed her face against Jenny's arm:

"She looked so miserable, poor thing. She hung on his arm, and he seemed sullen and angry. I can quite imagine it. I am sorry for her — fancy allowing herself to become dependent on him in such a way. He has brought her to her knees, I am sure. How could she be such an idiot, when she knew him? Oh, but think of it, Jenny! He is going to have a child by somebody else — oh, my God! my God!"

Jenny sat on the arm of the chair. Cesca nestled close to her: "I suppose you are right — I have no instincts. Perhaps I never loved him really, but I should have liked to have a child by him. And yet I could not make up my mind. Sometimes he wanted me to marry him straight off, go to the registry office, but I wouldn't. They would have been so angry with me at home, and people would have said we were obliged to marry, if we had done it that way. I did not want that either, although I knew they thought the worst of me all the same, but that did not worry me. I knew I was ruining my reputation for his sake, but I did not care, and I don't care now, I tell you.

"But he thought I refused because I was afraid he would not marry me afterwards. 'Let's go to the registry office first, then, you silly girl,' he said, but I would not go. He thought it was all sham. 'You cold!' he said; 'you are not cold any longer than you choose to be.' Sometimes I almost thought I wasn't. Perhaps it was only fright, for he was such a brute; he beat me sometimes — nearly tore the clothes off me. I had to scratch and bite to protect myself — and cry and scream."

"And yet you went back to him?" said Jenny.

"I did, that is true. The porter's wife did not want to do his rooms any longer, so I went and tidied up for him. I had a key. I scrubbed the floor and made his bed — Heaven only knows who had been in it."

Jenny shook her head.

"Borghild was furious about it. She proved to me that he had a mistress. I knew it, but I did not want proof. Borghild said he had given me the key, because he wanted me to take them by surprise, and make me jealous, so that I should give in, as I was compromised anyway. But she was not right, for it was me he loved — in his way — I know he loved me as much as he could love anybody.

"Borghild was angry with me because I pawned the diamond ring I had from our grandmother. I have never told you about it. Hans said he had to have money — a hundred kroner — and I promised to get it. Where I didn't know. I dared not write to father, for I'd spent more than my allowance already, so I went and pawned my watch and a chain bracelet and that ring — one of those old ones, you know, with a lot of little diamonds on a big shield. Borghild was angry because it had not been given to her, being the eldest, but grandmother had said I should have it, as I was named after her. I went down one morning as soon as they opened; it was hateful, but I got the money and I took it to Hans. He asked where I had got it from, and I told him.

Then he kissed me and said: "Give me the ticket and the money, puss ' — that is what he used to call me — - and I did. I thought he meant to redeem it, and said he need not. I was very much moved, you see. 'I will settle it in another way,' said Hans, and went out. I stayed in his rooms and waited. I was very excited, for I knew he wanted the money, and I decided to go and pawn the things again the next day. It would not be so horrid a second time — nothing more would be difficult. I would give him everything now. Then he came — and what do you think he had done?" She laughed amidst the tears. "He had redeemed the things from the loan-office and pawned them with his private banker, as he called him, who gave more for them.

"We went about all day together — champagne and all the rest of it — and I went home with him at night. He played to me — my God, how he played! I lay on the floor and cried. Nothing mattered as long as he played like that, and to me alone. You have not heard him play; if you had, you would understand me. But afterwards it was awful. We fought like mad, but I got away at last. Borghild was awake when I came home. My dress was torn to tatters. 'You look like a street-girl,' she said. I laughed. It was five o'clock.

"I should have given in in the end, you know, if it hadn't been for one thing he had said. Sometimes he used to say: 'You are the only decent girl I have met. There is not a man who could get round you. I respect you, puss.' Fancy, he respected me for refusing to do what he begged and worried me about constantly. I wanted to give in, for I would have done anything to please him, but I could not get over my scare; he was so brutal, and I knew there were others. If only he had not frightened me so many times, I might have given up the struggle but then, of course, I should have lost his respect. That is why I broke with him at last — for wanting me to act in such a way that he would despise me."

She nestled close to Jenny, who caressed her. "Do you love me a little, Jenny?"

"You know I do, darling child."

"You are so kind. Kiss me once more! Gunnar is kind, too — and Ahlin. I shall be more careful. I don't wish him any harm. Besides, I may marry him, as he is so fond of me. Ahlin would never be brutal — I know that. Do you think he would worry me? Not much. And I might have children. Some day I will come into money, and he is so poor. We could live abroad and we could both work. There is something refined about all his work, don't you think? That relief of the boys playing, for instance, and the cast for the Almquist monument. Not very original, perhaps, in composition, but so beautiful, so noble and restful, and the figures so perfectly plastic."

Jenny smiled a little and stroked the hair from Francesca's forehead; it was wet with tears.

"I wish I could work like that — always — but I have those eternal pains in my heart and my head. My eyes hurt me too, and I am dead tired always."

"You know what your doctor says — only nerves — every bit of it. If you only would be sensible!"

"I know. That is what they all say, but I am afraid. You say that I have no instincts — not in the way you mean, but I have them all right in another way. I have been a devil all this week — I know it perfectly well — but I have been waiting all the time for something awful I knew was going to happen. You see, I was right."

Jenny kissed her again.

"I was down at S. Agostino tonight. You know that image of the Madonna that works miracles; I knelt before it and prayed to the Virgin. I think I should be happier if I turned Catholic. A woman like the Virgin Mary Avould understand. I ought really never to marry. I ought to go into a convent — Siena, for instance. I might paint copies in the gallery and earn some money for the convent. When I copied that angel for Melozzo da Forli in Florence there was a nun painting every day. It wasn't so bad." She laughed. "I mean, it was awful. I hated it. But they all said my copies were so good — and so they were. I believe I should be happy in that way. Oh, Jenny, if I only felt well and were at peace in my mind, but I am so bewildered and frightened. If I were well, I could work, work — always. And I'd be so good and nice — you don't know how good I could be. I know I am not always good. I give in to every mood when I feel as I do at present. I am going to stop it, if only you will love me, all of you, but you especially. Let us ask that Gram here. Next time I see him I'll be so nice and sweet to him, you see. We'll ask him here and take him out, and I will do anything to amuse him. Do you hear, Jenny? Are you pleased with me now?"

"Yes, Cesca dear."

"Gunnar does not think I can be serious," she said pensively.

"Oh yes, he does; he only thinks you are very childish. You know what he thinks of your work. Don't you remember what he said in Paris about your energy and your talent? Great and original, he said. He did not think lightly of you that time."

"Gunnar is a nice boy, but he was angry with me because of Douglas." "Any man would have been angry with you. I was, too."

Francesca sighed and sat quiet an instant. "How did you get rid of Gram? I thought you would never be able to shake that fellow off. I thought that he would come home with you and sleep here on the sofa."

Jenny laughed. "Oh no! He went with me to the Aventine and had breakfast; then he went home. I rather like him, you know."

"Dio mio! Jenny, you are abnormally good. Have you not got enough to mother already, with us? Or have you fallen in love with him?"

Jenny laughed again. "I don't think there is much chance for me. I suppose he will fall in love with you, like the rest, if you are not careful."

"They all do, it seems — Heaven only knows why. But they soon get cured, and then they're angry with me afterwards." She sighed.

They heard steps on the stairs.

"That is Gunnar. I am going into my room a little. I must bathe my eyes."

She passed Heggen in the door with a short greeting as she hurried away. He shut the door and came into the room.

"You are all right, I see — but so you always are. You are an extraordinary girl, Jenny. I suppose you have been working all the morning — and she?" He pointed towards Cesca's room.

"In a bad state, poor little thing."

"I saw it in the papers when I looked in at the club. Have you finished the study? Show me. It is very good." Heggen held the picture to the light and looked at it for some time. "This part stands out beautifully. It is powerful work. Is she lying on her bed crying, do you think?"

"I don't know. She has been crying in here. She had a letter from her sister."

"If ever I meet that cad," said Hebben, "I shall find some pretext to give him a sound thrashing."

V

O NE afternoon Helge Gram sat in the club reading Norwegian newspapers. He was alone in the reading-room when Miss Jahrman entered. He stood up and bowed, but she came up to him with a smile and shook hands: "How are you getting on? Jenny and I have been wondering why we never see you; we were determined to come here on Saturday to see if we could find you and ask you to go out with us somewhere. Have you got rooms yet?"

"No, I am sorry to say. I am still at the hotel. All the rooms I have seen are so expensive."

"But it is not cheaper at the hotel, is it? I suppose you have to pay three lire a day at least? I thought so. It is not cheap in Rome, you know. You must have rooms to the south in winter. You don't speak Italian, of course, but why did you not ask us to help you? Jenny or I would willingly have gone with you to look for rooms."

"Thank you very much. I would not dream of troubling you about that."

"It is no trouble whatever. How are you getting on? Have you met any people?"

"No. I came here on Saturday, but I did not speak to anybody. I read the papers. The day before yesterday I saw Heggen in a café on the Corso and exchanged a few words with him. I have also met two German doctors I knew in Florence, and I went with them to Via Appi one day."

"Ugh! German doctors are not nice, are they?" Helge smiled, embarrassed.

"Perhaps not, but we have some interests in common, and when one goes about without having anybody to talk to. . . ."

"Yes, but you must make up your mind to speak Italian; you know the language, don't you? Come for a walk with me and we will talk Italian all the way. I shall be a very strict maestra, you will see."

"Thank you very much, Miss Jahrman, but I am afraid you will not find me very entertaining — except unwittingly perhaps."

"Rubbish! Look here, I've got an idea! Two old Danish ladies left for Capri the day before yesterday. Their room may be vacant still. I am sure it is. A nice little room and cheap. I don't remember the name of the street, but I know where it is. Shall I go with you and have a look at it? Come along."

41

On the stairs she turned round and smiled awkwardly at him:

"I was awfully rude to you the other evening, Mr. Gram. Please accept my apologies."
"My dear Miss Jahrman!"
"I was out of sorts that day. You cannot imagine what a scolding I got from Jenny, but I deserved it."

"Not at all. I was to blame for forcing my company upon you, but it was so tempting to speak to you when I saw you and heard that you were Norwegians."
"Of course, an adventure like that could be great fun, but I spoilt it with my bad temper. I was ill, you see. My nerves worry me; I can't sleep and I can't work, and then I get horrid sometimes."

"Are you feeling better now?"

"Not really. Jenny and Gunnar are working — everybody works but myself. Is your work getting on all right? Aren't you pleased? Every afternoon I sit to Jenny for my picture. I am having a day off today. I think she does it only to prevent me from being alone with my thoughts. Sometimes she takes me for a ride outside the walls. She is like a mother to me — Mia cara mammina."

"You are very fond of your friend?"

"I should think so! She is so good to me. I am delicate and spoilt, and nobody but Jenny could stand me in the long run. She is so clever too, intelligent and energetic. And pretty — don't you think she is lovely? You should see her hair when it is let down! When I am good she lets me do it for her. Here we are," she said.

They mounted a pitch-dark staircase.

"You mustn't mind the stairs; ours are still worse: you will see for yourself when you pay us a visit. Come one evening. We'll get hold of the others and all go for a proper rag. I spoilt the last one for you."

She rang a bell on the top floor. The woman who opened the door looked nice and tidy. She showed them a room with two beds. It looked out over a grey backyard with washing hanging in the windows, but there were plants on the balconies; loggias and terraces with green shrubs rose above the grey roofs.

Francesca went on talking to the woman while she examined the beds and looked into the stove, and explained things to Helge:

"There's sun here all the morning. When one bed's moved out, the room will look bigger;

and the stove is all right. The price is forty lire without light and fire, and two for servizio. It is cheap. Shall I say you take it? You can move in tomorrow, if you like."

"Don't thank me. I just loved to help you," she said, as they walked down the stairs. "I hope you will like it. Signora Papi is very clean, I know." "It is not a common virtue here, I suppose?"
"No, indeed. But I don't think the people who let rooms in Christiania are much better. My sister and I lived once in rooms in Holbergsgate and I had a pair of patent leather shoes under the bed, but I never dared to take them out. Sometimes I peeped at them under the bed; they looked like two little white woolly lambs."

"I have no experience in that way. I have always lived at home."

Francesca burst out laughing all of a sudden. "The signora thought I was your moglie, do you know, and that we were going to live there together. I said I was your cousin, but she did not catch on. Cugina — it is not an accepted relationship anywhere in the world, it seems."

Both laughed.

"Would you care to go for a walk?" asked Miss Jahrman suddenly. "Shall we go to Ponte Molle? Have you been there? Is it too far? We can come back by tram."
"Is it not too far for you? You're not well."

"It does me good to walk. ' You must walk more,' says Gunnar always — Mr. Heggen, you know."

She chatted all the time, looking at him now and again to see if he was amused. They took the new road along by the Tiber; the yellow-grey river rolled between the green slopes. Small, pearl-tinted clouds sailed over the dark shrubbery of Monte Mario and the blocks of villas between the evergreen trees.

Francesca nodded to a policeman and said laughingly to Gram:

"Do you know, that man has proposed to me. I used to walk here very often alone, and sometimes I spoke to him, and one day he proposed. The son of our tobacconist has also proposed to me. Jenny says it was my own fault, and I suppose it was."

"Miss Winge seems to scold you very often. She is a strict mamma, I can see."

"No, she isn't. She only scolds me when I need scolding: I wish somebody had done it long before." She sighed. "But nobody ever did."

43

Helge Gram felt quite free and easy in her company. There was something very soft about her — her lissom gait, her voice, and her face under the big mushroom hat. He did not quite like Jenny Winge when he thought of her now; she had such determined grey eyes and such an enormous appetite. Cesca had just told him that she herself could hardly eat anything at present.

"Miss Winge is a very determined young lady, I should think," he said.

"No doubt about that! She has a very strong character; she has always been wanting to paint, but she had to go on teaching, teaching! She has had a hard time, poor Jenny. You would not believe it when you see her now. She is so strong, she never gives in. When I first met her at the art school I thought she was very reserved, almost hard — armour-plated, Gunnar called it. She was very retiring; I did not know her really till we came out here. Her mother is a widow for the second time — she is a Mrs. Berner — and there are three more children. They had only three small rooms, imagine, and Jenny had to live in a tiny servant's room, work and study to complete her education, besides helping her mother in the house and with money as well. They could not afford a servant. She knew nobody and had no friends. She shuts herself up, as it were, when things go badly, and does not want to complain, but when she is in luck she opens her arms to everyonethat needs comfort and support."

Francesca's cheeks were burning. She looked at him with her big eyes.

"All the bad luck I have had has been my own doing. I am a bit hysterical, and give way to all sorts of moods. Jenny gives me a talking-to; she says that if anything irreparable happens to you it is always your own fault, and if you cannot train your will to master your moods and impulses and so on, and have not complete control of yourself, you might as well commit suicide at once."

Helge smiled at her. "Jenny says," and "Gunnar says," and "I had a friend who used to say." How young and trusting she seemed!

"Don't you think it possible that Miss Winge's principles might not apply to you? You are so different, you two. No two people have the same views on life itself even."

"No," she said quietly. "But I am so fond of Jenny. I need her so."
They came to the bridge. Francesca bent over the railing. Farther up the river there was a factory; its tall chimney stood reflected in the swift yellow water. Behind the undulating plain, far away, lay the Sabine mountains, mud-grey and bare, and behind them, farther still, rose snowclad peaks.

"Jenny has painted this with strong evening light on it. The factory and the chimney are quite red. It was on a hot day, when you cannot see the mountains for mist, but only a few white snow-peaks in the heavy metallic blue of the sky, and the clouds above the snow. It is very pretty. I must ask her to show it to you."

"Shall we have some wine here?" he asked.

"It'll soon be getting cold, but we might sit down a little." She led the way across the round piazza behind the bridge. She chose an osteria with a small garden. Behind a shed with chairs and tables stood a seat under some bare elms. At the back of the garden was a meadow, and on the opposite side of the river the slope appeared dark against the limpid sky. Francesca broke a twig from an elder that grew by the fence; it had small green shoots, with tops blackened by the cold.

"All the winter they stand like that, shivering with cold, but when spring comes they have not been harmed."

When she dropped the twig he picked it up and kept it. They had white wine. Francesca mixed hers with water, and hardly drank any of it. She smiled imploringly:

"Will you give me a cigarette?"

"With pleasure, if you think you can stand it."

"I scarcely ever smoke now. Jenny has almost given it up for my sake. I suppose she is making up for it tonight, though. She is with Gunnar." She laughed. "You must not tell Jenny that I smoked, promise me."

"I won't," he said, laughing too.

She smoked in silence for a while: "I wish she and Gunnar would marry, but I am afraid they won't. They have always been such friends. You don't easily fall in love with a friend, do you? One you knew so well before. They are very much alike in character, and it is just the contrast that attracts you, people say. It is stupid it should be so, I think, for it would be much better to fall in love with somebody akin to you, as it were; it would save all the misery and disappointment, don't you think?

"Gunnar's home is a small farm in the country. He came to Christiania, to an aunt, who took care of him, because they were so poor at home. He was only nine then, and had to carry the washing; his aunt kept a laundry. Later he got into a factory. He's taught himself all he knows by sheer hard work. He reads a lot; he takes an interest in everything, and wants to get to the bottom of it. Jenny says he even forgets to paint. He has learnt Italian thoroughly; he can read any book — poetry, too.

45

"Jenny is the same. She has learnt heaps because it interested her. I can never learn out of books; reading always give me a headache. But when Jenny or Gunnar tell me things, I remember them. You are very clever too; do tell me about the things you are studying. There is nothing I love more, and I store it in my memory.

"Gunnar has taught me- to paint too. I always loved to draw; it came naturally. Three years ago I met him in the mountains at home. I had gone there to sketch. I made very nice pictures, quite correct, but not an ounce of art in them. I could see it myself, but I could not understand the reason why. I saw there was something missing in my pictures — something I wanted to put into them — but did not quite know what it was, and had not the least idea how to get it there.

"I spoke to him about it, showed him my tilings. He knew less than I about technique — he is only a year older than I — but he could make better use of what he had learnt. Then I made two pictures of a summer night in that wonderful chiaro-scuro, where all the colors are so deep and yet with such a strong light. They were not good, of course, but they had something of what I had wanted. I could see they were done by me and not by any little girl who had just learnt something about drawing. You see what I mean?

"I've a subject out here — on the other way to the city. We'll go there another time. It is a road between two vine- yards — quite a narrow one. In one place there are two baroque gates with iron gratings, each of them with a cypress beside it. I have made a couple of coloured drawings. There is a heavy dark blue sky above the cypresses and clearness of green air, and a star, and a faint outline of houses and cupolas in the distant city. I wanted the picture to be sort of stirring, you see."

Twilight began to fall upon them. Her face looked pale under the brim of her hat. "Don't you think I ought to get well, and be allowed to work?"
"Yes," he said in a low voice; "dear. . . ."

He could hear that she was breathing heavily. They were both quiet for a moment, then he said :

"You are very fond of your friends, Miss Jahrman?"

"I want to like everybody, you see," she said quietly, taking a long breath.

Helge Gram bent suddenly forward and kissed her hand, which rested white and small on the table.

"Thank you," said Francesca in a low voice, and after a short pause: "Let us go back now; it is getting cold."

The next day when he moved into his new room a majolica vase with small blue iris was standing in the sunlight on his table. The signora explained that his "cousin" had brought them. When Helge was alone he bent over the flowers and kissed them one by one.

VI

H ELGE GRAM liked his lodgings by the Ripetta. It seemed easy to do good work at the little table by the window that looked out on the yard with washing and flower-pots on the balconies. The people opposite had two children — a boy and a girl about six and seven. When they came out on their balcony they nodded and waved to him, and he waved back. Lately he had taken to greeting their mother too, and his nodding acquaintance with these people made him feel more at home in the place. Cesca's vase stood in front of him; he kept it always filled with fresh flowers. Signora Papi was quick at understanding his Italian. It was because she had had Danish lodgers, Cesca said — Danes can never learn foreign languages.

Whenever some errand brought the signora to his room she always stayed a long while chatting by the door. Mostly about his cousin, "che bella," said Signora Papi. Once Miss Jahrman had paid him a visit alone and once she came with Miss Winge, each time to invite him to tea. When Signora Papi at last discovered that she prevented him from working, she broke off the conversation and left. Helge leaned back in his chair, resting his neck on his folded hands. He thought of his room at home, beside the kitchen, where he could hear his mother and sister talking about him, being anxious about him or disapproving of him. He heard every word, as probably they meant him to do. Every day out here was a precious gift. He had peace at last and could work, work.

He spent the afternoons in libraries and museums. As often as he could do so without inflicting his company too much upon them, he went to late tea with the two girl artists at Via Vantaggio. As a rule they were both in; sometimes there were other visitors. Heggen and Ahlin were nearly always there.

Twice he found Miss Winge alone, and once Francesca. They were always in Jenny's room, which was cosy and warm, although the windows stood wide open until the last rays of light had faded. The stove glowed and sparkled, and the kettle on the spirit-lamp was singing. He knew every article in the room now — the drawings and photographs on the walls, the flower vases, the blue tea-set, the bookshelf by the bed, and the easel with Francesca's portrait. The room was always a little untidy; the table by the window was littered with tubes and paint-boxes, sketch-books and sheets of drawing-paper; Jenny kicked brushes and painting rags under it as she was laying the tea. There was often a litter of needlework or half-darned stockings on the sofa to be put away before sitting down to butter the biscuits. A spirit-lamp and toilet trifles were frequently left lying about and had to be removed.

While these preparations were going on, Gram would sit by the stove and talk to Francesca, but sometimes Cesca would take it into her head to be domesticated and let Jenny be lazy. Jenny begged to be spared, but Cesca hustled about like a whirlwind, putting all the stray articles where Jenny could not find them afterwards, and ended up by putting drawing-pins into pictures that would not hang straight, or curled themselves on the wall, using her shoe as a hammer.

Gram could not understand Miss Jahrman at all. She was always nice and friendly to him, but never as intimate and confidential as on the day they had walked to Ponte Molle.Sometimes she was strangely absent; she seemed not to grasp what he said, although she answered kindly enough. Once or twice he thought he bored her. If he asked how she was, she hardly answered, and when he mentioned her picture with the cypresses she said sweetly: "You must not be offended, Mr. Gram, but I don't care to speak of my work before it is finished. Not now anyway."

He noticed that Ahlin did not like him, and this egged him on. The Swede, then, considered him a rival? He was under the impression that Francesca had of late been less friendly with Ahlin. When he was by himself Helge turned over in his mind what he was going to say to Francesca — in his imagination he held long conversations with her. He longed for a talk like the one they had that day at Ponte Molle; he wanted to tell her all about himself, but when he saw her he felt nervous and awkward. He did not know how to lead the conversation on to what he wanted to say, and he was afraid of being pressing or tactless; afraid to do anything that made her like him less. She noticed his embarrassment, and came to the rescue with chatter and laughter, and made it easy for him to joke and laugh with her. He was grateful for the moment; she filled the pauses with small talk and helped him along when he made a start, but when he came home and thought it all over, he was disappointed. Their conversation had again been about all sorts of amusing trifles, nothing more.

When he was alone with Jenny Winge they always talked seriously — about solid things, so to speak. Sometimes he was slightly bored with these discussions on abstract matters, but more often he liked to talk to her, because the conversation frequently turned from general matters to things concerning himself. Gradually he got into the way of telling her a great deal about himself — about his work, the difficulties he encountered in life and those in himself. He noticed that Jenny avoided talking about Francesca Jahrman with him, but not that she scarcely ever talked about herself.

It did not occur to him that the reason why he could not talk to Francesca as he talked to Jenny was that he wanted to appear far more important, confident, and strong to her than he really believed himself to be.

On Christmas Eve they all went to the club, and afterwards to the midnight mass at S. Luigi de Franchesi. Helge found it very impressive. The church was in semi-darkness, in spite of the lighted chandeliers ; they hung so high that their blaze of light was lost. The altar was one solitary wall of light from the flashing golden flames of hundreds of wax candles, and the subdued sound of the organ and the singing of the choir floated through the church. He sat beside a lovely young Italian woman, who took a rosary of lapis lazuli from a velvet case and prayed fervently. Gradually Francesca began to mutter more and more audibly. She was sitting beside Jenny in front of him.

"Let's go, Jenny. You don't think this gives you any sort of real Christmas feeling, do you? It's like an ordinary concert, and a bad one at that. Listen to that man singing now — absolutely no expression. His voice is absolutely done. Ugh!" "Hush, Cesca! Remember you are in church."
"Church! It's a concert, I tell you — didn't we have to get tickets and a program? I can't stand it. I shall lose my temper soon."

"We'll go after this if you like, but do keep quiet while we are here."

"New Year's night last year was quite different," said Francesca. "I went to Gesu. They had the Te Deum; it was very beautiful. I knelt beside an old peasant from the Campagna and a young girl; she looked ill — but oh, so pretty! Everybody sang; the old man knew the whole Te Deum by heart. It was very solemn."

As they made their way slowly down the crowded aisle, the Ave Maria sounded through the church.
"Ave Maria." Francesca sniffed. "Can't you hear how indifferent she is to what she sings — exactly like a gramophone? I cannot bear to hear that kind of music ill-treated."

"Ave Maria," said a Dane walking beside her — "I remember how beautifully it was sung by a young Norwegian lady — a Miss Eck."

"Berit Eck. Do you know her, Mr. Hjerrild?"

"She was in Copenhagen two years ago studying under Ellen Beck. I knew her quite well. Do you know her?"

"My sister knew her," said Francesca. "I think you met my sister Borghild in Berlin. Do you like Miss Eck — or Mrs. Hermann as she is now?"

"She was a very nice girl — and good-looking. Extraordinarily gifted, too, I think."
Francesca and Hjerrild lagged behind.
Heggen, Ahlin, and Gram were to accompany the ladies home and have supper.
Francesca had got a big parcel from home, and the table was laid with Norwegian Christmas fare, decorated with daisies from the Campagna and candles in seven-branched candlesticks.

Francesca came in last and brought the Dane with her. "Wasn't it nice, Jenny, of Mr. Hjerrild to come too?"

There were butter and cheese, cold game and brawn and ham on the table, as well as drinks for the men. Francesca sat by Hjerrild, and when the conversation became more animated and general she turned to speak to him.

"Do you know the pianist, Mr. Hermann, who married Miss Eck?"

"Yes; I know him very well. I lived at the same boarding-house with him in Copenhagen, and I saw him in Berlin on my way here."

"What do you think of him?"

"He is a handsome fellow, tremendously talented. He gave me some of his latest compositions — very original, I call them. I like him very much."

"Have you got them here? May I have a look at them? I should like to try them on the piano at the club. I knew him years ago," said Francesca.

"Oh yes. I remember now, he has a photo of you. He would not say who it was." Heggen's attention was drawn to their conversation.
"Yes," said Francesca inaudibly; "I think I gave him a photo once."

"All the same, he is too much of a bully for me," said Hjerrild, "unpardonably rude, but perhaps that is why he is irresistible to women. Rather too plebeian for my taste."

"That was exactly what . . ." — she searched for the right words — "what I admired in him was that he had made his way from the bottom of the ladder to where he now stands such a struggle must necessarily make one brutal, it seems to me. Don't you think that a great deal — almost anything — can be excused from that point of view?"

"Nonsense, Cesca," said Heggen suddenly. "Hans Hermann was discovered when he was thirteen, and has been helped along ever since."
"Yes, but to have to accept help always, to have to thank other people for everything and always be afraid of being ignored, neglected, reminded of being — as Hjerrild just said — of plebeian origin."

"I might say the same about myself — the last, I mean."

"No, you cannot, Gunnar. I'm sure you have always been superior to your surroundings. When you came among people of higher social standing than the one you were born to, you were superior even there. You were cleverer; you had greater knowledge and a finer mind. You could always feel strong in the consciousness of having done it all yourself. You were never obliged to thank people that you knew looked down upon you because of your low birth, who snobbishly sup- ported a talent which they did not understand, and who were inferior, though believing they stood above you. You did not have to thank people you could not feel grateful to. No, Gunnar, you cannot speak of the feelings of a man of the people, because you have never had them — you don't know what they are."

"A man who accepts the kind of help you speak of from people he cannot be grateful to is decidedly a plebeian, it seems to me."

"Oh, but can't you understand that one does such a thing when one knows one has talent — perhaps genius — that craves to be developed? It seems to me that you, who call yourself a democrat, should not speak like that about lower-class individuals."

"A man who respects his talent does not want to see it prostituted. As to being a democrat — social democracy is the craving for justice, and justice claims that men of his type should be subjugated, pressed down to the very bottom of the community, chained and forgotten. The real, legitimate lower class must be thoroughly subdued."

"A most peculiar socialism," laughed Hjerrild.

"There is no other for grown-up people. I don't take into account those blue-eyed, childish souls who believe that every- body is good and that all evil is the fault of the community. If everyonewere good, the community would be a paradise, but the vulgar souls spoil it. You find them in every grade of life. If they are masters, they are cruel and brutal; if they are servants, they are servile and cringing — and stupid. I have found them among the socialists too, for that matter — well, Hermann calls himself a socialist. If they find hands stretched out to lift them up, they grasp them — and stamp on them afterwards. If they see a troop marching past, they join it to get part of the booty, but loyalty and fellowship they have none. They laugh secretly at the aim, the ideal, and they hate justice, for they know that if it were to prevail they would come off badly.

"All those who are afraid of justice I call legitimately lower-class, and they should be fought without mercy. If they have any power with the poor and weak, they frighten and tyrannize them till they too become the same. If they are poor and weak themselves, they give up the struggle, and make their way by begging and flattering — or plundering if they have an opportunity.

"No, the ideal is a community governed by upper-class individuals, for they never fight for themselves; they know their own endless resources, and they give with open hands to those who are poorer. They endeavor to bring light and air to every possibility for good and beauty in the inferior souls — those who are neither this nor that; good when they can afford it, bad when the proletariat forces them to be so. The power should be in the hands of those who feel the responsibility for every good impulse that is killed."

"You are wrong about Hans Hermann," said Cesca quietly. "It was not for his own sake alone that he rebelled against social injustice. He, too, spoke of the good impulses that

52

were wasted. When we walked about it the east end and saw the pale little children, he said he would like to set fire to the ugly, sad, crowded barracks where they lived."

"Mere talk. If the rent had been paid to him. ..." "For shame, Gunnar!" said Cesca impetuously.
"All the same he would not have been a socialist if he had been born rich — but still a true proletarian."

"Are you sure you would have been a socialist yourself," said Cesca, "if you had been born a count, for instance?"

"Mr. Heggen is a count," said Hjerrild, laughing, "of many airy castles."

Heggen sat silent for a minute. "I have never felt I was born poor," he said, speaking as if to himself.

"As to Hermann's love for children," said Hjerrild, "there was not much of it for his own child. And the wav he treated his wife was disgraceful. He begged and pleaded till he got her, but when she was going to have the baby, she had to beg and implore him to marry her."

"Have they got a little boy?" whispered Francesca.

"Yes; he arrived after they had been married six weeks, just the day I left Berlin. When they had been married a month Hermann left her and went to Dresden. I don't see why they did not marry before, as they had agreed to divorce anyhow. She wanted it."

"How disgraceful," said Jenny, who had been listening to the conversation. "To marry with the intention to divorce!"

"Well," said Hjerrild, smiling. "When people know each other in and out, and know they cannot get on, what else is there to do?"

"Not marry at all, of course."

"Naturally. Free love is much better, but she had to marry. She is going to give concerts in Christiania in the autumn and try to get pupils. She could not do it, having the child, unless she had been married."

"Perhaps not, but it is hateful all the same. I have no sympathy with free love, if it means that people should take up with each other although they presume they will tire of one another. It seems to me that even to break an ordinary platonic engagement is a slight stain on the one who breaks it. But if one has been unfortunate enough to make a mistake, and then goes through the marriage ceremony for the sake of what people say, it is a blasphemy to stand there and make a promise that one has agreed beforehand not to keep."

By dawn the visitors left. Heggen stayed a second after the others had gone. Jenny opened the balcony doors to let out the smoke. The sky was grey, with a pale, reddish light appearing above the housetops. Heggen went up to her:

"Thanks so much. We've had a pleasant Christmas. What are you thinking of?" "That it is Christmas morning. I wonder if they got my parcel at home in time."

"I daresay they did. You sent it on the eleventh, didn't you?"

"I did. It was always so nice on Christmas morning to go in and look at the tree and the presents in daylight — but I was young then," she added, smiling. "They say there's been lots of snow this winter. I suppose the children are tobagganing in the mountains today."

"Yes, probably," said Heggen. "You are getting cold. Good-night, and thanks again." "Good-night, and a happy Christmas to you, Gunnar."

They shook hands. She stayed by the window a little while after he had gone.

One day during Christmas week Gram went into a overcoat, he heard Heggen say: "I don't like that man."
"No; he is disgusting," said Jenny, sighing.

"It is not good for her either — with this sirocco blowing She will be a rag tomorrow. I suppose she does not work at all — only walks about with that fellow?"

"Work, no! But I can do nothing. She walks from here to Viterbo with him in those thin slippers of hers, in spite of the cold and the sirocco — only because the man can tell her about Hans Hermann."

Gram greeted them as he passed. They made a movement as if inviting him to sit at their table, but he pretended not to see, and sat down farther up the room with his back to them. He understood that they were speaking about Francesca.

VII

Heggen and Jenny were sitting at a table, but they did not see him. As he was taking off his He was almost a daily visitor now at the Via Vantaggio; he could not help it. Miss Winge was always alone, reading or sewing, and seemed pleased to see him. He thought she had changed a little of late; she was not so determined or so ready with her opinions as she used to be; not so inclined to argue and to lay down the law. She seemed almost a little sad. He asked her once if she were not quite well.

"Yes, I am very well, thank you. Why do you ask?"

"I don't know — you seem so quiet nowadays."

She had lighted the lamp meanwhile, and he noticed that she blushed.

"I may have to go home soon. My sister is ill with pneumonia, and my mother is so upset about it. I am very sorry to go," she added after a pause. "I should have liked to stay for the spring at least."

She sat down to her needlework. He wondered in his mind if it was Heggen — he had never been able to find out if there was an understanding between them. For the present, Heggen, who was said to be rather impressionable generally, was very much attached to a young Danish nurse staying in Rome with an elderly lady. It seemed so strange that she should blush; it was not like her.

Francesca came in that evening before he left. He had not seen her much since Christmas Eve, but enough to understand that he was quite indifferent to her. She was never in a temper, or childishly impetuous; she went about as if she did not see anybody, her mind completely absorbed by something or other. At times she seemed almost to walk in a trance.

He saw a great deal of Jenny; he went to the trattoria where she used to have her meals, and also to her rooms. He scarcely knew why, but he felt he wanted to see her.

One afternoon Jenny went into Francesca's room to look for some turpentine. Francesca always took whatever she needed from Jenny's belongings, but she never put the things back.

Cesca was lying on the bed sobbing, with her head deep in the pillow. Jenny had not heard her come in.

"My dear, what is the matter? Are you ill?"

"No, but please go away, Jenny, do! I won't tell you; you'll only say it's my own fault." Jenny understood it was no good talking to her when she was in that state, but at tea-time she knocked at her door. Cesca thanked her, but did not want any tea.

That night, when Jenny was reading in bed, Cesca suddenly came into the room in her nightdress. Her eyes were red and swollen with crying.

"May I sleep with you tonight? I don't want to be alone."

Jenny made room for her. She did not like the idea of sharing her bed, but Cesca used to come when she was very unhappy and ask to be allowed to sleep with her.

"Go on reading, Jenny; I won't disturb you. I shall lie very still here by the wall."

Jenny pretended to read for some time. Now and then a high like a sob was heard from Francesca.

"Shall I put out the lamp, or would you like it burning?" Jenny asked. "No, put it out, please."
In the dark she put her arm round Jenny and told her, sobbing, that she had been to the Campagna again with Hjerrild, and he had kissed her. At first she had just scolded him a little, thinking it was only fun, but he soon became so disgusting that she got angry. "And he wanted me to go and stay at an hotel with him tonight. He said it exactly as he would have asked me to go to a confectioner's with him. I was furious, and he got very angry and said some nasty, horrid things." She shivered as in a fever. "He spoke about Hans — he said that Hans, when he showed him my picture, had spoken to him about me in such a way as to make Hjerrild believe — you know what I mean ?" She nestled close to Jenny. "Can you understand it — for I don't — that I still care for that cad of a man? Hans had not mentioned my name, though, and he did not imagine, of course, that Hjerrild would meet me or know me from the photograph; it was taken when I was eighteen."

Jenny's birthday was on the seventeenth of January. She and Francesca were having a dinner-party in the Campagna, in a small osteria in the Via Appia Nuova. Ahlin, Heggen, Gram, and Miss Palm, the Danish nurse, made up the party.

From the tram terminus they walked two and two along the sunny, white road. Spring was in the air, the brown Campagna had a greyish-green tinge; the daisies, which had been blossoming more or less all the winter, began to spread all over in silvery spots, and the impatient clusters of tender green shoots on the elder bushes along the fences had grown.

The larks hung trembling high up in the blue-white sky, and there was a haze over the city and the ugly, red blocks of houses it had sprinkled over the plain. Beyond the massive arches of the canal, the Alban mountains, with small white villages, showed faintly through the mist.

Jenny walked in front with Gram, who carried her grey dustcoat. She was radiantly beautiful in a black silk dress; he had never seen her in anything but her grey dress or coat and skirt. It seemed to him almost as if he walked with a new and strange woman. Her waist was so small in the shiny black material that her form above it seemed round and supple; the bodice was cut open in a deep square in front, and her hair and skin were dazzlingly fair. She wore a big black hat, in which he had seen her before, but without specially noticing it. Even her pink beads looked quite different with the black dress.

They ate out of doors in the sunshine under the vine, which threw a shadow in the form of a fine bluish net over the tablecloth. Miss Palm and Heggen wanted to decorate the table with daisies; the macaroni was quite ready, but the others had to wait until they came back with the decorations. The food was good and the wine was excellent; Cesca had brought fruit, and coffee, which she was going to make herself, to make sure it should be good. After dinner Miss Palm and Heggen investigated marble reliefs and inscriptions that had been found on the site and fitted into the masonry of the house.

After a while they disappeared round a comer. Ahlin remained sitting at the table smoking, his eyes half shut against the glare.

The osteria lay at the foot of a small hill. Gram and Jenny walked up the slope at random. She picked small wild flowers that grew in the yellow earth.

"There are masses of these at Monte Testaccio. Have you been there, Mr. Gram?"

"Yes, several times. I went there yesterday to have a look at the Protestant cemetery. The camelia trees are covered with blossoms, and in the old part I found anemones in the grass."

"Yes, they are out now. Somewhere at Via Cassia, beyond Ponte Molle, there are lots of them. Gunnar gave me some almond blossoms this morning; they have them already at the Spanish stairs, but I daresay they are forced."

They reached the top and began strolling about. Jenny walked with her eyes on the ground; the short grass was springing up everywhere, and variegated thistle-leaves and some big, silver-grey ones were basking in the sun. They walked towards a solitary wall, which rose out of a mound of gravel; the Campagna extended around them in every direction, grey-green below the light spring skies and the warbling larks. Its boundaries were lost in the haze of the sun. The city beyond them seemed a mirage only, the mountains and the clouds melted together, and the yellow arches of the canal appeared, only to vanish again in the mist. The countless ruins were reduced to small, glistening pieces of walls, strewn about on the green, and pines and eucalyptus trees by the red or ochre houses stood solitary and dark on this fine day of early spring.

"Do you remember the first morning I was here, Miss Winge? I imagined I was disappointed, and I believed it to be because I had longed so much and dreamt so much that everything I was going to see would be colorless and poor, compared to my dreams. Have you noticed how on a summer day, when you lie in the sun with your eyes closed, all colors seem grey and faded when you first open them? It is because the eyes are weakened by not being used and cannot at once grasp the complexity of the colors as they really are; the first impression is incomplete and poor. Do you understand what I mean?"

Jenny nodded.

"It was my case in the beginning here. I was overwhelmed by Rome. Then I saw you passing by, tall and fair and a stranger. I did not pay any attention to Francesca then — not till we were in the tavern. When I sat there with you, who were all strange to me — it was really the first time such a thing happened to me. Up till then my association with strangers had been only an occasional meeting on my way between school and home. I was confused; it seemed impossible to speak to people. I almost longed for home and all it meant — and I longed for Rome as I knew it from hearsay and from pictures. I thought I could not settle down to anything but look at pictures made by others — read books the men had written — made the best use of the work of others and live in a world of fiction. I felt desperately lonely among you. You once said something about being lonely; I understand now what you meant.

"Do you see that tower over there? I went there yesterday. It is the remnant of a fortress from the Middle Ages, from feudal times. There are a good many of them in the city and round about. You see sometimes an almost windowless wall built in between the houses in a street. It is a bit of the Rome of the robber barons. We know comparatively little about that time, but I am very interested in it at present. I find in the records names of dead people, of whom sometimes nothing is known but their names, and I long to know more about them. I dream of Rome in the Middle Ages, when they fought in the street with fierce cries, and the town was full of robber-castles, where their womenfolk were shut up — daughters of those wild beasts and with their blood in their veins. Sometimes they broke away from their prison and mixed in the life, such as it was, inside the red-black walls. We know so little about those times, and the German professors do not take great interest in them, because they cannot be remade so as to convey abstract ideas; they are simply naked facts.

"What a mighty current of life has washed over this country! — breaking into billows round every spot with town and castle on it. And yet the mountains rise above it bare and desolate. Think of the endless number of ruins here in the Campagna only; of the stacks of books written on the history of Italy — and on the history of the whole world for that matter — and think of the hosts of dead people we know. Yet the result of all these waves of life, rolling one after the other, is very, very small. It is all so wonderful!

"I have talked to you so often and you have talked to me; yet I don't really know you. You are just as much a mystery to me as that tower. — I wish you could see how your hair shines where you are standing now. It is glorious.

"Has it ever struck you that you have never seen your face? Only the reflection of it in the glass. We can never see what our face looks like when we sleep or shut our eyes — isn't it odd? It was my birthday the day I met you; today it is yours. Are you glad to be twenty-eight, you who think that every year completed is a gain?"

"I did not say that. I said that you may have had so much to go through the first twenty-five years of your life that you are glad they are over."

"And now?" "Now?"

"Yes; do you know exactly what you want to attain during the next year — what use you are going to make of it? Life seems to me so overwhelmingly rich in possibilities that even you, with all your strength, cannot avail yourself of them. Does it ever occur to you, and does it make you sad, Jenny?"

She only smiled in answer, and looked down. She threw the end of her cigarette on the ground and put her foot on it; her white ankle showed through the thin black stocking. She followed with her eyes a pack of sheep running down the opposite slope.

"We are forgetting the coffee, Mr. Gram — I am sure they are waiting for us."

They returned to the osteria in silence; on the slope, which stretched right down to where they had been lunching, they noticed that Ahlin was lying forward over the table, his head on his arms. Francesca in her bright green gown bent over him, her arms round his neck, trying to lift his head.

"Oh, don't, Lennart! Don't cry. I will love you. I will marry you — do you hear? — but you must not cry like that. I will marry you, and I think I can be fond of you, only don't be so miserable."

Ahlin sobbed: "No, no — not if you don't love me, Cesca; I don't want you to. . . ."

Jenny turned and went back along the slope. Gram noticed that she flushed a deep red down to her neck. A path took them down by the other side of the house into the orchard.

Heggen and Miss Palm were chasing each other round the little fountain, splashing each other with water. Miss Palm shrieked with laughter. Helge saw the color again mount to Jenny's face and neck as he walked behind her between the vegetable beds. Heggen and Miss Palm had made peace.

"The same old round," said Helge; "take your partners." Jenny nodded, with the shadow of a smile.

The atmosphere at the coffee-table was somewhat strained. Miss Palm alone was in good spirits. Francesca tried to make conversation while they were sipping their liqueurs, and, as soon as she decently could, proposed that they should go for a walk.

The three couples made for the Campagna, the distance between them increasing, until they lost sight of one another altogether among the hills. Jenny walked with Gram.

"Where are we going really?" she said.

"We might go to the Egeria grotto, for instance."

The grotto lay in quite an opposite direction to the one chosen by the others. They started to walk across the scorched slopes to the Bosco Sacro, where the ancient cork trees stretched their dark foliage to the burning sun.

"I ought to have put on my hat," said Jenny, passing a hand over her hair. The ground of the sacred grove was covered with bits of paper and other litter; on the stump of a tree near the edge two ladies were seated, doing crochet work, and some little English boys played hide-and-seek behind the massive trunks. Jenny and Gram turned out of the grove and walked down the slope towards the ruin.

"Is it worth-while going down?" said Jenny, and without waiting for an answer, sat down on the slope.

"No; let us stay here," and Helge lay down at her feet on the short, dry grass, took off his hat, and, steadying himself on his elbow, looked up at her in silence.

"How old is she?" he asked suddenly. "I mean Cesca."

"Twenty-six." She sat looking at the view in front of her.

"I am not sorry," he said quietly. "You have noticed it, I daresay. A month ago I might have. . . . She was so sweet to me once, so kind and confidential, and I was not used to that kind of thing. I took it as — well, as l'invitation à la valse, you see, but now ... I still think she is sweet, but I don't mind in the least if she dances with somebody else."

He was lying looking at her: "I believe it is you, Jenny, I am in love with," he said suddenly.

She turned half-way towards him, with a faint smile, and shook her head.

"Yes," said Helge firmly; "I think so. I don't know for certain, for I have never been in love before — I know that now — although I have been engaged once." He smiled to himself.

"It was one of my blunders in the old foolish days.

"This, I am sure, is love. It was you, Jenny, I saw that evening — not her. I noticed you already in the afternoon when you crossed the Corso. I stood there thinking that life was new, full of adventure, and just then you passed me, fair and slender, and stranger. Later, when I had wandered about in this foreign town, I met you again. I also noticed Cesca, of course, and no wonder I was a little flustered for a moment, but it was you I saw first. And now we are sitting here together — we two."

Her hand was close to him as she sat leaning on it ; suddenly he stroked it — and she drew it away.

"You are not cross with me, are you? It is really nothing to be cross about. Why should I not tell you that I believe I am in love with you? I could not resist touching your hand — I wanted to feel that it was real, for it seems to me so wonderful that you are sitting here. I do not really know you, though we have talked about many things. I know that you are clever, level-headed, and energetic — and good and truthful, but I knew that the moment I saw you and heard your voice. I don't know any more about you now, but there is of course a great deal more to learn — and perhaps I shall never learn it.

But I can see for myself, for instance, that your silk skirt is glowing hot, and that if I laid my face in your lap I should burn myself."

She made an involuntary movement with her hand across her lap.

"It attracts the sun; there are sparks in your hair, and the sunrays filter through your eyes. Your mouth is quite trans- parent; it looks like a raspberry in the sun."

She smiled, looking a little embarrassed. "Will you give me a kiss?" he said suddenly.

"L' invitation à la valse?'" She smiled lightly.

61

"I don't know — but you cannot be cross with me because I ask you for one single little kiss — on a day like this. I am only telling you what I am longing for, and, after all, why could you not do it ?"

She did not move.

"Is there any reason why not? — I shall not try to kiss you, but I cannot see why you should not bend down for a second and give me a tiny little kiss as you sit there with the sun right on your lips. It is no more to you than when you pat a bambino on the head and give him a soldo. It is nothing to you, Jenny, and to me it is all I wish for — just this moment I long for it so much," he said, smiling.

She bent suddenly down and kissed him. Only for a second did he feel her hair and lips brush his cheek, and he saw the movement of her body under the black silk as she bent down and rose again. Her face, he noticed, which was smiling serenely as she kissed him, now looked embarrassed, almost frightened. He did not move, but lay still, musing contentedly in the sunshine. She became herself again.

"There, you see," he said at last laughingly, "your mouth is exactly as before; the sun is shining on your lips, right into the blood. It was nothing to you — and I am so happy you must not believe that I want you to think of me — I only want you to let me think of you, while you may sit and think of anything in the world. Others may dance — to me this is much better — if only I may look at you."

They were both silent. Jenny sat with her face turned away, looking at the Campagna bathing in the sun.

As they walked back to the osteria, Helge chatted merrily about all sorts of things, telling her about the learned Germans he had met in the course of his work. Jenny stole a glance at him now and again; he used not to be like that, so free and easy. He was really handsome as he walked, looking straight ahead, and his light brown eyes were radiant like amber in the sun.

VIII

JENNY did not light the lamp when she got in, but, putting on an evening cloak in the dark, she went out to sit on the balcony. The night was cold, the skies stretched over the roofs like black velvet, covered with glittering stars. He had said when they parted: "I may come up tomorrow and ask you to go with me for a trip in the Campagna?"

Well, nothing had really happened — she had merely given him a kiss, but it was the first kiss she had ever given to a man, and it had not happened in the way she had expected. It was almost a joke — kissing him like that. She was not in love with him, yet she had kissed him. She had hesitated and thought: I have never kissed, and then a strange sensation of indifference and soft languor stole over her. Why be so ridiculously solemn about it? — and she did it — why not? It did not matter; he had asked for it quite handily, because he thought he was in love with her and the sun was bright. He had not asked her to love him, and he had made no further advances; he had not claimed anything, only that one little kiss, and she had given it without a word. It was altogether beautiful; she had done nothing to be ashamed of. She was twenty-eight, and she would not deny to herself that she longed to love and to be loved by a man, to nestle in his arms, young, healthy, and good to look upon as she was. Her blood was hot and she was yearning, but she had eyes that saw clearly, and she had never lied to herself. She had met men now and then and had asked herself: Is he the man? — one or two of them she might have loved if she had tried, if she could have closed her eyes to the one little thing that always was there, making her feel an opposition which she had to master. She had not met anyone whom she felt compelled to love, so had not risked it. Cesca would let one man after another kiss and fondle her, and it made no difference; it merely grazed her lips and skin. Not even Hans Hermann, whom she loved, could warm her strangely thin, chilly blood.

She herself was different; her blood was red and hot, and the joy she coveted should be fiery, consuming, but spotlessly clean. She would be loyal and true to the man to whom she gave herself, but he must know how to take her wholly, to possess her body and soul, so that not a single possibility in her would be wasted or left neglected in some corner of her soul — to decay and fester. No, she dared not, would not be reckless — not she. Yet she could understand those who did not trouble their heads about such things; who did not subdue one instinct and call it bad, and give in to another, calling it good, or renounce all the cheap little joys of life, saving up all for the great joy that after all might never come. She was not so sure herself that her road led to the goal — not sure enough not to e impressed sometimes by people who quite cynically admitted that they had no road, no goal, and that to have ideals and morals was like trying to catch the moon on the water.

Once, many years ago, a man had asked her one night to go with him to his rooms, much in the same way as he would have offered to take her out to tea. It was no temptation to her — she knew, besides, that her mother was waiting up for her, which made it quite impossible. She knew the man very slightly, did not like him, and was cross because he was to see her home; and it was not because her senses were stirred, but from purely mental curiosity, that she turned the question for a moment over in her mind: what if she did? — what would be her feelings if she threw overboard will, self-control, and her old faith? A voluptuously exciting shiver ran through her at the thought. Was that kind of life more pleasant than her own? She was not pleased with hers that evening; she had again sat watching those who danced, she had tasted the wine and had listened to the music, and she had felt the dreadful loneliness of being young and not knowing how to dance or how to speak the language of the other young people and share their laughter, but she had tried to smile and look and talk as if she enjoyed it. And when she walked home in the icy-cold spring night she knew that at eight o'clock next morning she had to be at the school to act as substitute for one of the teachers. She was working that time at her big picture, but everything she did seemed dull and meaningless, and at six o'clock she had to go home and teach mathematics to her private pupils. She was very hard worked; she sometimes felt her nerves strained to the utmost, and did not know how she would be able to carry on till the long vacation.

For an instant she felt herself drawn by the man's cynicism — or thought she was — but she smiled at him and said "no" in the same dry and direct way that he had asked her.

He was a fool, after all, for he began preaching to her — first commonplace flattery, then sentimental nonsense about youth and spring, the right and freedom of passion, and the gospel of the flesh, until she simply laughed at him and hailed a passing cab.

And now — she was old enough now to understand those who brutally refused to deny themselves anything in life — who simply gave in and drifted, but the greenhorns, who boasted of having a mission to fill, when they enjoyed life after their fashion, the champions of the eternal rights of nature, who did not trouble to brush their teeth or clean their nails — they could not impose on her.

She would be true to her own old moral code, which aimed at truth and self-control, and originated from the time she was sent to school. She was not like the other children; even her clothes were unlike theirs, and her little soul was very, very different. She lived with her mother, who had been left a widow at the age of twenty, and had nothing in the world but her little daughter. Her father had died before she was old enough to remember him. He was in his grave and in heaven, but in reality he lived with them, for his picture hung above the piano and heard and saw everything they said and did. Her mother spoke of him constantly, telling her what he thought of everything and what Jenny might or must not do because of father. Jenny spoke of him as if she knew him, and at night, in bed, she spoke to him, and to God as one who was always with father and agreed with him about everything.

She remembered her first day at school, and smiled at the recollection. Her mother had taught her herself until she was eight years old. She used to explain things to Jenny by comparison; a cape, for instance, was likened to a small point near the town, which Jenny knew well, so when the teacher asked her in the geography lesson to name some Norwegian capes, she answered without hesitation: "Naesodden." The teacher smiled and all the pupils laughed. "Signe," said the teacher, and another girl stood up briskly to answer: "Nordkap,

Lindesnaes, Stat." Jenny smiled in a superior way, not heeding their laughter. She had never had child friends, and she never made any.

She had smiled indifferently at their sneering and teasing, but a quiet, implacable hatred grew in her towards the other children, who to her mind formed one compact mass, a many-headed savage beast. The consuming rage which filled her when they tormented her was always hidden behind a scornful, indifferent smile. Once she had nearly cried her eyes out with rage and misery, and when on one or two occasions she had lost control of herself, she had seen their triumph. Only by putting on an air of placid, irritating indifference could she hold her own against them.

In the upper form she made friends with one or two girls; she was then at an age when no child can bear to be unlike others, and she tried to copy them. These friendships, however, did not give her much joy. She remembered how they made fun of her when they discovered that she played with dolls. She disowned her beloved children and said they belonged to her little sisters.

There was a time when she wanted to go on the stage. She and her friends were stage-struck; they sold their school books and their confirmation brooches to buy tickets, and night after night they went to the gallery of the theatre. One day she told her friends how she would act a certain part that interested them. They burst out laughing; they had always known she was conceited, but not that she was a megalomaniac. Did she really believe that she could become an artist, she, who could not even dance? It would be a pretty sight indeed to see her walk up and down the stage with that tall, stiff skeleton of hers.

No, she could not dance. When she was quite a child her mother used to play to her, and she twisted and turned, tripped and curtseyed as she liked, and her mother called her a little linnet. She thought of her first party, how she had arrived full of anticipation, happy in a new white dress which her mother had made after an old English picture. She remembered how she stiffened all over when she began to dance. That stiffness never quite left her; when she tried to learn dancing by herself her soft, slim body became stiff as a poker. She was no good at it. She was very anxious to go to a dancing class, but it never came to anything.

She laughed at the recollection of her school friends. She had met two of them at the exhibition at home, the first time she had got one of her pictures hung and a few lines of praise in the papers. She was with some other artists — Heggen was one of them — when they came up to congratulate her: "Didn't we always say you'd be an artist? We were all sure that some day we should hear more of you."

She had smiled: "Yes, Ella; so was I."

Lonely! She had been lonely ever since her mother met Mr. Berner, who worked with her in the same office. She was about ten at that time, but she understood at once that her dead father had departed from their home. His picture was still hanging there, but he was gone, and it dawned upon her what death really meant. The dead existed only in the memory of others, who had the power conditionally to end their poor shadow life — and they were gone for ever.

She understood why her mother became young and pretty and happy again; she noticed the expression on her face when Berner rang the bell. She was allowed to stay in the room and listen to their talk; it was never about things the child could not hear, and they did not send her out of the room when they were together in her home. In spite of the jealousy in her little heart, she understood that there were many things a grown-up mother could not speak about with a little girl, and a strong feeling of justice developed in her. She did not wish to be angry with her mother, but it hurt very much all the same.

She was too proud to show it, and when her mother in moments of self-reproach suddenly overwhelmed her child with tenderness and care, she remained cold and passive. She said not a word when her mother wanted her to call Berner father and said how fond he was of her. In the night she .tried to speak to her own father, with a passionate longing to keep him alive, but she felt she could not do it alone; she knew him only through her mother. By and by Jens Winge became dead to her too, and since he had been the center of her conception of God, and heaven, and eternal life, all these faded away with his picture.

She remembered quite distinctly how, at thirteen, she had listened to the Scriptures at school without believing anything, and because the others in her form believed in God and were afraid of the devil, and yet were cowardly and cruel, and mean and common — in her opinion at least — religion became to her something despicable, cowardly, something associated with them.

She got to like Nils Berner against her will; she preferred him almost to her mother in the first period of their married life. He claimed no authority over his step-daughter, but by his wise and kind, frank ways he won her over. She was the child of the woman he loved — that was reason enough for him to be fond of Jenny.

She had much to thank her stepfather for; how much, she had not understood till now. He had fought and conquered much that was distorted and morbid in her. When she lived alone with her mother in the hothouse air of tenderness, care, and dreams, she had been a nervous child, afraid of dogs, of trams, of matches — afraid of everything — and she was sensitive to bodily pain. Her mother dared scarcely let her go alone to school.

The first thing Berner did was to take the girl with him to the woods; Sunday after Sunday they went to Nordmarken, in broiling sunshine or pouring rain, in the thaws of spring, and in winter on ski. Jenny, who was used to conceal her feelings, tried not to show how tired and nervous she was, and after a time she did not feel it.

Berner taught her to use map and compass, he talked to her as to a friend, and he taught her to observe the signs of wind and clouds, which brought about a change in the weather, and to reckon time and distance by the sun. He made her familiar with animals and plants — root and stalk, leaf and bud, blossom and fruit. Her sketch-book and his camera were always in their knapsack.

All the kindness and devotion her stepfather had put into this work of education she appreciated now for the first time — for he was a well-known ski-runner and mountaineer in the Jotunheim and Nordlandstinderne.

He had promised to take her there too. The summer when she was fifteen, she went with him grouse-shooting. Her mother could not go with them: she was expecting the little brother by that time.

They stayed in a solitary mountain saeter below Rondane. She had never been so happy in all her life as when she awoke in her tiny bunk. She hurried out to make coffee for her step- father, and he took her to the Ronde peaks, into the Styg mountains, and on fishing tours; and they went down together to the valley for provisions. When he was out hooting, she bathed in the cold mountain brooks and went for endless walks on the moors; or sat in the porch knitting and dreaming, weaving romances about a fair saeter maiden and a huntsman, who was very like Berner, but young and handsome, and who could tell about hunting and mountaineering like Berner used to do in the evening by the fire. And he should promise to give her a gun and take her up to unknown mountain-tops.

She remembered how tormented, ashamed, and unhappy she was when she knew that her mother was going to have a baby. She tried to hide her thoughts from her mother, but she knew she only partly succeeded. Berner's anxiety about his wife as the time drew near brought a change in her feelings. He spoke to her about it: "I am so afraid, Jenny, because I love your mother so dearly," and he told her that when she herself was born her mother was very ill. The belief that her mother's condition was unclean and unnatural left her when he spoke, but with it went also the feeling that the bond between her mother and

herself was mysterious, supernatural. It became everyday, commonplace; she had been born and her mother had suffered; she had been small and needed her mother, and because of that her mother had loved her. Another little child was soon coming, who needed her mother more. Jenny -felt she had grown up all at once; she sympathized with her mother as well as with Berner, and comforted him in a precocious way: "It will pass off quite well; it always does, you know.
They scarcely ever die of it."

When she saw her mother with the new child, who took all her time and care, Jenny felt very forlorn, and she cried, but by and by she became very fond of the baby, especially when little Ingeborg was over a year old and was the sweetest, darkest little gipsy doll you could imagine — and her mother had another tiny infant.

She had never considered the Berner children as her sisters; they were exactly like their father. Her relationship to them was more that of an aunt — she felt herself almost as an elderly, sensible aunt to her mother as well as to the children. When the accident happened, her mother was younger and weaker than she. Mrs. Winge had become young again in her second happy marriage, and she was a little tired and worn after her three confinements in the comparatively short time. Nils was only five months old when his father died.

Berner fell one summer when out mountaineering, and w r as killed on the spot. Jenny was then sixteen. Her mother's grief was boundless; she had loved her husband and been worshipped by him. Jenny tried to help her as much as she could. How deeply she herself mourned her stepfather she never told anybody; she knew that she had lost the best friend she had ever had.

When she had finished school, she began to take drawing lessons, and helped her mother in the house. Berner had always been interested in her drawings; he had been the first to teach her perspective and such things — all he knew about it himself. He had believed she had some talent.

They could not afford to keep his dog. The two little puppies were sold, and Mrs. Berner thought Leddy ought to be sold too — it cost so much to feed her. But Jenny objected; nobody should have the dog, which was mourning for its master, if they could not keep it, and she had her way. She took the dog herself one evening to Mr. Iversnaes, Berner's friend, who shot and buried Leddy.

What Berner had been to her — a friend and a comrade — she tried to be to his children. As the two girls grew up, the relations between them and Jenny became less intimate, though still quite friendly, but the great difference in age made a breach between them which Jenny never tried to cross.

They were now quite nice little girls in their teens, with anæmia, small flirtations, friendships, parties, and all the rest of it — a merry pair, but somewhat indolent. The friendship between Nils and her had grown in strength as time went on. His father had called the tiny baby Kalfatrus; Jenny had adopted the name, and the boy called her Indiana.

During all those sad years now behind her, the rambles in Nordmarken with Kalfatrus were the only occasions when she could breathe freely. She enjoyed them specially in spring or autumn, when there were few people about, and she and the boy sat quietly gazing into the burning pile of wood they had made, or lay on the ground talking to one another in their particular slang, which they dared not use at home for fear of vexing their mother. Her portrait of Kalfatrus was the first of her paintings to please her; it was really good.

Gunnar scolded her for not exhibiting it; he thought it would have been bought for the picture gallery at home. She had never painted so good a picture since.
She was to have painted Berner — papa. She had begun to call him thus when his own children started to talk, and also to call her mother mamma. This marked to her mind the change that had taken place in the relations between her and the mother of her brief childhood.

The first part of the time out here, when at last she was freed from the constant strain, was not pleasant. She realized that her every nerve was quivering from the strain, and she thought it impossible ever to regain her youth. From her stay in Florence she remembered only that she had been cold, felt lonely, and been unable to assimilate all that was new around her. Little by little the endless treasure of beauty was revealed to her, and she was seized by a great longing to grasp it and live in it, to be young, to love and be loved. She thought of the first spring days when Cesca and Gunnar took her to Viterbo — of the sunshine on the bare trees and the masses of anemones, violets, and cowslips in the faded grass. Of the steppe-like plain outside the city, with fumes of boiling, strongly smelling sulphur springs wafted through the air, and the ground all round white with curdling lime. The thousands of swift emerald-green lizards in the stone walls, the olive trees in the green meadows, where white butterflies fluttered about. The old city with singing fountains and black mediaeval houses, and the towers in the surrounding wall with moonlight on them. And the yellow, slightly effervescent wine, with a fiery taste from the volcanic soil on which it was grown.

She called her new friends by their names. In the night Francesca made a confession of her young, eventful life, and crept into her bed at last to be comforted, repeating time after time: "Fancy, you being like this! I was always afraid of you at school. I never thought you could be so kind!"

Gunnar was in love with both of them. He was full of fire, like a young faun in spring-time, and Francesca let herself be kissed, and laughed and called him a silly boy.

But Jenny was afraid, though not of him. She dared not kiss his hot, red mouth, for the sake of something intangible, intoxicating, frivolous, which would last only while they were there amid sun and anemones — something irresponsible. She dared not put aside her old self; she felt that she could not take a flirtation light-heartedly, and neither could he. She had already seen enough of Gunnar Heggen to know that in his affairs with other women he was such as they were — and yet not quite — for in his inmost self he was a good man, much better than most women are. His infatuation had soon turned into friendship, and during the lovely, peaceful time in Paris, when they had worked hard, and afterwards out here, it had grown stronger and stronger.

It was quite a different matter with Gram. He did not arouse any adventurous fancies or wild longings in her. He was not at all stupid, as she had thought at first; it was only that he seemed almost stunted, checked in mental growth, when he came out here, and she at least ought to have understood it. There was something gentle and young and sound bout him, which she liked — he seemed more than two years her junior. His talk of being in love with her was nothing but a surplus of the joy he felt at the freedom of his new life. There was no danger in it, either for him or for her. They were fond of her at home, of course, and Gunnar and Francesca were fond of her too, but did any one of them think of her tonight? She was not altogether sorry to know that there was someone who did.

IX

WHEN she awoke in the morning she told herself that he would very likely not come at all, and so much the better — but when he knocked at her door she was pleased all the same.

"I have had nothing to eat yet, Miss Winge. Could you give me a cup of tea and some bread?"

Jenny looked about her in the room. "Yes, but the room isn't done yet."
"I'll shut my eyes while you lead me on to the balcony," said Gram from behind the door. "I am dying for a cup of tea."

"Very well, half a minute." Jenny covered her bed with the counterpane, tidied the dressing-table, and changed her dressing-jacket for a long kimono. "Come in, and please go and sit on the balcony while I get your tea." She brought out a stool and placed some bread and cheese on it.

Gram looked at her bare, white arms in the long, fluttering sleeves of the dark blue kimono with a pattern of yellow and purple iris.

"What a pretty thing you have on. It looks like a real geisha dress."

"It is real. Cesca and I bought these in Paris to wear at home in the morning."

"It is a capital idea, I think, to go about like that and look pretty when you are alone. I like it."

He lit a cigarette and gazed at the smoke as it rose in the air.

"Ugh! At home the maid and my mother and sister used to look like anything in the morning. Don't you think women ought always to make themselves look as pretty as possible?"

"Yes, but it isn't always possible when you have to do housework."

"Perhaps not, but they might at least do their hair before breakfast and put on a thing like that, don't you think?"

He was just in time to save a cup, which she was on the point of brushing down with her sleeve.

"You see how practical it is. Now, drink your tea; you said you were thirsty."

She discovered suddenly that Cesca's whole stock of coloured stockings were hanging to dry on the balcony, and she removed them a little nervously.

While he was having his tea, he explained:

"I lay awake last night thinking, almost until dawn, and then, of course, I overslept, so had no time to stop at the latteria on my way. I think we should go to Via Cassia to that anemone place of yours."

"Anemone place." Jenny laughed. "When you were a boy did you, too, have special places for violets and bluebells, and kept them a secret from the others and went there all alone every year?"

"Of course I had. I know a beech grove by the old road to Holmenkollen, where there are real scented violets."

"I know it too," she interrupted triumphantly, "to the right, just before the road branches off to Sorkedal."

"Exactly. I had some other places too, on Fredriksborg and" "I must go in and put on my dress," said Jenny.
"Put on the one you had yesterday, please!" he called after her.

"It will get so dusty" — but she changed her mind in the same moment. Why should she not make herself look nice? The old black silk had been her best for a good many years; she need not treat it with such deference any more.

"I don't care! but it fastens at the back, and Cesca's not in."

"Come out here and I'll button it for you. I am an expert at it. It seems to me I have done nothing all my life but fasten mother's and Sophy's buttons at the back."

She could manage all but two, and she allowed Gram to help her with them. As she stood by him in the sunshine while he fastened her dress, he became aware of the faint, mild fragrance of her hair and her body. He noticed one or two small rents in the silk, which were carefully darned, and the sight of it filled his heart with an infinite tenderness towards her.

"Do you think Helge a nice name?" he asked, when they were having lunch at an osteria far out on the Campagna.

"Yes; I like it."

"Do you know that it is my Christian name?"

"Yes; I saw you had written it in the visitors' book at the club." She blushed slightly, thinking he might believe that she had looked it up on purpose.

"I suppose it is nice. On the whole, there are few names that are nice or ugly in themselves; it all depends if you like the people or not. When I was a boy we had a nurse called Jenny; I could not bear her, and ever since I thought the name was hideous and common. It seemed to me preposterous that you should be called Jenny, but now I think it so pretty; it gives one an idea of fairness. Can you not hear how delicately fair it sounds? — Jenny — a dark woman could not be called that, not Miss Jahrman, for instance. Francesca suits her captially, don't you think? It sounds so capricious, but Jenny is nice and bright."

"It is a name we've always had in my father's family," she said, by way of an answer. "What do you think of Rebecca, for instance?"

"I don't know. Rather harsh and clattering, perhaps, but it is pretty, though."

"My mother's name is Rebecca," said Helge. "I think it sounds hard, too. My sister's name is Sophy. She married only to get away from home, I am sure, and have a place of her own. I wonder mother could be so delighted to get her married, considering the cat-and-dog life she herself has led with my father. But there was no end of a fuss about the Rev. Arnesen, when my sister got engaged to him. I can't stand my brother-in-law, neither can father, I believe, but mother!…

"My fiancée — I was engaged once, you know — her name was Catherine, but she was always called Titti. I saw she had that name put into the papers, too, when her marriage was announced.

"It was a stupid thing altogether. It was three years ago. She was giving some lessons in the school where I was teaching. She was not a bit pretty, but she flirted with everybody, and no woman had ever taken any notice of me — which you can easily understand, when you think of me as I was here at first. She always laughed at everything — she was only nineteen. Heaven knows why she took to me.

"I was jealous, and it amused her. The more jealous she made me, the more in love was I. I suppose it was less love than male vanity, having a sweetheart very much in demand. I was very young then. I wanted her to be exclusively taken up with me — a very difficult proposition as I was then. I have often wondered what she wanted me for.

"My people wanted our engagement to be kept secret, because we were so young. Titti wanted it made public, and when I reproached her for being too much interested in other men, she said she could not spend all her time with me, as our engagement was a secret.

"I took her home, but she could not get on with my mother. They always quarreled, and Titti simply hated her. I suppose it would have made no difference to mother if I had been engaged to somebody else; the fact that I was going to marry was enough to put her against any woman. Well — Titti broke it off."

"Did it hurt you very much?" Jenny asked quietly. "Yes, at the time. I did not quite get over it till I came here, but I think it was mostly my pride that suffered. Don't you think that if I had loved her really, I should have wished her to be happy when she married another? But I didn't."

"It would have been almost too unselfish and noble," said Jenny, smiling.

"Oh, I don't know. That is how you ought to feel if you really love. Don't you think it is strange that mothers never care for their sons' sweethearts? They never do."

"I suppose a mother thinks no woman is good enough for her boy."

"When a daughter gets engaged it is quite different. I saw that in the case of my sister and the fat, red-haired clergyman. There was never much sympathy between my sister and myself, but when I saw that fellow making love to her, and thought that he . . . Ugh!

"I sometimes think women who have been married some time become more cynical than we men ever are. They don't give themselves away, but you notice it all the same. marriage to them means merely business. When a daughter marries they are pleased to have her saddled on to some one who can feed and clothe her, and if she has to put up with the shady side of marriage in return, it's not worth making a fuss about. But if a son takes upon himself the same kind of burden for a similar return, they are not so enthusiastic about it. Don't you think there is something in it?"

"Sometimes," said Jenny.

When she came home that evening she lit the lamp and sat down to write to her mother to thank her for the birthday greetings and tell her how she had spent the day.

She laughed at herself for having been so solemn the night before. Heaven knows, she had had difficulties and been lonely, but so had most of the young people she knew.

Some of them had been worse off than she. She thought of all the young girls — and the old ones — who had taught at the school; nearly all of them had an old mother to support, or sisters and brothers to help. And Gunnar? — and Gram? Even Cesca, the spoilt child from a rich home, had fought her way, since she had left home at twenty-one and kept herself on the little money left her by her mother.

As to loneliness, she had chosen it herself. All said and done, she had perhaps not been quite sure about her own powers, and to deaden her doubts, had held by the idea that she was different from other people — and they had been repelled. She had made some headway since, had proved to herself that she could do something, and had grown more friendly, less reserved, than before. She was obliged to admit that she had never made any advances, either as a child or since; she had always been too proud to take the first step. All the friends she had — from her stepfather to Gunnar and Cesca — had first stretched out their hands to her. And why had she always imagined that she was passionate? Such nonsense! She who had reached twenty-eight without ever having been the least in love. She believed that she would not be a failure as a woman, if once she were fond of a man, for she was healthy, good looking, and had sound instincts, which her work and outdoor life had developed. And very naturally she longed to love and be loved — longed to live. But to imagine that she would be able, from sheer rebellion of her senses, to fall into the arms of any man who happened to be near at a critical moment was utter nonsense. It was only because she would not admit to herself that she was dull sometimes and wished to make a conquest and flirt a little just like other girls — a pastime which in reality she did not approve of — that she preferred to imagine she was consumed by a thirst for life and clamoring senses. Such high-flown words were only invented by men, poor things, not knowing that women generally are simple and vain, and so stupid that they are bored unless there is a man to entertain them. That is the origin of the legend of the sensual woman — they are as rare as black swans, or disciplined, educated women. Jenny moved Francesca's portrait on to the easel. The white blouse and the green skirt looked hard and ugly. It would have to be toned down. The face was well drawn, the position good.

This episode with Gram was really nothing to be serious about. It was time she became reasonable. She must do away with those silly notions that she was afraid of every man she met — as with Gunnar in the beginning — afraid of falling in love with him, and almost more of his falling in love with her: a thing she was so unused to that it bewildered her.

Why could one not be friends with a man? If not, the world would be all a muddle. She and Gunnar were friends — a solid, comfortable friendship.

There was much about Gram that would make a friendship between them quite natural. They had had much the same experiences. He was so young and so full of confidence in her; she liked his "Is it not?" and "Don't you think?" He had talked yesterday about being in love with her — he thought at least he was, he said. She smiled to herself. A man would not speak to her as he had done if he had really fallen in love with a woman and wanted to win her.

"He is a dear boy; that's what he is."

Today he had not broached the subject. She liked him when he said that if he had been really fond of the girl he would have wished her happiness with the other man.

X

JENNY and Helge were running hand in hand down Via Magnanapoli. The street was merely a staircase, leading to the Trajan Forum. On the last step he drew her to him and kissed her.

"Are you mad? You mustn't kiss people in the street here."

And they both laughed. One evening they had been spoken to by two policemen on the Lateran piazza for walking up and down under the pines along the old wall kissing each other.

The last sunrays brushed the bronze figures on top of the pillar and burned on the walls and on the tree-tops in the gardens. The piazza lay in the shade, with its old, rickety houses round the excavated forum below the street level.

Jenny and Helge leaned over the railing and tried to count the fat, lazy cats which had taken their abode among the stumps of pillars on the grass-covered plot. They seemed to revive a little as the twilight began to fall. A big red one which had been lying on the pedestal of the Trajan pillar stretched himself, sharpened his claws on the masonry, jumped down on to the grass, and ran away.

"I make it twenty-three," said Helge.

"I counted twenty-five." She turned round and dismissed post card seller, who was recommending his wares in fragments of every possible language.

She leaned again over the railing and stared vaguely at the grass, giving way to the pleasant languor of a long sunny day and countless kisses out in the green Campagna. Helge held one of her hands on his arm and patted it — she moved it along his sleeve until it rested between both of his. Helge smiled happily.

"What is it, dear?"

"I am thinking of those Germans." She laughed too — quietly and indifferently, as happy people do at trifles that do not concern them. They had passed the Forum in the morning and sat down a moment on the high pedestal of the Focas pillar, talking in whispers. Beneath them lay the crumbled ruins, gilded by the sun, and small black tourists rambled among the stones. A newly married German couple were walking bythemselves, seeking solitude in the midst of the crowd of travelers. He was fair and ruddy of face, wore knickerbockers and carried a kodak, and read to his wife out of Baedeker. She was very young, plump, and dark, with the inherited stamp of hausfrau on her smooth, floury face.

She sat down on a tumbled pillar, posing to her husband, who took a snapshot of her. And the two who sat above, under the Focas pillar, whispering of their love, laughed, heedless of the fact that they were sitting above the Forum Romanum.

"Are you hungry?" asked Helge. "No; are you?"

"No — but do you know what I should like to do?" "Well?"

"I should like to go home with you and have supper. What do you say to that?" "Yes, of course."

They walked home arm in arm through small side streets. In her dark staircase he drew her suddenly to him, and kissed her with such force and passion that her heart began to beat violently. She was afraid, and at the same time angry with herself for being so, and whispered in the dark: "My darling," to prove to herself that she was calm.

"Wait a moment," whispered Helge, when she was going to light the lamp, and he kissed her again. "Put on the geisha dress; you look so sweet in it. I will sit on the balcony while you change."

Jenny changed her dress in the dark; she put the kettle on and arranged the anemones and the almond sprigs before she called him in and lighted up.

He took her again in his arms and said:

"Oh, Jenny, you are so lovely. Everything about you is lovely; it is heavenly to be with you. I wish I could be with you always."

She took his face between her two hands.

"Jenny — you wish it — that we could be always together?" She looked into his beautiful brown eyes:
"Yes, Helge; I do."

"Do you wish that this spring — our spring — never would end?"

"Yes — oh yes." She threw herself suddenly into his arms and kissed him; her half-open lips and closed eyes begged for more kisses; his words about their spring, that should never cease, awoke a painful anxiety in her heart that the spring and their dream would come to an end. And yet behind it all was a dread, which she did not try to explain to herself, but it came into existence when he asked if she wished they could always be together.

78

"I wish I were not going home," said Helge sadly.

"But I am going home soon too," she said softly, "and we shall probably come back here together."

"You are quite determined to go? Are you sorry that I have upset all your plans in this way?"

She gave him a hurried kiss and ran to the kettle, which was boiling over.

"No, you silly boy. I had almost made up my mind before, because mamma wants me badly." She gave a short laugh. "I am ashamed of myself — she is so pleased that I am coming home to help her, and it is really only to be with my lover. But it is all right. I can live cheaper at home even if I help them a little, and I may be able to earn something. What I can save now, I shall want here later."

Helge took the cup she gave him and seized her hand: "But next time you come here you will come with me; for
I suppose you will — you mean — that we should marry?"

His face was so young and so anxiously inquiring that she had to kiss him several times, forgetting that she had been afraid of that word, which had not been mentioned between them before.
"I suppose that will be the most practical plan, you dear boy, since we have agreed to be together always."

Helge kissed her hand, asking quietly: "When?"

"When you like," she answered as quietly — and firmly. Again he kissed her hand.

"What a pity we can't be married out here," he said a moment after in a different voice. She did not answer, but stroked his hair softly. Helge sighed : "But I suppose we ought not to, as we are going home so soon in any case. Your mother would feel hurt, don't you think, at such a hurried marriage?"

Jenny was silent. It had never occurred to her that she owed her mother any account of her doings — her mother had not consulted her when she had wanted to marry again.

"It would hurt my people, I know. I don't like to admit it, but it is so, and I should much prefer to write and tell them that I am engaged. As you are going home before me, it would be nice of you to go and see them."

Jenny bent her head as if to shake off a disagreeable sensation, and said: "I will, dear, if you wish me to — of course."

"I don't like it at all. It has been so lovely here — only you and I, nobody else in all the world. But mother would be so vexed, you see, and I don't want to make things worse for her than they are already. I don't care for my mother any longer — she knows it, and is so grieved at it. It is only a formality, I know, but she would suffer if she thought I wanted to keep her out in the cold. She would think it was vengeance for the old story, you know. When we are through with all that, we will get married, and nobody will have anything more to say. I wish so much that it would be soon — don't you?"

She kissed him in answer.

"I want you," he whispered, and she made no resistance when he caressed her. But he let her go suddenly and, buttering his biscuit, began to eat.

Afterwards they sat by the stove smoking, she in the easy-chair and he on the floor with his head in her lap.

"Isn't Cesca coming back tonight either?" he asked suddenly.

"No; she is staying in Tivoli till the end of the week," Jenny answered a little nervously. "You have such pretty, slender feet."

"You are so lovely — oh, so lovely — and I am so fond of you. You don't know how I love you, Jenny — I should like to lie down on the floor at your feet."

"Helge! Helge!" His sudden violence frightened her, but then she said to herself: he is my own darling boy. Why should I be afraid of him.

"No, Helge — don't. Not the shoes I stamp about with in those dirty streets."

Helge rose — sobered and humble. She tried to laugh the whole matter away. "There may be many dangerous bacilli on those shoes, you know."

"Ugh! What a pedant you are. And you pretend to be an artist." He laughed too, and to hide his embarrassment, he went on boisterously: "A nice sweetheart you are. Let me smell: I thought so — you smell of turpentine and paint."
"Nonsense, dear; I have not touched a brush for three weeks. But you will have to wash, sir."

"Have you any carbolic, in case of infection?" While he was washing his hands he said : "My father used to say that women are utterly destitute of poetry."

80

"Your father is quite right."

"And they can cure people by ordering cold baths," he said, with a laugh.

Jenny became suddenly serious. She went to him, put her hands on his shoulders, and kissed him : "I did not want you at my feet, Helge."

When he had gone she was ashamed of herself. He was right. She did want to give him a cold bath, but she would not do it again, for she loved him. She had played a poor part tonight. She had thought of Signora Rosa. What would she have said if anything had happened? It was rather humiliating to realize that she had been afraid of a scene with an angry signora — and tried to get out of her promise to her lover. In accepting his love and responding to his kisses she had as good as bound herself over to give him all he asked. She, of all people, would not play a game where she took everything and gave but little — not more than she could easily withdraw, if she changed her mind.

It was only nerves — this dread of something she had never tried. But she was glad he had not asked for more than she could willingly give, for there would come a moment, she thought, when she herself would wish to give him all.

It had all come so slowly and unnoticeably — just like spring in the south — and as steadily and surely. No sudden transition, no cold and stormy days that made one long desperately for the sun, for wealth of light and consuming heat. There had been none of those tremendously clear, endless, maddening spring nights of her own country. When the sunny day was past, night came quietly, the cold and darkness bringing peaceful sleep between the bright, warm days — each new day a little warmer than the one before, each day with more flowers on the Campagna, which did not seem greener than yesterday, yet was much more green and mellow than the week before.

Her love for him had come in the same way. Every night she looked forward to the next sunny day with him on the Campagna, but gradually it was more himself and his young love that she longed for. She had let him kiss her because it gave her pleasure, and from day to day their kisses had grown more frequent, till at last words faded away and kisses took their place.

He had become more manly and mature from day to day; the uncertainty and the sudden despondency of the earlier days had quite left him. She herself was brighter, friendlier, more sure of herself, not the coldness of youth, always ready to fight, but more a calm confidence in herself. She was not disappointed with life now because it would not shape itself according to her dreams, but accepted each day, trusting that the unknown was right and could be turned to advantage.

Why should not love come in the same way, slowly, like the warmth that grows day by day, thawing and tempering, and not as she had always believed it would come — as a storm that would change her at once into a woman she did not know, and whom her will could not control.

Helge accepted this slow, sound growth of her love quite naturally and calmly. Every night when they parted her heart was filled with gratitude to him, because he had not asked for more than she could give that day.
Oh, if they could have stayed here till May — till summer — the whole of summer, so that their love might ripen until they belonged to one another completely. They would go together to the mountains in the summer; the marriage could take place here later, or at home in the autumn, for they would marry, of course, in the ordinary way, since they were fond of each other.

When she thought of her journey home, she was almost afraid that she would awake as from a dream, but she told herself such thoughts were nonsense, since she loved him and he loved her. She did not like the disturbing elements of engagements, visiting relations, and so on, though they were trifles after all.

Heaven be praised for this blessed spring in Rome that had brought them together — they two alone on the green Campagna among the daisies.

"Don't you think Jenny will be sorry some day that she ever got engaged to that Gram?" asked Francesca one evening when she was sitting in Heggen's room.

He shook the ashes from his cigarette without answering. He discovered all of a sudden that it had never struck him as in- discreet to speak about Francesca's affairs to Jenny. But to speak about Jenny's to Francesca was quite another matter.

"Can you understand what she wants with him?" she asked again.

"Well, it's hard to say. We don't always understand what you women want with this or that man. We imagine that we choose for ourselves, but we are more like our brothers, the dumb animals, than we care to think. Some say we are disposed to love — because of our natural state — place and opportunity do the rest."

"Ugh!" said Francesca, shrugging her shoulders. "If that is so, you, I should say, are always disposed."

Gunnar laughed reluctantly: "Or I have never been disposed enough; I have never thought of any woman as the only one — and so on, and that is an essential condition in love — because of our natural state."

Francesca stared thoughtfully in front of her.

"I daresay you are right. But it happens sometimes that one falls in love with somebody for some special reason — not only because time and circumstances are favorable. I for one love him — you know who I mean — because I don't understand him. It seems to me impossible that anybody could really be what he appeared to be. I always expected something would happen that would explain what I saw. I searched for the hidden treasure. You know how desperately anxious one gets to find the longer one seeks. Even now, when I think that some other woman may find it, I . . . But there are some who love because the loved one is perfect to them — can give them all they need. Have you ever been in love with any woman to such an extent that you thought everything in her was right and good and beautiful — that you could love everything in her?

"No," he said briskly.

"But that is real love, don't you think? And that is how I thought Jenny would love, but it is impossible for her to love Helge Gram like that."

"I don't know him really. I know only that he is not so stupid as he looks — as the saying goes — I mean, there is more in him than you'd think at first sight. I suppose Jenny has found out his real value."

Cesca was quiet. She lit a cigarette and watched the flame of the wax vesta till it burnt out.

"Have you noticed that he always asks, 'Don't you think?' and 'Is it not?'? Has it not struck you that there is some- thing effeminate, something unfinished, about him?"

"Perhaps so. Possibly that's what attracted her. She is strong and independent herself, and might love a man weaker than herself."

"I'll tell you what I think. I don't believe that Jenny really is so strong and independent. She's only been forced to be. At home she had to help and support, and there was nobody to support her. She had to take care of me, because I needed her — now it is Gram. She is strong and determined, and she knows it, and nobody asks her in vain for help, but nobody can go on forever giving help and never getting any themselves. Don't you see that it will make her very lonely, always being the strongest? She is lonely now, and if she marries that fellow she will never be anything else. We all talk to her about ourselves, and she has nobody she could talk to in the same way. She ought to have a husband she could look up to, whose authority she should feel, one to whom she could say: This is how I have lived and worked and fought, for I thought it right, and who could judge if it was right? Gram cannot, because he is her inferior. How can she know if she has been in the right, when she has nobody with authority to confirm it? Jenny should ask, 'Is it not?' and 'Don't you think?' — not he."

They sat both quiet a while, then Heggen said:

"It is rather curious, Cesca, that when it is a question of your own affairs you cannot make head or tail of it, but when it concerns somebody else, I think you often can see clearer than any of us."

"Perhaps. That is why I think sometimes I ought to go into a convent. When I am outside a trouble I seem to understand it all, but when I am mixed up in it myself I can't see a thing."

XI

T HE juicy, blue-grey giant leaves of the cactus were scarred by names, initials, and hearts carved in the flesh. Helge was carving an H and a J, and Jenny stood with her arms round his shoulder, looking on.

"When we come back here our initials will be a brown scar like all the others," said he. "Do you think we shall be able to find them?"

She nodded.

"Among all the others?" he inquired in doubt. "There are so many. We will go and look for them, won't we?"

"Of course we will."

"You do think we shall come back here, don't you? And stand as we are now." He put his arm round her.

"Yes; I don't see why we should not, dear."

With arms encircled they went to the table and sat down, looking in silence out over the Campagna.

The sunlight seemed to move and the shadows wandered along the hillocks. Sometimes the rays came in thick bunches between white clouds, sailing in the sky. On the horizon, where the dark eucalyptus grove by the Fontane peeped over the farthest hill, rose a pearl-yellow haze, which would grow towards evening and cover the whole sky.

Far on the plain the Tiber hurried to the sea, golden when the sunshine fell on it, but silvery grey like the side of a fish when it mirrored the clouds. The daisies on the hill looked like new-fallen snow; on the field behind the osteria pale-grey, silky wheat was coming up, and two almond trees were covered with light pink blossoms.

"Our last day in the Campagna," said Helge. "It's quite sad!"

"Till next time," she said, kissing him and trying not to give in to her own sad mood. "Yes. Have you thought of it, Jenny, that when we sit here again it cannot be exactly the same as now? One changes day by day; we shall not be the same when we sit here again. Next year — next spring — is not this spring? — we shall not be the same either. We may be just as fond of one another, but not exactly in the same way as now."

Jenny shivered: "A woman would never say that, Helge."

"You think it strange that I should say it? I cannot help thinking it, because these months have made such a change in me — and in you, too. Don't you remember, you told me on that first morning how different you are now from the time you first came here? You could not have been fond of me as I was when we first met — could you, now?"

She stroked his cheek: "But, Helge, dear boy, the great change is just that we have got so fond of one another, and our love will ever increase. If we change, it will be only because our love has grown, and that is nothing to be afraid of, is it? you remember the day at Via Cassia — my birthday — when the first fine threads between us were spun? They have grown stronger now, and grow stronger every day. Is there anything in that to make you afraid?"
He kissed her neck: "You are leaving tomorrow...." "And you are coming to me in six weeks"

"Yes; but we are not here. We cannot go about in the Campagna. We have to leave in the midst of spring"

"It is spring at home too — and larks are singing there as well. Look at those driving clouds — just like those at home. Think of Nordmarken. We shall go there together. Spring is lovely at home, with strips of melting snow on all the hills round the deep blue fjords, the last runs on ski when the snow is melting and the brooks are rushing down the mountain-side; when the sky is green and clear at night with large, bright golden stars, and the ski scrape and sing on the icy crust of the snow. We may be able to go there together yet this spring."

"Yes, yes — but I have been to all these places — Vester Aker, Nordmarken — so often alone that I dread them. It seems to me almost as if fragments of my old discarded souls were hanging on every shrub up there."

"Hush, hush, dear. I should love to go there with my dearest friend, after being there alone and sad so many a spring."

They wandered hand in hand in the green Campagna — the haze had risen towards evening, and a slight breeze blew in their direction. From the road came the creaking of hay-carts, pulled by white oxen, and the tinkling of bells on the red harness of mules in front of blue vine carts.

Jenny looked tenderly at everything, bidding farewell in her mind to all the things she knew so well, and that were so dear to her. She had seen it all day after day with him, without knowing she had noticed it, and now suddenly she understood that it was all imprinted in her mind together with the memories of those happy days: here was the slope, where the short grass had grown softer and greener from day to day, and the faithful daisies in the meager soil; the thorny hedges along the roads and the rich green leaves of the calla under the bushes; the unceasing warble of the larks in the sky, and the innumerable concertinas that played to the dancers in the osterias on the plain — concertinas with the peculiar, glassy sound, for ever playing the same short Italian tunes. Why must she leave it all now?

The wind chilled her like a bath, till her body felt like a cool rich leaf, and she longed to give it to him.

They said good-bye for the last time at her door, and they could not part. "Oh, Jenny, if only you could be mine!"
She nestled closer in his arms and whispered: "Why not?"

His arms closed tight about her shoulders and her waist, but she trembled the instant she had said it. She did not know why she was afraid; she did not want to be, and she repented of having made a movement, as if she wished to get out of his passionate embrace, and he let her go.

"No, no; I know it is impossible."

"I would like you to," she said humbly.

He kissed her: "I know. But I must not. Thank you for everything. Oh, Jenny, my Jenny! Good-night! Thank you for loving me!"

The tears streamed down her cheeks as she lay in bed. She tried to tell herself that there was no sense in crying like that, as if something were gone forever.

PART TWO

I

THERE was a wait of several minutes at Frederikshald — time for a cup of coffee. Jenny hurried along the platform; then suddenly she stopped to listen. Somewhere, nearby, a lark was singing overhead. Once back in her compartment she leaned back in her corner and closed her eyes, her heart heavy with longing for the south.

The train rushed past small rocks of red granite, torn as it were from the mountain range, and between them dazzling glimpses of deep-blue fjords met the eye. Spruce trees clung to the mountain-side, with the afternoon sun on their reddish trunks and dark green, shiny needles. Everything in nature seemed conspicuously clear and clean after its bath of melting snow. The naked branches of foliferous trees stood out distinctly against the thin air, and little streamlets gurgled alongside the line.

It was all so different from the southern spring, with its slow, sound breathing and softly blended colors — she missed it so much. The sharp coloring now before her eyes reminded her of other springs, when she had been filled with longing for a joy far different from her present restful happiness.

Oh! for the spring out there, with the sprouting vegetation on the immense plain and the firm, severe lines of the encircling mountains, which, man has robbed of their woods, to build stone-grey cities on the spurs and plant olive groves on the slopes. For thousands of years, life has been teeming on the sides of the mountain, borne by it in patience, yet it raises its crown in eternal solitude and quiet towards heaven. Its proud outlines and subdued green and silvery grey coloring, the ancient cities and the slowly advancing spring — in spite of all that can be said of the tumultuous life of the south — make one's own life run with a calmer, healthier beat, that meets the coming of spring with greater equanimity than here, where it comes in such mighty waves.

Oh, Helge! She longed to be out there with him. It was so far away, and so long since it all happened. Not quite a week, yet it seemed almost a dream, as if she had never been away at all. But she had been there — not here to see and feel how the white, frosty, peaceful winter yielded and the dry, strong, light blue air, drenched with mist in the middle of the day, hung quivering over the ground. Every outline was blurred or broken, but the colors were vivid and sharp — naked, as it were — until evening came, when everything froze under a sky of pale green, everlasting light.

— You dear boy of mine — what are you doing now? I miss you so, and I want to be with you. I can scarcely believe that you are mine, and I can't bear to be alone, longing for you, all this bright, long spring. —

As the train proceeded on its way the scenery changed. Strips of snow showed among the trees and along the fences; the soft, shaded brown of the faded meadows and the ploughed fields met the eye, and the intense blue of the sky toned down near the horizon. The undulating line of the forest-clad mountain slopes lay far away; the branches of detached groups of trees in the fields gave the effect of lattice-work against the sky.

The old grey houses of the farms shone like silver, and the new barns were glowing red. The pine needles formed an olive green background for the purple buds of the beeches and the light green of the aspens.

Such is spring: glowing colors that last a little while, then everything turns a golden green, swelling with the sap of life, and ripens in a few weeks into full summer — spring, when no joy is great enough. Evening fell, the last long red sunrays vanished behind a ridge, and the golden light in the cloudless sky faded slowly.

When the train left Moss, the mountain ridge stood dark against the clear sky, and the reflection of it in the green fjord was black and transparent. One single large, bright star rose behind the range; its light was mirrored in a filmy golden thread on the water.

It reminded her of Francesca's nocturnes; she was fond of reproducing the colorings after sunset. Jenny wondered how things were going with Cesca, and she felt a pang of conscience when she realized that she had seen very little of her in the two last months. Cesca was working hard and was perhaps in difficulties, but all Jenny's intentions to have a good long talk with her had come to nothing.

It was dark when she arrived at her destination; her mother, Bodil, and Nils were at the station to meet her.

It was as if she had seen her mother a week ago, but Mrs. Berner cried when she kissed her daughter: "Welcome home, my darling child — God bless you!" Bodil had grown, and looked very smart in a long coat and skirt. Kalfatrus greeted her shyly.

As she came out of the station she smelt the odor peculiar to the railway square of Christiania — a mixture of sea-water, coal smoke, and dried herring. The cab drove along Carl Johan, past the old familiar houses. Mrs. Berner asked about the journey, and where she had spent the night. It seemed all so commonplace to Jenny, as if she had never been away from it. The two young people on the back seat said never a word.

Outside a garden gate in Wergelandsveien a young couple stood kissing each other good-night. A few stars twinkled in the clear deep blue sky above the naked trees in the Castle gardens. A smell of moldering leaves came through the carriage window, reminding her of melancholy springs of old.

The cab stopped at the house where they lived. There was light still in the dairy on the ground floor; the woman came out on the doorstep, when she heard the cab, and said: "Good evening; welcome back," to Jenny. Ingeborg came rushing down the stairs to embrace her, and hurried up again, carrying her sister's bag. Supper was laid in the sitting-room, and Jenny saw her napkin with her father's silver ring in her old place beside Kalfatrus. Ingeborg hurried into the kitchen, and Bodil went with Jenny to her old room at the back, which had been Ingeborg's during her absence, and still harbored some of her belongings. On the walls were some picture cards of actors; Napoleon and Madame Récamier in mahogany frames hung on either side of Jenny's old empire mirror above the antique chest of drawers.

Jenny washed and did her hair; she felt an irritation in her skin from the journey, and passed the powder-puff a couple of times over her face. Bodil sniffed the powder to see if it was scented. They went to supper. Ingeborg had a nice hot meal ready; she had been to a cookery school that winter. In the light of the lamp Jenny saw that her young sisters had their thick curly hair tied up with silk bows. Ingeborg's small, dark face was thinner, but she did not cough any longer. She saw, too, that mamma had grown older — or had she perhaps not noticed, when she was at home and saw her every day, that the small wrinkles in her mother's pretty face increased, that the tall, girlish figure stooped a little, and that the shoulders lost their roundness? Since she grew up she had always been told that her mother looked like an elder and prettier sister of hers.

They spoke about everything that had happened at home during the year.

"Why didn't we take a taxi?" said Nils suddenly. "How stupid of us to ride home in an old four-wheeler!"

"Well, it's too late now; no good crying over spilt milk," laughed Jenny.

The luggage arrived; her mother and sisters watched the unpacking with interest. Ingeborg and Bodil carried the things into Jenny's room and put them in the drawers; the embroidered underlinen, which Jenny told them she had bought in Paris, was handled almost with reverence. There was great joy over the gifts to themselves: shantung for summer dresses and Italian bead necklaces. They draped themselves in the stuff before the glass, and tried the effect of the beads in their hair. Kalfatrus alone showed some interest in her pictures, trying to lift the box that contained her canvases.

"How many have you brought?"

"Twenty-six, but they are mostly small ones."

"Are you going to have a private exhibition — all by yourself?" "I don't know yet — I may, some day."
While the girls were washing up and Nils was making his bed on the sofa, Mrs. Berner and Jenny had a chat in Jenny's room over a cup of tea and a cigarette.

"What do you think of Ingeborg?" asked Mrs. Berner anxiously.

"She looks well and bright, but, of course, she will need looking after. We must send her to live in the country till she gets quite strong again."

"She is so sweet and good always — bright and full of fun, and so useful in the house. I am so anxious about her; I think she has been out too much last winter, dancing too much, and keeping late hours, but I had not the heart to refuse her anything. You had such a sad childhood, Jenny — I know you missed the company of other children, and I was sure you and papa would think it right to let the child have all the pleasure she could." She sighed. "My poor little girls, they have nothing to look forward to but work and privations. What am I to do if they get ill besides? I can do so little."

Jenny bent over her mother and kissed the tears from her pretty, childish eyes. The longing to give and to receive tenderness, the remembrance of her early childhood, and the consciousness that her mother did not know her life — its sorrows before and its happiness now — melted into a feeling of protecting love, and she gathered her mother into her arms.

"Don't cry, mother dear. Everything will come all right. I am going to stay at home for the present, and we have still something left of Aunt Katherine's money."

"No, Jenny, you must keep that for yourself. I understand now that you must not be hampered in any way in your work. It was such a joy to us all when your picture at the exhibition was sold last autumn."

Jenny smiled. The fact that she had sold a picture and had two or three lines in the papers about it made her people look upon her work in quite a different light.

"Don't worry about me, mother. It is all right. I may be able to earn something while I am here. I must have a studio, though," she said, after a pause, adding as an explanation: "I must finish my pictures in a studio, you see."

"But you will live at home, won't you?" asked the mother anxiously. Jenny did not answer.
"It won't do, my dear child, for a young girl to live alone in a studio." "Very well," said Jenny; "I shall live at home."

When she was alone she took out Helge's photo and sat down to write to him. She had been home only a couple of hours, and yet everything she had lived through out there, where he was, seemed so far away and altogether apart from her life here, before or now. The letter was one single cry of yearning.

II

J ENNY had hired a studio and was arranging it to her taste. Kalfatrus came in the afternoons and helped her. "You have grown so tall that I almost thought I could not call you by the old name any longer."

The boy laughed.

Jenny asked about all his doings while she had been away, and Nils told her of the extraordinary adventures he and two boy friends had had while they lived for some weeks in the log huts in Nordmarken. As she listened, it crossed her mind that her trips up there with him were now things of the past.

She went in the mornings to the outskirts of the city — to walk by herself in the sunshine. The fields lay yellow with dead grass, there was still snow under the pines, but tiny buds were coming out on the foliage trees and from underneath the dead leaves peeped downy shoots of the blue anemone. She read Helge's letters again and again; she carried them about her wherever she went. She longed for him impatiently, madly — longed to see him and touch him and convince herself that he was hers.

She had been back twelve days and had not yet been to see his parents; when he asked her a third time if she had been, she made up her mind to go next day. The weather had changed in the night; a strong north wind was blowing, the sun shone with a sharp light, and clouds of dust were whirling in the streets. Then came a hail-storm so violent that she had to take refuge in a doorway. The hard white grains rebounded from the pavement on to her shoes and frivolous summer stockings. Next moment the sun came out again.

The Grams lived in Welhavensgate. At the comer Jenny stopped for a moment to look about; the two rows of grey houses stood almost completely in the raw, icy shade; on the one side a narrow strip of sun fell on the top floor; she was pleased to think that Helge's parents lived there.

Her way to school had been along this street for four years. She knew it well — the smell shops, the black marks of snow on the plaster ornaments of the front entrances, the plants in majolica pots or coloured tissue paper in the windows, the fashion-plates against the panes at the dressmaker's, and the narrow gateway leading to dark back-yards, where small heaps of dirty snow made the air still more raw. A tramcar rolled heavily up the hill.

Close to where she stood, in the other street, was a large house with a dark yard; they had lived there when her stepfather died.

Outside a door with a brass plate, with "G. Gram" engraved on it; she stood still for a moment, her heart beating. She tried to laugh at herself for this senseless feeling of oppression each time she had to face anything new, for which she had not prepared her mind in advance. Why should she consider her future parents-in-law of such importance? They could not hurt her. . . . She rang the bell.

She heard somebody coming through the hall; then the door opened. It was Helge's mother; she knew her from a photograph.

"Are you Mrs. Gram? I am Miss Winge." "Oh yes — please come in."

Jenny followed her through a long, narrow hall encumbered with cupboards, boxes, and outdoor clothes.

Mrs. Gram opened the door to the drawing-room. At this moment the sun came in, showing up the moss-green plush furniture, curtains and portiéres of the same material, and the vivid colors of the carpet. The room was small and very full — photographs and sundry fancy articles stood in every possible place.

"I am afraid it is very untidy here. I have not had time to dust for several days," said Mrs. Gram. "We don't use this room every day, and I have no servant just now. I had to dismiss the one I had — she was so dirty and always answering back, but it's hard to get another at all, and just as well, for they're all alike as far as that goes. Keeping house nowadays — it's simply dreadful. Helge told us you would be coming, but we had almost given up hope of seeing you."

When she talked and laughed she showed big, white front teeth and a black hole on either side, where two were missing.

Jenny sat looking at the woman who was Helge's mother — how different it all was from what she had imagined.

She had formed a picture in her mind of Helge's home and mother from his descriptions, and she had pitied the woman whom the husband did not love and who had loved the children so much that they had rebelled and longed to get away from this tyrannic mother-love that could not bear them ever to be anything but her children. In her heart she had taken the mother's part. Men did not understand to what extent a woman could change who loved and got no love in return except the love of small children; they could not understand what a mother would feel at seeing her children grow up and glide away from her, or how she could rise in defiance and anger against the inexorable life that let little children grow up and cease to feel their mother everything to them, while they were everything to her as long as she lived.

Jenny had wanted to love Helge's mother — and she could not do it; on the contrary, she felt an almost physical antipathy towards Mrs. Gram as she talked on and on.

The features were the same as Helge's — the high, slightly narrow forehead, the beautifully carved nose, and the even, dark brows, the same small mouth with thin lips, and the pointed chin. But there was an expression about her mouth as if everything she said were spiteful, and a malicious and scornful look about the fine wrinkles of the face. The remarkably well-shaped eyes, bluish in the white, were hard and piercing. They were large, dark brown eyes — much darker than Helge's.

She had been uncommonly pretty; yet Jenny was convinced she was right in thinking that Gert Gram had not been anxious to marry her. She was no lady as far as language and manners went — but many pretty girls of the middle classes soon turned harsh and sour when they had been married some time and shut up in a home, with worries of housekeeping and servants to spoil their life.

"Mr. Gram asked me to go and see you and give you the latest news about him," said Jenny. She felt she could not speak about him as Helge.

"I understand that he spent his time exclusively with you lately — he never mentioned anybody else in his letters. I thought he was in love with a Miss Jahrman at first."

"Miss Jahrman is my friend — there were several of us always together at first, but she has been very busy lately working at a large picture."

"Is she the daughter of Colonel Jahrman of Tegneby? Then I suppose she has money?"

"No; she is studying on a small inheritance from her mother. She is not on very good terms with her father — that is to say, he did not like her wanting to become an artist, so she refused to accept any help from him."

"Very stupid of her. My daughter, Mrs. Arnesen, knows her slightly — she stayed with us at Christmas. She said there were other reasons why the Colonel did not want to have anything to do with her; she is said to be very good looking, but has a bad reputation."

"There is not the least truth in it," said Jenny stiffly.

"You have a good time, you artists." Mrs, Gram sighed. "I cannot see how Helge could work at all — it seems to me he never wrote about anything else but going here and there in the Campagna with you."

"Oh," said Jenny. It was very painful to hear Mrs. Gram speak of things out there. "I think Mr. Gram worked very hard, and one must have a day off now and again."

"Possibly — but we housewives must get along without it. Wait till you get married, Miss Winge. Everybody wants holidays, it seems to me. I have a niece who has just become a school teacher — she was to study medicine, but she was not strong enough, so had to give it up and begin at the seminary instead. She is always having a day off, it seems to me, and I tell her there is no danger of her being overworked."

Mrs. Gram left the room, and Jenny rose to have a look at the pictures.

Above the sofa was a large view of the Campagna; one could easily see that Gram had studied in Copenhagen. The drawing was good and thorough, but the coloring thin and dry. The background with two Italian women in national dress and the miniature plants round the tumbled pillar was poor. The model study of a young girl below was better. She had to smile — no wonder Helge had found some difficulty in accepting Rome as it was, and had been disappointed at first, after having grown up with all this Italian romance on the walls at home.

There were several well-drawn small landscapes from Italy, with ruins and national costumes, and some copies — Correggio's "Danae" and Guido Reni's "Aurora" — which were not good, and other copies of baroque pictures which she did not know, but a study of a priest was good.

There was also a large light green summer landscape — an experiment in impressionism — but thin and plain as far as coloring went. The one over the piano was better, the sun above the ridge and the air quite good. A portrait of Mrs. Gram hung beside it — very good indeed — better than any of the other things. The figure and the hands were perfectly drawn, the bright red dress, draped at the sides, the openwork black mittens, and the high black hat with a red wing were very effective; the pale face with the dark eyes below the curls on her forehead was good, but unfortunately she stood as glued on to the grey-blue background. The portrait of a child drew her attention — near the frame was written "Bamsey, four years old." Was that pretty little frowning child in a white shirt Helge? How good he was!

Mrs. Gram returned with some cake and wine on a tray. Jenny muttered something about giving trouble: "I have been looking at your husband's paintings."

"I don't understand much about it, but I think they are beautiful. He says himself that hey are no good, but it is only a way of talking, I think," she said, with a short, harsh laugh. "My husband is pretty easy-going, you see, and painting pictures could not pay our way when we had married and had children, so he had to do something useful besides. But he was too lazy to paint as well, and that is why he pretended that he had no talent. To me his pictures are much prettier than all the modern paintings, but I suppose you think differently?"

96

"Your husband's pictures are very pretty, especially your portrait, which I think beautiful."

"Do you? — but it is not very like me, and certainly not flattering." She laughed again, the same slightly bitter laugh. "I think he painted much better before he began to imitate those who were modern then — Thaulow and Krogh and others."

Jenny sipped her wine in silence while Mrs. Gram went on talking.

"I should like to ask you to stay to lunch, Miss Winge, but I have to do everything myself, you see, and we were not prepared for your coming. I am sorry, but I hope you will come another time."

Jenny understood that Mrs. Gram wished to get rid of her — it was quite natural, as she was without a servant and had to get the lunch — so she took her leave. On the stairs she met Mr. Gram — she thought so at least. As she passed him she had the impression that he looked very young and that his eyes were very blue.

III

T WO days later, in the afternoon, when Jenny was painting in her studio, Helge's father called. As he stood with his hat in his hand, she saw that his hair was grey — so grey that she could not make out what the original color had been, but he still looked young. He was thin, and had a slight stoop — not the stoop of an old man, but rather of one too slender for his height. His eyes too were young, though sad and tired and so big and blue that they gave one a curious impression of being wide open, surprised, and at the same time suspicious.

"I was very anxious to meet you, Jenny Winge," he said, "as you can understand for yourself. No; don't take off your overall, and tell me if I disturb you."

"Not in the least," said Jenny warmly. She liked his smile and his voice. She threw her overall on a chair : "The light is almost gone already. It was very good of you to come and see me."

"It is a very long time since I was in a studio," said Gram, sitting down on the sofa.

"Don't you ever see any of the other painters — your contemporaries?" asked Jenny.

"No, never," he answered curtly.

"But" — Jenny bethought herself — "how did you find your way up here? Did you ask them at home for my address, or at the artists' club?"

Gram laughed.

"No; I met you on the stairs the other day, and yesterday, as I was going to the office, I saw you again. I followed you. I was half a mind to stop you and introduce myself. Then I saw you go in here, and I knew there were studios in this house, so I thought I would pay you a visit."

"Do you know," said Jenny, with a merry laugh, "Helge too followed me in the street — I was with a friend. He had lost his way in the old streets by the rag market, and he came and spoke to us. That is how we made his acquaintance. We thought it rather cool at the time, but it seems to run in the family."

Gram frowned, and sat quiet an instant. Jenny realized that she had said the wrong thing, and was thinking what to say next.

"May I make you some tea?" she asked, and without waiting for an answer lit the spirit-lamp under the kettle.

"Miss Winge, you must not be afraid that Helge is like me in other things. I don't think he takes after his father in anything — fortunately." He laughed. Jenny did not know what to say to this, and busied herself with the tea.

"It's rather bare in here, as you see, but I live at home with my mother." "I see. This a good studio, is it not?"

"I think so."

After a moment he said : "I have been thinking of you very much lately, Miss Winge — I understood from my son's letters that you and he. . . ."

"Yes, Helge and I are very fond of each other," said Jenny, looking straight at him. He took her hand and held it an instant.

"I know my son so little — his real self is almost unknown to me, but as you are fond of him you must know him far better. I have always believed that he was a good boy, and clever in a way, and the fact that you love him proves to me that I have reason to be pleased — and proud of him. Now that I know you, I can understand that he loves you, and I hope he will make you happy."

"Thank you," said Jenny, giving him her hand again.

"I am fond of the boy — he's my only son — and I think he likes me too."

"I know he does. Helge is very fond of you and of his mother." She blushed as if she had been tactless.

"Yes, I believe so; but he must have seen long ago that his father and mother did not care for one another. Helge has not had a happy home, Jenny. I don't mind telling you this, for if you have not already understood it, you will soon see it for yourself. You are a sensible girl. Helge's experience of his own home will teach him, perhaps, to value your love and try to keep it."

Jenny poured out the tea: "Helge used to come and have tea with me in the afternoon in Rome — it was really during these visits we learnt to know each other, I think." "And you became fond of each other?"

"No, not at once. Perhaps we were, though — even then — but we believed that we were great friends only. He came to tea afterwards too, of course." They both smiled.

"Tell me something about Helge from the time he was a boy — when he was quite small, I mean."

Gram smiled sadly and shook his head: "No; I cannot tell you anything about my son. He was always good and obedient, and did well at school. He was not particularly clever, but he worked steadily and diligently. He was very reserved as a boy — and later, too, for that matter — with me, anyhow. You, I am sure, have more to tell me."

"About what?"

"About Helge, of course. Tell me what he looks like to the girl who loves him. You are no ordinary girl either — you are an artist — and I believe you are intelligent and good.

Will you not tell me how you came to like him — what it was that made you choose him?"

"Well," she said laughingly — "it is not so easy to say — we just got fond of each other."

He laughed too. "Well, it was a stupid question, I admit.

One would say I had quite forgotten what it was to be young and in love, don't you think?"

"Don't you think! — Helge says that so often, too. It w r as one of the things that made me like him. He was so young.

I saw that he was very reserved, but gradually thawed a good deal."

"I can understand he would — to you. Tell me more!

Oh, but don't look so frightened. I don't mean that you should tell me the whole story. Only tell me something about yourself and about Helge, about your work — and about Rome. I am an old man. I want to feel again what it is like to be an artist — and free. To work at the only thing you care for — to be young — and in love — and happy."

He stayed for two hours. When he was ready to go and stood with his hat in his hand, he said in a low voice: "It is no use trying to hide from you the state of things at home. When we meet there, it would be better if we pretended not to have met before. I don't wish Helge's mother to know that I have made your acquaintance in this way — for your sake, so as not to expose you to any disagreeable, malicious words from her. It is enough for her to know that I like somebody — especially if it is a woman — to turn her against them. You think it strange, I am sure, but you understand, don't you?"

"Yes," said Jenny quietly.

"Good-bye. I am happy about you for Helge's sake — believe me, Jenny."

She had written to Helge the night before about her visit to his home, and when she read her letter through, she realized how very cold and poor was the part about her meeting with his mother. When writing to him that night she told him about his father's visit, but she tore the letter up and began another. It was so difficult to tell him about his father's call and not to mention hers to Mrs. Gram. She did not like having secrets with one from the other. She felt humiliated on Helge's behalf at having been initiated all at once in the misery of his home, and she ended by not saying a word about it in her letter — it would be easier to explain when he came.

IV

TOWARDS the end of May Jenny had not heard from Helge for several days, and was beginning to fear that something had happened. If no letter came the next day she would send a wire. In the afternoon, when she was in her studio, there was a knock at the door. When she opened she was seized and hugged and kissed by a man who stood on the landing.

"Helge!" She was overjoyed. "Helge! how you frightened me, you dear boy. Let me look at you. Is it really and truly you?" and she pulled the cap-cap off his head.

"I hope it could not be anybody else," he said laughingly. "But what does all this mean?"

"I will tell you," he said, pressing his face against her neck. "I wanted to give you a surprise, and so I did, it seems." After the first tender greetings were over they sat down hand in hand on the sofa.

"Let me look at you, Jenny — oh, how lovely you are! At home they believe I am in Berlin. I am going to an hotel for the night. I mean to stay a few days in town before telling them. Won't it be fun! It is a pity you live at home now. We could have been together all day."

"When you knocked I thought it was your father coming." "Father?"

"Yes." She felt a little embarrassed; it seemed suddenly so difficult to explain the whole thing to him. "You see, your father came one day to call, and he has been to tea sometimes in the afternoon. We sit and talk about you."

"But, Jenny, you never wrote a word about it; you have not even mentioned that you had met father."

"No; I preferred to tell you. You see, your mother does not know about it; your father thought it better not to mention it."

"Not to me?"

"Oh no, we never meant that. He believes most likely that I have told you. It was only your mother who was not to know. I thought it was — well, I did not like to write you that I had a secret from your mother. You understand?"

Helge was silent.

"I did not like it myself," she continued. "But what could I do? He called on me, you see, and I like him very much. I am getting quite fond of your father."

"Father can be very attractive, I know — and then you are an artist, too." "He likes me for your sake, dear. I know it is so."

Helge did not answer.

"And you have only seen mother once?"

"Yes — but are you not hungry ? Let me give you something to eat."

"No, thanks. We'll go out and have supper somewhere together."

There was a knock at the door again. "It is your father," whispered Jenny. "Hush — sit still — don't open!"
They heard retreating steps on the landing. Helge frowned. "What is it, dear?"
"Oh, I don't know — I hope we won't see him. We don't wish to be disturbed, do we? Not to see anybody."

"No," she kissed his mouth, and, bending his head, she kissed him again on the neck behind the ear.

After dinner, when they were having coffee and liqueurs, Jenny said suddenly: "I cannot get over this about Francesca."

"Did you not know before? I thought she had written to you." Jenny shook her head.

"Never a word — you could have knocked me down with a feather when I got her letter. Only a few words: 'Tomorrow I am going to marry Ahlin.' I had not the least suspicion of it."

"Neither had we. They were very much together, of course, but that they were going to marry even Heggen did not know until she asked him to give her away."

"Have you seen them since?"

"No. They went to Rocca di Papa the same day, and they were still there when I left Rome."

Jenny sat a while thinking.

"I thought she was all taken up with her work," she said. "Heggen told me she had finished the big picture of the gate, and that it was very good. She had begun several small ones too, but then she got married all of a sudden. I don't know if they had been properly engaged even. And what about you, Jenny — you wrote you had begun a new picture?"

Jenny led him to the easel. The big canvas showed a street with a row of houses — offices and factories — in grey-green and brick-red coloring. To the right were some workshops; behind them rose the walls of some big houses against a rich blue sky, with a few departing rain clouds, leaden grey in color, but shining white where the sun came through. There was a strong light on the shops and the wall, and on the young foliage of some trees in a yard. A few men, some wagons and fruit barrows stood about in the street.
"I don't know much about it, but is it not very good? I think it is fine — it is beautiful."
"When I was wandering about waiting for my own boy — after walking here so lonely and sad many a spring before — and saw the maples and the chestnuts opening out their tender leaves against the smoky houses and red walls under a golden spring sky, I wanted to paint it."

"Where did you get the view?"

"Stenersgaten. You see, your father spoke about a picture of you as a boy, which he kept in his office. I went down there to have a look at it, and then I saw this view from his office window. They let me stand in the box factory next door to paint it, but I had to change it a bit — compose a little."

"You have been a good deal with father, I see," said Helge after a pause. "I suppose he is very interested in your picture?"

"Yes. He often came over to look while I was working on it, and gave me some good advice. He knows a lot about painting, of course."

"Do you think father had any talent?" asked Helge.

"Oh yes, I believe so. The pictures hanging in your home are not particularly good, but he let me see some studies he keeps in his office, and I think they show a refined and quite original talent. He would never have been a great artist; he is too susceptible to influence, but I think it is because of his readiness to appreciate and love the good work of others. He has a great understanding and love of art."

"Poor father!" said Helge.

"Yes" — Jenny nestled closer to him — "your father is perhaps more to be pitied than you or I understand."

They kissed — and forgot to speak any more of Gert Gram. "Your people don't know about it yet?" Helge asked.
"No," said Jenny.

"At first, when I was sending all my letters to your home address, did your mother never ask who wrote to you like that every day?"

"No. My mother is not that kind."

"My mother," repeated Helge hotly. "You mean to say that mother would have done so — that she is tactless. I don't think you are just to my mother — surely, for my sake, you ought not to speak like that of her."

"Helge! What do you mean?" Jenny looked at him, astonished. "I have not said a word about your mother."

"You said, my mother is not like that." "I did not. I said my mother."

"No; you said my mother. You may not like her — although I cannot see what reason you have so far not to — but you should remember that you speak about my mother, and that I am fond of her as she is."

"Oh, Helge! I don't understand how. . . ." She stopped, as she felt tears filling her eyes. It was so strange a thing for Jenny Winge to shed tears that she felt ashamed of it, and was quiet.

But he had seen it: "Jenny, my darling, have I hurt you?

Oh, my own girl — what a misery it is! You can see for yourself — no sooner have I come back, but it begins again."

He clenched his hands and cried: "I hate it — I hate my home!"

"My darling boy, you must not say so. Don't let it upset you like that." She took him in her arms. "Helge, dearest, listen to me — what has it to do with us? — it cannot make any difference in us" — and she kissed and petted him till he stopped crying and shivering.

V

JENNY and Helge were sitting on the sofa in his room, silent, with arms encircled. It was a Sunday in June; Jenny had been for a walk with Helge in the morning and had dined at the Grams'. After dinner they all sat in the drawing-room, struggling through the tedious afternoon, until Helge got Jenny into his own room on the pretext of reading her something he had written.

"Ugh!" said Jenny at last.

Helge did not ask why she said it. He only laid his head in her lap and let her stroke his hair; neither spoke.

Helge sighed: "It was nicer at your place in the Via Vantaggio, was it not?"

The sound of plates and of fat spluttering in a pan came from the kitchen. Mrs. Gram was getting supper. Jenny opened the window wide to let out the smell that had penetrated into the room. She stood a moment looking out on the yard. All the windows were kitchen or bedroom windows with blinds half drawn, except one large one in each corner. Ugh! How well she knew those dining-rooms with a single corner window looking on to the yard, dark and dismal, with never a glimpse of sun. Soot came in when one aired the rooms, and the smell of food was permanent. The playing of a guitar came from a servant's room, and a high soprano voice -was singing a doleful Salvation Army hymn.

The guitar reminded her of Via Vantaggio, and Cesca, and Gunnar, who used to sit on her sofa with his legs on a stool, strumming on Cesca's guitar and singing Cesca's Italian songs. And she was seized with a sudden, desperate longing for everything out there. Helge came to her side: "What are you thinking of?"

"Of Via Vantaggio."

"Oh yes. What a lovely time we had there!"

She put her arm round his neck and drew his head on to her shoulder. It had struck her the moment he spoke that he was not a part of that which filled her heart with longing. She raised his head again and looked into his amber brown eyes, wishing to be reminded of all the glorious days in the Campagna, when he lay among the daisies looking at her. And she wanted to shake off the intense, sickening feeling of discomfort which always came over her when she was in his home.

Everything was unbearable here. The first evening she was invited to the house after Helge's official arrival, when Mrs. Gram had introduced her to her husband, she had to pretend not to know him, while Helge stood looking on at this comedy, knowing they had deceived his mother. It was dreadful — but something still worse had happened. She had been left alone with Gram for a few minutes and he mentioned that he had been to the studio to see her one afternoon, but she had not been in. "No, I was not at the studio that day," she had answered, turning very red. He looked at her in great surprise, and almost without knowing why she did so she blurted out: "I was, but I could not let you in, because there was somebody with me." Gram had smiled and said: "Yes, I heard quite distinctly that somebody was moving in the studio." In her confusion she had told him that it was Helge, and that he had been a few days in town incognito.

"My dear Jenny," Gram had said, and she saw that he was hurt, "you need not have kept it secret from me. I would certainly not have intruded on you — but I will say that it would have given me much pleasure if Helge had told me."

She found nothing to say, and he continued: "I shall be careful not to tell him."

She had never meant to keep it a secret from Helge that she had told his father, but she had not yet been able to tell him — afraid that he would not like it. She was worried and nervous about all these mysteries, one after the other.

It is true, she had not told them anything at home either, but that was quite different. She was not used to speak to her mother about anything concerning herself; she had never expected any understanding from her, and had never asked for it. Her mother, besides, was very anxious about Ingeborg just at present. Jenny had got her to rent a cottage a little way out of town; Bodil and Nils came to school by train every day, and Jenny lived in the studio.

Yet she had never been so fond of her mother and her home as she was now. Once or twice when she had been worried about things, and out of spirits, her mother had tried to help and comfort her without asking any questions. She would have blushed at the mere thought of forcing herself into the confidence of any of her children. To grow up in a home like Helge's must have been a torture. It seemed almost as if the gloom of it hung about them even when they were together elsewhere.

"Dearest," she said, caressing him.

Jenny had offered to help Mrs. Gram wash up and to get the supper, but she had said, with her usual smile: "No, my dear, you have not come here for that — certainly not, kiss Winge."

Perhaps she did not mean it, but Mrs. Gram always smiled in a spiteful way when she talked to her. Poor woman, it was probably the only smile she had.

Gram came in; he had been for a walk. Jenny and Helge went to sit with him in his study. Mrs. Gram came in for an instant.

"You forgot to take your umbrella, dear — as usual. You were lucky to escape a shower. Men want such a lot of looking after, you know," she said, turning to Miss Winge.

"You manage it very well," said Gram. His voice and manners were always painfully polite when he spoke to his wife.

"You are sitting in here too, I see," she said to Helge and Jenny.

"I have noticed that the study is the nicest room in every house," said Jenny. "It was in our house, when my father was alive. I suppose it is because they are made to work it."

"The kitchen ought in that case to be the very nicest room in every house," said Mrs. Gram. "Where do you think more work is done, Gert — in your room or mine" — for I suppose the kitchen is my study."

"Undoubtedly more useful work is done in your room."

"I believe, after all, that I must accept your kind offer of help, Miss Winge — it is getting late."

They were at table when the bell rang. It was Mrs. Gram's niece, Aagot Sand. Mrs. Gram introduced Jenny.

"Oh, you are the artist with whom Helge spent so much of his time in Rome. I guessed that much when I saw you in Stener sgaten one day in the spring. You were walking with Uncle Gert, and carried your painting things."

"You must be mistaken, Aagot," said Mrs. Gram. "When do you imagine you saw them?"

"The day before Intercession Day, as I was coming back from school."

"It is quite true," said Gram. "Miss Winge had dropped her paintbox in the street, and I helped her to pick the things up."

"A little adventure, I see, which you have not confessed to your wife," said Mrs. Gram, laughing. "I had no idea you knew each other before."

Gram laughed too: "Miss Winge did not recognize me.

108

It was not very flattering to me — but I did not wish to remind her. Did you not suspect when you saw me that I was the kind old gentleman who had helped you?"

"I was not sure," said Jenny feebly, her face turning purple. "I did not think you recognized me." She tried to smile, but she was painfully conscious of her blushing and unsteady voice.

"It was an adventure, indeed," said Mrs. Gram. "A most peculiar coincidence."

"Have I said something wrong again?" asked Aagot when they went into the drawing-room after supper. Mr. Gram had retired to his study and Mrs. Gram had gone into the kitchen. "It is detestable in this house. You never know when there's going to be an explosion. Please explain. I don't understand anything."

"Mind your own business," said Helge angrily.

"All right, all right- — -don't bite me! Is Aunt Rebecca jealous of Miss Winge now?" "You are the most tactless woman. . . ."

"After your mother, yes. Uncle Gert told me so one day."

She laughed. "Have you ever heard anything so absurd! Jealous of Miss Winge." She looked inquisitively at the two others.

"You need not bother about things that only concern us, Aagot," said Helge curtly. "Indeed? I only thought — but never mind; it does not matter."

"No; it does not in the least."

Mrs. Gram came in and lit the lamp. Jenny looked almost scared at her angry face. She stood a moment, staring with hard, glittering eyes, then she bent down and picked up Jenny's scissors, which had fallen on the floor.

"It looks as if it were a specialty of yours to drop things. You should not let things slip through your fingers, Miss Winge. Helge is not as gallant as his father, it seems." She laughed. "Do you want your lamp? . . She went into the study and pulled the door after her. Helge listened an instant — his mother spoke in a low but angry voice in the other room.

"Can't you leave that wretched business alone for once?" came distinctly through the door; it was Gram speaking.

Jenny turned to Helge: "I am going home now — I have a headache."

"Don't go, Jenny. There will be such a scene if you go. Stay a little longer. Mother will only be more angry if you run away now."

"I cannot stand it," she whispered, nearly crying.

Mrs. Gram walked through the room. Gram came in and joined them. "Jenny is tired; she is going now. I will see her home."

"Are you going already? Can't you stay a little longer?" "I have a headache and I am tired," murmured Jenny.
"Please stay a little," he whispered to her. "She" — he indicated the kitchen with his head — "does not say anything to you, and while you are here we are spared a scene."

Jenny sat down quietly and took up her needlework again. Aagot crocheted energetically at a hospital shawl.
Gram went to the piano. Jenny was not musical, but she understood that he was, and by and by she became calm as he played softly — all for her, she felt.

"Do you know this one, Miss Winge?" "No."

"Nor you either, Helge? Did you not hear it in Rome?

In my time it was sung everywhere. I have some books with Italian songs." He rose to look for them; as he passed Jenny he whispered: "Do you like me to play?"
"Yes."

"Shall I go on?"

 "Yes, please."

He stroked her hand: "Poor little Jenny. You had better go now — before she comes."
Mrs. Gram brought a tray of cakes and dessert.

"How nice of you to play to us, Gert. Don't you think my husband plays beautifully, Miss Winge? Has he played to you before?" she asked innocently.

Jenny shook her head: "I did not know that Mr. Gram played the piano."

"What a beautiful worker you are." She looked at Jenny's embroidery. "I thought you artists did not condescend to do needlework. It is a lovely pattern — where did you get it? Abroad, I suppose?"

"I designed it myself."

"Oh well, then it is easy to get nice patterns. Have you seen this, Aagot? Isn't it pretty? You are very clever" — and she patted Jenny's hand.

What loathsome hands she had, thought Jenny — small, short fingers, with nails broader than long, and splayed out wide.

Helge and Jenny saw Aagot to her rooms and walked slowly down Pilestaedet in the pale night of June. The chestnuts in bloom along the hospital wall smelt strongly after the afternoon shower.

"Helge," said Jenny, "you must try and arrange so that we need not go with them the day after tomorrow."

"It is impossible. They have asked you and you have accepted. It is for your sake they have arranged this picnic."

"But can you not understand how miserable it will be? I wish we could go alone somewhere, you and I, as in Rome."

"There is nothing I would like better, but if we refuse to be a party to their midsummer outing it will only make things more unpleasant at home."

"Not more than usual, I suppose," she said scornfully.

"Yes, much more. Can you not put up with it for my sake? Hang it all, you are not obliged to be in the midst of it always, or to live and work there!" He was right, she thought, and reproached herself for not being patient enough. He, poor boy, had to live and work in a home she could scarcely endure for two hours. He had grown up in it and lived his whole youth in it.

"I am horrid and selfish, Helge." She clung to him, tired, worried, and humiliated. She longed for him to kiss her and comfort her. What did it really matter to them? They had each other, and belonged somewhere far away from the air of hatred, suspicion, and anger in his home.

The scent of jessamine was wafted from the old gardens that still remained.

"We can go off by ourselves another day — just you and I," he said, to comfort her. "But how could you be so silly?" he said suddenly. "I cannot understand it. You ought to have known that mother would get to know it — as sure as anything."

"Of course she does not believe the story your father told," said Jenny timidly. — Helge sniffed. — "I wish he would tell her everything just as it happened."

"You may rest assured he won't do that. And you cannot do it — you must just go on pretending. It was awfully stupid of you."

"I could not help it, Helge."

"Well — I had told you enough about things at home for you to know. You could have prevented father from coming again, and all your visits to the office — as well as the meetings in Stenersgate."

"Meetings? — I saw the view and knew I could make a good picture of it — and so I have."

"Yes, yes, you have. The fault, no doubt, is mostly father's. Oh, the way he speaks of her." Helge fumed. "You heard what he had said to Aagot — and what he said to you tonight.

"She" — imitating his father — "does not say anything to you! "Remember it is our mother he speaks of like that."
"I think your father is much more considerate and courteous to your mother than she is to him."

"That consideration of father's — I know it. Do you call it considerate the way he has won you over to his side? And his politeness — if you knew how I have suffered under it as a child, and since. He used to stand and listen very politely without saying a word, and if he spoke, it was in an icy cold, extremely civil manner. I almost prefer mother's loud anger and scoldings. Oh, Jenny, it is all so miserable."

"My poor, darling boy."

"It is not all mother's fault. Everybody prefers father.

You do — quite naturally — I do myself, but I understand her being as she is. She wants to be first with everybody, and she never is. Poor mother."

"I am sorry for her," said Jenny, but her heart remained cold to Mrs. Gram. The air was heavy with scent from leaf and blossom as they went through the square. On the seats under the trees there was whispering and murmuring in the clear summer night.

Their solitary steps echoed on the pavement of the deserted business quarter where the tall buildings slept — the pale blue sky was reflected in the shop windows.

"May I come up?" he whispered as they stood at her entrance. "I am tired," said Jenny softly.

"I should like to stay a while with you — don't you think it would be nice to be by ourselves a little?"

She said nothing, but began to walk up the stairs, and he followed.

Jenny lighted the seven-armed candlestick on her writing-table, took a cigarette, and held it to the flame: "Will you smoke?"

"Thanks." He took the cigarette from her lips.

"The thing is, you see," he said suddenly, "that there was once some story about father and another woman. I was twelve then, and I don't know exactly how much truth there was in it. But mother! ... it was a dreadful time. It was only because of us that they remained together — father told me so himself. God knows, I don't thank him for it! Mother is honest at least, and admits that she means to hold on to him by hook or by crook and not let go."

He sat down on the sofa. Jenny went and sat beside him, kissing his eyes. He sank on his knees and laid his head in her lap.

"Do you remember the last evening in Rome, when I said good-night? Do you still love me as you did then?"

She did not answer. "Jenny?"

"We have not been happy together today — it's the first time."

He lifted his head: "Are you vexed with me?" he said in a low voice. "No, not vexed."

"What, then?"

"Nothing — only. . . ." "Only what?"

"Tonight" — she hesitated — "when we walked here, you said we would go somewhere alone — some other day. It was not as it was in Rome; now it is you who decide what I must do and not do."

"Oh no, Jenny."

"Yes — but I don't mind; I like it so. I only think that, if such is the case, you ought to help me out of all this trouble."

"You don't think I did help you today?" he asked slowly.

"Ye — s. Well, I suppose there was nothing you could do."

"Shall I go now?" he whispered after a pause, drawing her close to him.

"Do as you wish," she said quietly.

"You know what I wish. What do you wish — most?"

 "I don't know what I want." She burst into tears.

"Oh, Jenny darling." He kissed her softly time after time.

When she recovered herself he took her hand: "I am going now. Sleep well, dear; you are tired. You must not be cross with me."

"Say good-night nicely to me," she said, clinging to him.

"Good-night, my sweet, beloved Jenny." He left, and she fell to crying again.

VI

THESE are the things I wanted you to see," said Gert Gram, rising. He had been on his knees, looking for something on the lower shelf of his.

Jenny pushed the sketch-books aside and pulled the electric lamp nearer. He wiped the dust from the big portfolio and placed it before her.

"I have not shown these to anybody for a great many years, or looked at them myself, but I have been wanting you to see them for some time — in fact, from the day I called on you at your studio. When you came here to look at Helge's picture I meant to ask you if you cared to see them, and all the time you were working close by here I had it in my mind.

"It is strange to think, Jenny, that here in this little office I have buried all my dreams of youth. There in the safe they lie like corpses in their tomb, and I myself go about a dead and forgotten artist."

Jenny said nothing. Gram sometimes used expressions that were rather too sentimental, she thought, although she knew that the bitter feelings which dictated them were real enough. In a sudden impulse she bent forward and stroked his grey hair.

Gram bowed his head as if to prolong the slight caress — and without looking at her, untied the portfolio with trembling hands.

She realized in surprise that her own hands shook as she took the first sheet from him, and she felt a strange fear and oppression at heart, as of a danger threatening. She was suddenly afraid when she realized that she did not want anybody to know of her visit and that she dared not tell Helge about it. At the mere thought of her lover she became depressed; she had long since consciously stopped analyzing her real feelings for him. She did not want to heed the foreboding that crossed her mind at this moment, not to let herself be disturbed by inquiring into Gert Gram's feelings for her.

She turned over the sheets of the portfolio with the dreams of his youth; it was a melancholy business. He had told her about this work often when they were alone, and she understood that he thought he had been born an artist for the sake of this and nothing else. The pictures hanging in his home he called the amateur work of a conscientious and diligent pupil, but these — they were his own. They were illustrations to Landstad's Folksongs.

At first sight these big sheets with frames of Roman foliage and ornate black-letter writing were good enough. The coloring was pure and effective in most of them, in some

115

really fine, but the figures in the vignettes and borders were without style and life, although the miniature drawings were correct in every detail. Some of them were naturalistic, others approaching Italian mediaeval art to such an extent that Jenny recognized certain Annunciation angels and madonnas in the cloaks of knights and maidens, and the leaves in gold and purple she remembered having seen in a book of mass in the San Marco library. The words of the songs looked very strange, hand-printed in elegant monastic Latin types. In some of the larger full-page illustrations the composition was baroque, a direct copy of Roman altar pictures. It was an echo of all he had seen and lived among and loved — an echo of the melody of Gert Gram's youth; not a single note was his own, but this melody of many notes was resounded in a particularly soft, melancholy tone.

"You don't quite like them," he said. "I can see you don't."

"Yes, I like them. There is much that is pretty' and delicate about them, but, you know" — she searched for the right expression — "the effect is a little strange on us, who have seen the same subjects treated differently and so perfectly, that we cannot conceive them treated in another way."

He sat opposite her, resting his chin in his hand. By and by he looked up, and she was sad at heart to meet his eyes.

"I seem to remember them as being much better than they are," he said quietly, trying to smile. "I have not opened this portfolio for many a year, as I told you."

"I have never quite understood that you were so attracted by the later renaissance and the baroque," she said, to divert the conversation.

"I am not surprised, Jenny dear, that you don't understand it." He looked into her face with a melancholy smile. "There was a time when I believed in myself as an artist, but not so completely that I did not have a slight doubt sometimes, not of succeeding to express what I wanted, but as to what I really wanted to express. I saw that romantic art had had its day and was on the decline — there was decadence and falsehood all along — and yet in my heart I was devoted to romance, not in painting alone, but in real life. I wanted the Sunday-peasants of romance, although I had lived long enough in the country as a boy to know they did not exist, and when I went abroad it was to the Italy of romance I turned my steps. I know that you and your contemporaries seek beauty in things as they are, tangible and real. To me there was beauty only in the transformation of reality, which had already been done by others. In the eighties there came a new art-creed. I tried to adopt it, but the result was lip-service only, for my heart rebelled against it."

"But reality, Gert, is not a fixed conception. It appears different to everyone who sees it. An English painter once said to me: ''There is beauty in everything; only your eyes see it or do not see it.''"

"I was not made to conceive reality, only the reflection of it in the dreams of others. I lacked entirely the capacity to form a beauty for myself out of the complexity of realities; I knew my own ineffectiveness. When I came to Italy the baroque took my heart and fancy. Can you not understand the agony of my soul on realizing my inefficiency? To have nothing new or personal wherewith to fill up form, only develop the technique in soaring fancies, break-neck foreshortenings, powerful effects of light and shade, and cunningly thought-out compositions. The emptiness of it all is to be hidden under the ecstasy — contorted faces, twisted limbs, saints, whose only true passion is the dread of their own engulfing doubt, which they try to drown in sickly exaltation. It is the despair of the good, the work of an epigon school wishing to fascinate — mostly themselves."

Jenny nodded. "What you say, Gert, is at least your own subjective view. I am not so sure that the painters you speak of were not highly pleased with themselves."

He laughed and said: "Perhaps they were — and perhaps this is my hobby-horse because for once I had — as you say — a subjective view,"

"But the picture of your wife in red is impressionistic, excellent.' The more I look at it, the more I like it."

"Yes, but that is a solitary instance." After a pause "When I painted it, she was all the world to me. I was very much in love with her — and I hated her intensely already."

"Was it because of her you gave up painting?" asked Jenny.

"No. All our misfortunes are of our own making. I know you have not what they call faith, neither have I — but I believe in a God, if you like, or a spiritual power which punishes justly.

"She was cashier in a shop in the High Street; I happened to see her there. She was remarkably pretty, as you can see still. One evening when she went home I waited for her and spoke to her. We made friends — and I seduced her," he said in a low and harsh voice.

"And you married her because she was going to have a child? — I thought so. F or twenty-seven years she has tormented you in return. Do you know what I think of the deity you believe in? — that it is rather relentless."

He smiled wearily. "I am not quite so old-fashioned as you may think. I don't consider it a sin if two young people, who love and believe in one another, join their lives in a lawful or unlawful way. But in my case I was the abductor. She was innocent when I met her — innocent in every way. I under- stood her better than she did herself. I saw that she was passionate, and would be jealous and tyrannical in her love, but I did not care. I was flattered that her passion was for me, that this beautiful girl was all mine, but I never meant to be hers alone, the way I knew she wanted it. I did not exactly mean to leave her, but I thought I should be able to arrange our life in such a way as not to share with her my interests, my work, my real life in fact, as I knew she would want to do. It was stupid of me, knowing that I was weak and she strong and ruthless. I thought that her great passion would give me, who was comparatively cold, a hold on her.

"Beyond her great faculty of loving there was nothing in her. She was vain and uneducated, envious and crude. There could be no mental fellowship between us, but I did not miss it; to possess her beauty and her passionate love was all I cared for."

He rose and went over to the side where Jenny was sitting. He took both her hands and pressed them against his eyes.

"What else but misery could I expect from a marriage with her? But we reap as we sow, and I had to marry her. I had a dreadful time of it. At first, when she come to my studio, she was proud to be my mistress, arrogant in her denunciation of old prejudices, declaring that the only life worth living was that of free love. The moment things went wrong she changed her tone. Then it was all about her respectable family in Frederikshald, her unstained virtue, and her good reputation. Many men had wanted her, but she had not listened to anybody, and I was a scoundrel and a wretch if I did not marry her at once. I had nothing to marry on; I had neglected my studies and had learnt nothing but painting. Some months went by — at last I had to apply to my father. My people helped me through. We got married, and two months later Helge arrived.

"I had had hopes of a great artistic work — my folklore illustrations — but I had to give up my dreams for the reality of making bread and butter. Once I had to come to an agreement with my creditors. She took her share of the struggle and poverty loyally and without complaint — she would willingly have starved for me and the children. Feeling as I did towards her, it was hard to accept what she gave in working, suffering, and renouncing for my sake.

"I had to sacrifice everything I loved; she forced me to give it up inch by inch. From the very first she and my father were mortal enemies. He could not bear his daughter-in-law, and that was a blow to her vanity, so she set about to make trouble between him and me.

My father was an official of the old school — a bit narrow and stiff maybe, but right-minded and loyal, noble and good at heart. You would have liked him, I am sure. We had been so much to one another, but our intimacy was put a stop to.

"As for my painting, I understood that I had not the talent I once had imagined, and I lacked energy to make continued efforts when I did not believe in myself — dead tired as I was of the struggle and of my life at her side, which became more and more of a caricature. She reproached me, but secretly she triumphed.

"She was jealous of the children too, if I was fond of them or they were fond of me. She would not share them with me nor me with them.

"Her jealousy has grown into a kind of madness as the years have gone by. You have seen it for yourself. She can scarcely bear to see me in the same room with you even when Helge is there."

Jenny went to him and laid her hands on his shoulders:

"I cannot understand," she said — "I really cannot — that you have been able to stand such a life."

Gert Gram bent forward, resting his head on her shoulder: "I don't understand it myself."

When he raised his head and their eyes met, she put her hand to his neck and, overwhelmed by a tender compassion, kissed him on the cheek and forehead.

She felt a sudden fear when she looked down at his face resting on her shoulder, with eyes closed, but the next moment he lifted his head and rose, saying:

"Thank you, Jenny dear."

Gram put the drawings back in their cover and straightened the table.

"I hope you will be very, very happy. You are so bright and courageous, so energetic and gifted. Dear child, you are everything I wanted to be, but never was." He spoke in a low, absent-minded voice.

"I think," he said a moment later, "that when relations between two people are new, before their life is perfectly accorded, there are many small difficulties to overcome. I wish you could live elsewhere, not in this town. You should be alone, far from your own people — at first at least."

"Helge has applied for a post in Bergen, as you know," said Jenny, and the feeling of despair and anguish again seized her when she thought of him.

"Do you never speak to your mother about it? Why don't you? Are you not fond of your mother?"

"Of course I am fond of her."

"I should think it would be a good thing to talk to her about it — get her advice."

"It is no good asking anybody's advice — I don't like to speak to anyone about these things," she said, wishing to dismiss the subject.

"No, you are perhaps. ..." He had been standing halfway turned to the window. Suddenly his face changed, and he whispered in a state of excitement:
"Jenny, she is down there in the street!" "Who?"
"She — Rebecca!"

Jenny rose. She felt she could have screamed with exasperation and disgust. She trembled; every fiber of her body was quivering with revolt. She would not be involved in all this — these wicked, odious suspicions, quarrels, spiteful words, and scenes — no, she would not.

"Jenny, my child, you are shivering — don't be afraid. I won't let her hurt you." "Afraid? Far from it." She steeled herself at once. "I have been here to fetch you; we have looked at your drawings, and we are now going to your house to supper."

"She may not have noticed anything."

"Heavens! we have nothing to hide. If she had not seen that I am here she will soon get to know it. I am going with you; we must do it for your sake as well as for mine — do you hear?"

Gram looked at her: "Yes, let us go, then."

When they got down in the street Mrs. Gram was gone. "Let us take the tram, Gert; it is late," she said, adding in a sudden temper: "Oh, we must stop all this — if only for Helge's sake."

Mrs. Gram opened the door. Gert Gram ventured an explanation; Jenny looked frankly into the angry eyes of his wife: "I am sorry Helge is out for the evening. Do you think he will be home early?"

"I am surprised you did not remember it," Mrs. Gram said to her husband. "It is no pleasure to Miss Winge to sit here with us two old people."

"Oh, that is all right," said Jenny.

"I don't remember hearing that Helge was going out this evening," said Gram.

"Fancy your coming without any needlework," said Mrs. Gram, when they were sitting in the drawing-room after supper. "You are always so industrious."

"I left the studio so late, I had no time to go home in between. Perhaps you could find me something?"

Jenny conversed with Mrs. Gram about the price of embroidery patterns at home and in Paris, and about books she had lent her. Gram was reading. Now and again she felt his eyes on her. Helge returned about eleven.

"What is the matter?" he asked, when they walked down the stairs. "Has there been a scene again?"

"No, not at all," she replied, in a short, irritated voice. "I suppose your mother did not like my coming home with your father."

"It seems to me, too, that you need not have done it," said Helge humbly.

"I am going home by tram." Overwrought, and unable to control herself, she pulled her arm out of his. "I cannot stand any more tonight, and I will not have these scenes with you every time I have been to your home. Good-night."

"Jenny! Wait! Jenny! . . ." He hurried after her, but she was already at the stop when the tram came, and got in, leaving him without a word.

VII

JENNY walked listlessly about in her studio next morning and could not settle down to anything. The pouring rain was beating against the big window. She stopped to look at the wet tiles of the roofs, the black chimneys, and the telephone wires, along which the small raindrops were rolling down like pearls until they gathered into one large one and fell off, to be replaced immediately by others.

She might go to her mother and the children in the country for a few days. She must go away from all this. Or she might go to a hotel in some other town and write for Helge to come and talk things over with her quietly. If they could only be together again — they two alone! She tried to think of their spring in Rome, of the silvery haze over the mountains, and of her own happiness in it all. But she could not reconstruct the picture of Helge from that time — as he had appeared to her enamored eyes.

Those days seemed already so far away; they were an isolated episode in her life, and although she knew they were a reality she could not connect them with her present existence.

Helge — her Helge was lost to her in the home at Welhavensgaten, and she herself could not fit in there. It seemed unthinkable that she should have anything to do with those people now and in all the time to come. Yes — Gram was right — they must go away.

And she would go at once — before Helge came, asking for an explanation of her behavior yesterday. She packed a bag, and as she was putting on her mackintosh somebody knocked at the door — again and again — she knew it was Helge. She stood absolutely still and waited till he had gone. After a while she took her bag, locked the studio, and went. Half-w T ay down the stairs she saw a man sitting in one of the windows. It was Helge. He had seen her too, so she went down to him. They looked at each other in silence.

"Why did you not open just now?" he asked. Jenny did not answer.

"Did you not hear me knocking?" He looked at her bag: "Are you going to your mother?"

She hesitated a little, then said: "No; I thought of going to Holmestrand for a few days and writing to you from there to come down, so that we could be together for a time without undue interference and scenes. I should like to talk matters over with you in peace and quiet."

"I am anxious to speak to you too. Can we not go up to your place?" She did not answer directly.

122

"Is there anybody there?" he asked.

Jenny looked at him: "Anybody in my studio when I have left?" "There might be somebody you do not wish to be seen with."

She turned purple in the face: "Why? How could I know that you were sitting there spying on me?"

"My dear Jenny, I don't mean to say that there was any harm in it, not on your part at least."

Jenny said nothing, but went up the stairs again. In the studio she placed her bag on the floor, and without taking off her things stood looking at Helge while he hung up his coat and put his umbrella in the corner.

"Father told me this morning that you had been to the office and that mother had been below in the street."

"Yes. It is a peculiar manner you people have — of spying, I mean. I must say, I find it hard to get accustomed to it."

Helge turned very red.

"Forgive me, Jenny — I had to speak to you, and the porter said he was sure you were in. You know very well that I don't suspect you."

"Really, I hardly know anything," she said, overcome with it all. "I cannot bear it any longer. All this suspicion and secrecy and discord. Good heavens, Helge! — can't you protect me from all this?"

"My poor Jenny." He rose and went to the window, where he remained standing with his back to her. "I have suffered more than you know. It is all so hopeless. Can you not see for yourself that mother's jealousy is not without foundation?"

Jenny began to shiver. He turned round and saw it.

"I don't believe father is aware of it himself. If he were, he would not give in like that to his desire to be with you. But he told me himself that we ought to go away from here, both of us. I am not so sure that your going away now is not his idea too."

"No; I decided myself to go to Holmestrand, but he spoke to me yesterday about leaving town, when — when we got married."

She went to him and put her hands on his shoulders.

"Dearest — if it is as you say, I will have to go away. Helge, Helge! What shall we do?"
"I am going," he said abruptly, lifting her hands from his shoulders and pressing them against his face.

They stood a moment in silence.

"But I must go too. Can you not understand? As long as I thought your mother absurd, even common, I could keep my countenance, but now it is different. You should not have said it, Helge — even if you are mistaken. I cannot go there any more with that on my mind. Whether she is justified or not, I cannot meet her eyes. I shall not be myself, and I shall look guilty."

"Come," said Helge, leading her to the sofa and sitting down beside her. "I am going to ask you a question. Do you love me, Jenny?"

"You know I do," she said quickly, as if frightened.

He took her cold hand between both of his: "I know you did once — though, God knows, I never understood why. But I knew it was true when you said so. You were loving and kind to me, and I was happy, but I was always afraid of a time coming when you would not love me any longer."

She looked up in his face, saying: "I am very, very fond of you, Helge."

"I know," he answered, with a shadow of a smile. "I don't think you turn cold all at once to somebody you have loved — you are not that kind. I know that you don't wish to make me suffer, and that you will suffer yourself the moment you understand that you don't love me any longer. I love you above everything."

He bent his head in tears. She put her arms round him. "Helge — my own darling boy." He raised his head and pushed her gently away from him: "Jenny, that time in Rome I could have made you mine — you wanted it yourself, for you believed that we could only find happiness in a life together. I was not so sure, I suppose, as I did not risk it. But here at home I have been wanting you more than ever. I wanted you to be mine entirely, for I was afraid of losing you, but I saw you were frightened every time you understood that I was longing for you."

She looked at him in awe. Yes, he was right — she had not wished to admit it, but it was so.

"If I asked you now — this moment — would you consent?" Jenny moved her lips; then came a quick and firm "Yes."

Helge smiled sadly, kissing her hand: "Gladly, because you wish to be mine? Because you cannot conceive of any happiness unless you are mine and I am yours? Not only because you want to be kind to me or don't want to break your word — tell me the truth."

She threw herself down on his knee and sobbed: "Let me go away for a time. I want to go up in the mountains. I must recover myself. I want to be your Jenny, as I was in Rome. I do want it, Helge, but I am so confused now. When I am myself again I will write you to come, and I will be your own Jenny again — yours only."

"I am my mother's son," said Helge quietly. "We have got estranged from one another. Will you not convince me that I am everything in the world to you, the only man, more than anything else? — more than your work and your friends, to whom I felt you belonged more than to me — just as you feel a stranger among the people I belong to."

"I did not feel a stranger towards your father."

"No, but my father and I are strangers to one another. There is one interest — your work — which I cannot share with you completely, and I know now that I should be jealous of it. You see, I am her son. If I am not convinced that I am everything in the world to you, I cannot help being jealous — anxiously fearing that someday there might come another whom you could love more, who could understand you better. I am jealous by nature."

"You must not be jealous, or everything will go to pieces. I cannot bear to be distrusted. I would rather you deceived me than doubted me — I could better forgive you that."

"I could not" — with a bitter smile.

Jenny stroked the hair from his forehead and dried his eyes. "We love one another, don't we, Helge? When we get away from all this and we both wish everything to be well and right, don't you think we can make one another happy?"

"I have seen too much. I dare not trust my good intentions or yours. Others have built their hopes on this and failed — I have seen what a hell two people can make life for each other. You will have to give me an answer to what I asked you. Do you love me? Do you wish to be mine — as you did in Rome? Do you wish it more than anything else in the world?"

"I love you very dearly, Helge," she said, crying piteously. "Thank you," he said, kissing her hand. "I know you cannot help it, poor darling, that you don't love me."

"Helge," she said imploringly.

"You cannot say that you wish me to stay because you would not be able to live without me. Dare you take the responsibility for everything that may happen if you say you love me — only so as not to send me away in sadness?"

Jenny sat looking down. Helge put on his overcoat.

"Good-bye, Jenny." He clasped her hand. "Are you going away from me, Helge?"

"Yes. I am going."

"And you will not come back?"

"Not unless you can say what I asked you to say." "I cannot say it now," she whispered in agony. Helge touched her hair lightly, and left.
Jenny remained on the sofa crying long and bitterly — her mind a perfect blank. Tired with crying, and worn out after all these months of petty, racking humiliation and quarrels, she felt her heart empty and cold. Helge was probably right.

After a while she began to feel hungry, and, looking at her watch, saw it was six. She had been sitting like this for four hours. When she rose to put on her coat she noticed that she had had it on all the time.

By the door she perceived a small pool of water running on to some of her pictures standing against the wall. She went for a duster to wipe it up, and, realizing suddenly that the pool was left from Helge's umbrella, she leaned her forehead against the door and cried again.

VIII

HER dinner did not take long. She tried to read a paper to divert her mind for a moment, but it was no good. She might just as well go home and sit there.

On the upper landing a man stood waiting. He was tall and thin. She took the last steps running, calling out Helge's name.

"It is not Helge," came the answer. It was his father. Jenny stood breathless before him, stretching out her hands: "Gert — what is it? — has anything happened?"

"Hush, hush!" He took her hand. "Helge has gone — he went to Kongsberg on a visit to a friend — a schoolfellow of his who lives there. Were you afraid, child, that something else had happened?"

"Oh, I don't know."

"My dear Jenny — you are quite beside yourself."

She went past him in the passage and opened her door. There was still daylight in the studio and Gert Gram looked at her. He was pale himself.

"Do you feel it so much? Helge said — at least that is what I understood him to say — that you have agreed to — that you both think you are not suited to each other."

Jenny was silent. Hearing somebody else say it, she wanted to protest. Up to now she had not quite realized that it was all over, but here was this man saying that they had agreed to part, and Helge had gone and her love for him was gone — she could not find it in her any more. It was all over, but, heavens! how was it possible, when she had not wanted it to end?

"Does it hurt so much?" he asked again. "Do you still love him?"

"Of course I love him." Her voice shook. "One does not cease all at once loving somebody one has been very fond of, and one cannot be indifferent to having caused suffering."

Gram did not speak at once; he sat down on the sofa, twisting his hat between his fingers: "I understand that it is very painful to both of you, but don't you believe, Jenny, when you think it over, that it is for the best?"

She did not reply.

"I cannot tell you how pleased I was when I met you and saw what kind of a woman my son had won. It looked to me as if my boy had got everything that I have had to renounce in life. You were so pretty and refined, I had an impression that you were as good as you were clever, strong, and independent. And you were a talented artist as well, with no hesitation as to your aim and means. You spoke of your work with joy and tenderness and of your lover in the same way.

"Then Helge came home. You seemed to change then — in a remarkably short time. The disagreeable things which are the order of the day in our home impressed you too much; it seemed impossible that an unsympathetic future mother-in- law could completely spoil the happiness of a young loving woman. I began to fear that there was some other deeper cause that you would see for yourself later on, and that perhaps you realized your love for Helge was not so strong as you had imagined. Or that you understood you were not really suited to each other, and that it was more a temporary emotion which had brought you together. In Rome you were both alone, young and free, happy in your work; in strange circumstances, without the pressure of everyday ties, and both with the youthful longing for love in your hearts. Was that not enough to awaken a mutual sympathy and understanding even if they did not penetrate to the very inmost of your being?" Jenny stood by the window looking at him. While he was speaking she felt an intense indignation at his words — although he might be right. Yet he did not understand, as he sat there plucking it all asunder, what it was that really hurt her:

"It does not make it easier even if there is some sense in what you say. Perhaps you are right."

"Is it not better anyhow that you have realized it now than if it had happened later, when the bonds would be stronger, and the suffering much greater in breaking them?"

"It is not that — it is not that." She interrupted herself suddenly: "It is that I — yes — I despise myself. I have given way to an emotional impulse — lied to myself; I ought to have known if I could keep my word before I said: I love.

I have always hated that kind of levity more than anything in the world. Now — to my shame — I find I have done that very thing."

Gram looked at her. Suddenly he turned pale — and then crimson. After a while he said, speaking with effort:

"I said it was better for two people who were not in perfect understanding to realize it before their relations had made such a change in their lives that neither of them — especially she — could ever obliterate the traces. If such be the case, they should try with some resignation and goodwill on either side to bring about harmony. Should this not be possible, then there is still the other way out. I don't know, of course, if you and Helge — how far you are affected. . . ."

Jenny laughed scornfully:

"I understand what you mean. To me it is just as binding that I have wanted to be his — promised it and cannot keep my promise — and just as humiliating as if I had really given myself to him — perhaps even more so."

"You will not speak like that when once you meet the man you can love with true, deep feeling."

Jenny shrugged her shoulders:

"Do you really believe in true and great love as you say?"

"Yes, I do. I know that you young people find the expression ludicrous, but I believe in it — for a good reason."

"I believe that everyoneloves according to his individuality; those who have a greater mind and are true to themselves do not fritter themselves away in little love affairs. I thought that I myself. . . . But I was twenty-eight when I met Helge, and I had never yet been in love. I was tired of waiting and wanted to try it. He was in love, young, warm-blooded, and sincere — and it tempted me. I lied to myself — exactly as all other women do. His intensity warmed me, and I was ready enough to imagine that I shared it, l though I knew such an illusion can only be kept alive as long as there is no claim on one to prove one's love.

"Other women live under this illusion quite innocently, because they do not know the difference between good and bad, and go on lying to themselves, but I can plead nothing of that kind in my defense. I am really just as small and selfish and false as other women, and you may depend upon it, Gert, I shall never know what that great and true love of yours is."

"Well, Jenny," said Gert, with his same melancholy smile — "God knows, I am neither great nor strong, and I've lived in lies and abominations for twelve years. But I was ten years older than you are now when I met a woman who taught me to believe in the feeling you speak of with such scorn, and my faith in it has never been shaken."

They were silent for a moment.

"And you remained with her?" said Jenny at last. "We had the children. I did not understand then that I should never have any influence on my own children, when another woman than their mother possessed my whole heart and soul.

"She was married too — very unhappily. Her husband was a drunkard. She had a little girl whom she could have brought with her. But we both stayed.

"It was part of the punishment, you see, for my relations with her who only gratified my senses, but was nothing to my soul. Our love was too beautiful to live on a lie; we had to conceal it like a crime.

"Believe me, Jenny, there is no other happiness than a great love."

She went up to him and he rose; they stood an instant close to one another without speaking.

"I must go now," he said abruptly, in a strained voice. "I must be back in time, or she will suspect something."

Jenny nodded, and followed him to the door.

"You must not believe that your heart is beyond love," he said; "it is a proud heart — and a warm one. Will you still count me among your friends, little girl?" "Yes, thank you," said Jenny, giving him her hand.

He bent over it and held it long to his lips — longer than ever before.

IX

GUNNAR HEGGEN and Jenny Winge were to have an exhibition together in November. He came to town for that purpose. He had been in the country that summer, painting red granite, green pines, and blue sky, and had lately been to Stockholm, where he had sold a picture.

"How is Cesca?" asked Jenny, when Heggen -was in her studio one morning having a drink.

"Cesca is all right." Gunnar took a gulp from his glass, smoked, and looked at Jenny, and she looked at him.

It was so nice to be together again and talk about people and things she had got so far away from. It seemed almost as if it had been in a remote country beyond all oceans that she had known him and Cesca, lived and worked with them, and been happy with them.

She looked at his open sunburnt face and crooked nose; it had been broken when he was a child. Cesca once said that the blow had saved Gunnar's face from being the most perfect fashion-plate type.

There was some truth in it. Looking at his features separately, they were exactly those of a rustic Adonis. His brown hair curled over a low, broad forehead and big steely blue eyes; the mouth was red, with full lips and beautiful white teeth. His face and his strong neck were tanned by the sun, and his broad, somewhat short body with well-knit muscles was almost brutally well shaped. But the sensual mouth and heavy eyelids had a peculiarly innocent and unaffected expression, and his smile could be most refined. The hands were regular working hands, with short fingers and strong joints, but the way he moved them was particularly graceful. He had grown thinner, but looked very well and contented, while she herself felt tired and dissatisfied. He had been working the whole summer, reading Greek tragedies and Keats and Shelley when he was not painting.

"I should like to read the tragedies in the original," said Gunnar, "and I am going to learn Greek and Latin."

"Dear me!" exclaimed Jenny. "I am afraid there are so many things you will want to study before you get any peace in your mind that you will end by not painting at all — except in your holidays."

"I have to learn those two languages because I am going to write some articles." "You!" cried Jenny, laughing. "Are you going to write articles too?"

"Yes; a long series of them about many different things. Amongst others, that we must introduce Latin and Greek into our schools again; we must see that we get some culture up here. We cannot go on like this any longer. Our national emblem will be a wooden porringer with painted roses on it and some carving, which is supposed to be a clumsy imitation of the poorest of all European styles, the rococo. That is how we are national up here in Norway. You know that the best praise they can give anybody in this country — artist or other decent fellow — is that he has broken away — broken away from school, tradition, customary manners, and ordinary civilized people's conception of seemly behavior and decency.

"I should like to point out for once that, considering our circumstances, it would be much more meritorious if somebody tried to get into touch with, appropriate, exchange, and bring home to this hole of ours some of the heaped-up treasures in Europe that are called culture.

"What we do is to detach a small part from a connective whole — a single ornament of a style, literally speaking — and carve and chip such an ugly and clumsy copy of it that it becomes unrecognizable. Then we boast that it is original or nationally Norwegian. And it is the same with spiritual movements."

"Yes, but those sins were committed even when classical education was the official foundation of all education."

"Quite so. But it was only a small part of the classics — a detached piece. A little Latin grammar and so on. We have never had a complete picture among the stories of our valued ancestors of what you might call the classical spirit. As long as we cannot have that, we are outside Europe. If we do not consider Greek and Roman history as the oldest history of our own culture, we have not got European culture. It does not matter what that history was in reality, but the version of it matters. The war between Sparta and Messene, for instance, was in fact only the fights between some half-savage tribes a very long time ago, but in the delivery of it, as we know it, it is the classic expression for an impulse which makes a sound people let themselves be killed to the last man rather than lose their individuality or the right to live their own life.

"Bless you, for many a hundred years we have not fought for our honor; we have lived merely to nurse our insides. The Persian wars were really trifles, but for a vigorous people Salamis, Thermopylae, and the Acropolis mean the bloom of all the noblest and soundest instincts, and as long as these instincts are valued, and a people believes that it has certain qualities to uphold, and a past, a present, and a future to be proud of, these names will be surrounded by a certain glamour. And a poet can write a poem on Thermopylae and imprint it with the feelings of his own time, as Leopardi has done in his ' Ode to Italy.' Do you remember I read it to you in Rome?" Jenny nodded.

"It is a bit rhetorical, but beautiful, is it not? Do you remember the part about Italia, the fairest of women, -who sits in the dust chained and with loosened hair, her tears dropping into her lap? And how he wishes to be one of the young Greeks who go to meet death at Thermopylæ, fearless and merry as if going to dance? Their names are sacred, and Simonides in dying sings songs of praise from the top of Antelos.

"And all the old beautiful tales, symbols, and parables that will never grow old. Think of Orpheus and Eurydice — so simple; the faith of love conquers death even; a single instant of doubt and everything is lost. But in this country they know only that it is the book of an opera.

"The English and the French have used the old symbols in making new and living art. Abroad, in certain good periods, there were people born with instincts and feelings so highly cultivated that they could be developed into an ability to make the fate of the Atrides understood and moving as a reality. The Swedes, too, have living connections with the classics — but we have never had them. What kind of books do we read here — and write? — feminine novels about sexless fancy-figures in empire dress, and dirty Danish books, which do not interest any man above sixteen, unless he is obliged to wear an electric belt. Or about some green youth, prattling of the mysterious eternal feminine to a little chorus girl who is impertinent to him and deceives him, because he has not sense enough to understand that the riddle can be solved by means of a good caning."

Jenny laughed. Gunnar was walking up and down the door.

"Hjerrild, I think, is working at a book on the ' Sphinx ' at present. As it happens, I also knew the lady once. It never went so far that I soiled my hands by giving her a thrashing, but I had been fond enough of her to feel it rather badly when I discovered her deceit. I have worked it off, you see. I don't think there is anything you cannot get over in time by your own effort."

Jenny sat silent for a second, then said: "Tell me about Cesca."

"Well, I don't think Cesca has touched a paint-brush since she married. When I went to see them she opened the door; they have no servant. She wore a big apron and had a broom in her hand. They have a studio and two small rooms; they cannot both work in the studio, of course, and her whole time is taken up with the house, she said. The first morning I was there she sprawled on the floor the whole time. Ahlin was out. First she swept, then she crept round and poked under the furniture with a brush for those little tufts of dust, you know, that stick in the corners. Then she scrubbed the floor and dusted the room, and you should have seen how awkwardly she did it all. We went out to buy food together; I was to lunch with them. When Ahlin came home she retired to the kitchen, and when the lunch was ready at last, all her little curls were damp — but the food was not bad. She washed up in the most unpractical way, going to the sink with every article to rinse it under the tap. Ahlin and I helped her, and I gave her some good advice, you know.

"I asked them to dine with me, and Cesca, poor thing, was very pleased at not having to cook and wash up.

"If there are going to be children — as I suppose there are — you may depend upon it that Cesca has done with painting, and it would be a great pity. I cannot help thinking it's sad."

"I don't know. Husband and children always hold the first place with a woman; sooner or later she will long to have them."

Gunnar looked at her — then sighed:

"If they are fond of one another, that is to say." "Do you think Cesca is happy with Ahlin?"

"I don't really know. I think she is very fond of him.

Anyhow it was 'Lennart thinks' and 'Will you?' and 'Shall I?' and 'Do you think the sauce is all right, Lennart?' and so on the whole time. She has taken to speaking a shocking mixture of Swedish and Norwegian. I must say that I don't quite understand their relations. He was very much in love with her, you remember, and he in not despotic or brutal — quite the contrary — but she has become so cowed and humble, our little Cesca. It cannot be housekeeping worries only, although they seemed to weigh heavily on her. She has no talent in that direction, but she is a conscientious little thing in her way, and they are rather badly off, I understand.

"Perhaps she has made some great mistake, profited by the wedding night, for instance, to tell him about Hans Hermann, Norman Douglas, and Hjerrild, and all the rest of her achievements from one end to the other. It might have been just a little overwhelming."

"Cesca has never concealed anything about her doings. I am sure he knew all her story before."

"H'm," said Gunnar, mixing himself a fresh drink. "There might have been one or two points she has kept quiet so far, and thought she ought to tell her husband."

"For shame, Gunnar," said Jenny.

"Well - — - you never really know what to think about Cesca. Her version of the Hans Hermann business is very peculiar, though I am sure Cesca has not done anything that I would call wrong. I cannot — on the whole — see what difference it makes to a man if his wife has had a liaison — or several — before, provided she had been true and loyal while it lasted. This claim of physical innocence is crude. If a woman has been really fond of a man and has accepted his love, it is rather mean of her to leave him without spending a gift on him.

"Naturally I should prefer my wife never to have loved anybody else before, so, perhaps, when it is your own wife you may think differently. Old prejudices and selfish vanity may count for something."

Jenny sipped at her drink, and was on the point of saying something when she checked herself. Gunnar had stopped by the window, standing with his back to her, his hands in his trouser pockets:

"Oh, I think it is sad, Jenny — I mean when once in a while you meet a woman who is really gifted in one way or another and takes a pleasure in developing her gift by energetic work — feels that she is an individual who can decide for herself what is right or wrong, and has the will to cultivate faculties and instincts that are good and valuable and eradicate others which are bad and unworthy of her; and then one fine day she throws herself away on a man, gives up everything, work, development — herself for the sake of a wretched male. Don't you think it sad, Jenny?"

"It is. But that is how we are made — all of us."

"I don't understand it. We men never do understand you, and I think it is because we cannot get it into our heads that individuals who are supposed to be reasonable beings are so completely devoid of self-esteem, for that is what you are. Woman has no soul — that is a true word. You admit more or less openly that love affairs are the only things that really interest you."

"There are men who do the same — at least in their behavior."'

"Yes, but a decent man has no respect for those effeminates. Officially at least we do not wish it to be considered anything but a natural diversion beside our work. Or a capable man wishes to have a family because he know T s he can provide for more than himself, and wants somebody to continue his work." "But surely woman has other missions in life."

"That is mere talk — unless she wants to be a reasonable being and work, and not content herself with being a female only. What is the good of producing a lot of children if they are not meant to grow up for any other purpose than continued production — if the raw material is not to be used?"

"It may be true to a certain extent," Jenny said, smiling.

"I know it is. I have seen enough of women to know, ever since I was a youngster and went to the workers' academy. I remember a girl at one of the English classes; she wanted to learn the language to be able to talk to the sailors on the foreign men-of-war. The only aim of the girls that counted for anything was to get a situation in England or America. We boys studied because we wanted to learn something for the sake of mental gymnastics and to complete as much as possible what we had learnt at school. The girls read novels.

"Take socialism, for instance. Do you think any woman has an idea what it really means, unless she has a husband who has taught her to see? Try to explain to a woman why the community must arrive at such a stage that every child born must have the opportunity to cultivate its faculties, if it has any, and to live its life in liberty and beauty — if it can bear liberty and has a sense of beauty. Women believe that liberty means no work and no restrictions as to their behavior. Sense of beauty they have none; they only want to dress up in the ugliest and most expensive things, because they are the fashion. Look at the homes they arrange. The richer, the uglier. Is there any fashion, be it ever so ugly or indecent, that they don't adopt if they can afford it? You cannot deny it.

"I won't mention their morals, because they haven't any. Let alone your treatment of us men, the way you treat one an- other is disgusting."

Jenny smiled. She thought he was right in some things and wrong in others, but she was not inclined to discuss them. Yet she felt she ought to say something:

"Aren't you rather hard on us?" she ventured.

"You shall see it all in print one day," he said complacently. "There is something in it, but all women are not alike; there is a difference even if it be only a difference in degree."

"Certainly, but what I have said applies to a certain extent to all of you, and do you know why? Because the principal thing to all of you is a man — one you have or one you miss. The only thing in life which is serious and worth anything — I mean work — is never a serious thing to you. To the best of you it is so for a short time, and I believe it is because you are sure when you are young and pretty that ' he ' will come along. But as time goes and he does not turn up, and you get on in years, you get slack and weary and dissatisfied."

Jenny nodded.

"Look here, Jenny. I have always placed you on the same level as a first-class man. You will soon be twenty-nine, and that is about the right age to begin independent work. You don't mean to say that now, when you should begin your individual life in earnest, you wish to encumber yourself with husband, children, housekeeping, and all those things which would only be so many ties and a hindrance in your work?"

Jenny laughed softly.

"If you had all those things and were going to die, surrounded by husband and kiddies and all that, and you felt you had not attained what you knew you might have done, don't you think you would repent and regret? I am sure you would."

"Yes, but if I had reached the farthest goal of my abilities and I knew, when dying, that my life and my work would live a long time after I had gone — and I were alone, with no living soul belonging to me, don't you think I should regret and repent then too?"

Heggen was silent a moment.

"Yes. Celibacy, of course, is not the same to women as to men. It often means that they are kept outside all those things in life which people make the most fuss about — simply that whole groups of organs, mental as well as physical, are wasting away unused. Ugh! Sometimes I almost wish you would be a little frivolous for once and have done with it all, so that you could work in peace and quiet afterwards."

"Women who have been a little frivolous, as you say, are not done with it. If they were disappointed the first time, they hope for better luck the next. One does not settle down disappointed, and before you know it you have had many a try."

"Not you," he said quickly.

"Thanks. It is quite new to hear you speak like that. You have always said that when women begin such a life they in- variably end by being dragged down completely."

"Most of them do. But there must be some exceptions. It applies to those who have no other instincts in life than a man — not to those who are something by themselves and not only of female sex. Why should you, for instance, not be true and loyal to a man even if you both saw that you could not give up everything to tie yourself down as his wife for the rest of your life? Love always dies sooner or later. Don't let yourself be deceived on that point."

"Yes; we know it — but still we won't believe it." She laughed. "No, my friend — either we love and believe it is the only thing worth living for, or we do not love — and are unhappy because we don't."

"Jenny, I don't like to hear you speak like that. No; to feel oneself in full vigor, with all faculties alert, ready to adopt and appropriate, to adapt and produce, make the utmost possible of oneself — work — that is the only thing worth living for, believe me."

X

J ENNY bent over Gert Gram's chrysanthemums: "I am so glad you like my pictures."
"Yes, I like them very much, especially the one of the young girl with the corals — as I told you already." Jenny shook her head.
"I think the coloring is so lovely," said Gram.

"It is not well finished. The scarf and the dress should have been more thoroughly worked up, but when I was painting it both Cesca and I were distracted by other things."

After a while she asked:

"Do you hear from Helge? How is he?"

"He does not write much. He is working at the essay for his doctor of science degree — you know he prepared himself for it in Rome. He says he is all right. He does not write to his mother at all, and she, of course, is very vexed about it. She has not improved as a companion, I am sorry to say, but she is not happy, poor thing, at present."

Jenny moved the flowers to her writing-table and began to arrange them:

"I am glad Helge is working again. He did not get much done in the summer." "Neither did you, dear."
"No, it is true, and the worst of it is that I have not been able to start yet. But I don't feel the least inclined to, and I was going to begin etching this winter, but. . . ."

"Don't you think it quite natural that a disappointment like yours should take some time to get over? Your exhibition is a success, and has been well spoken of in the papers. Don't you think that is enough to make you want to work again?
You have got a bid for the Aventine picture already — are you going to accept it?" She shrugged her shoulders: "Of course. I am obliged to accept. They always need money at home, as you know. Besides, I must go abroad; it is not good for me to stay here long."

"Do you want to go abroad?" said Gram gently, looking down. "Well, I suppose you are; it is only natural."

"Oh, this exhibition," said Jenny, sitting down in the rocking-chair — "all my pictures were painted such a long time ago, it seems to me, even the recent ones. The sketch of the Aventine was finished the day I met Helge, and I painted the picture while we were together — that of Cesca as well. And the one from Stenersgaten in your place, while I was waiting for him to come home. I have done nothing since. Ugh! So Helge is at work again?"

"It is only natural, my dear, that an experience like yours should leave deeper traces in a woman."

"Oh yes, yes — a woman; that is the whole misery of it. It is just like a woman to become uninterested and utterly lazy because of a love that does not even exist."

"My dear Jenny," said Gram, "I think it quite natural that it should take some time for you to get over it — to get beyond it, as it were; one always does, and then one understands that the experience has not been in vain, but that one's soul is the richer for it in some way or other."

Jenny did not reply.

"I am sure there is much you would not like to have missed — all the happy, warm, sunny days with your friend in that beautiful country. Am I not right?"

"Will you tell me one thing, Gert? — is it your own personal experience that you have been able to enrich your soul, as you say, by the incidents of your life?"

He gave a start as if hurt and surprised at her brutality; it was a moment before he answered her:

"It is quite a different thing. The experiences which are the results of sin — I don't mean sin in the orthodox sense, but the consequences of acting contrary to your understanding — are always far from sweet. I mean that my experiences have made my life in a way richer and deeper than a lesser misfortune might have done — since it was my fate not to attain the greatest happiness. I have a feeling that once it will be the case in a still higher degree, and will help me to understand the real meaning of life.

"In your case, I meant it in a different way. Even if your happiness proved to be of a passing nature, it was pure and guiltless while it lasted, because you believed in it implicitly and enjoyed it without any mental reservation. You deceived nobody but yourself."

Jenny did not speak. She would have had a great deal to say in opposition, but she felt dimly that he would not understand her.

"Don't you remember Ibsen's words:

"Though I ram my ship aground, it was grand to sail the seas?"

140

"I am surprised at you, Gert, for repeating those idiotic words. Nowadays we have too great a feeling of responsibility and too much self-esteem, most of us, to accept that kind of reasoning. If I am wrecked and sink, I will try not to wince, if I know that I have not run my ship aground myself. As far as I understand, the best sailors prefer to go down with their ship if the fault is theirs, rather than survive the disaster."

"I am of the opinion that, as a rule, one can thank oneself for every misfortune," said Gram, smiling, "but that one can nearly always draw some spiritual benefit out of it."

"I agree with you on the first point — and on the second on the condition that the misfortune does not consist in the diminution of one's self-esteem."

"You should not take this so seriously. You are quite excited and bitter. I remember what you said on the day Helge left, but, my dear child, you cannot really mean that one should quench every affection at its birth unless one can guarantee the moment it comes into life that it will last until one's death, endure all adversity, be ready for every sacrifice, and that it will understand the personality of its object as in a vision, show up its most sacred depths to prevent later change of opinion about him or her."

"Yes," said Jenny sharply.

"Have you ever felt this yourself?" asked Gram.

"No, but I know it, all the same. I have always known that it should be so. But when I was twenty-eight and still an old maid, longing to love and be loved, and Helge came and fell in love with me, I laid aside all claims on myself and my love, taking what I could get — to a certain extent in good faith. It will be all right, I thought — I am sure it will — although I did not feel assured in my inmost heart that nothing else could be possible. Let me tell you what my friend Heggen told me the other day. He despises women truly and honestly — and he is right. We have no self-esteem, and we are so lazy that we can never make up our mind in earnest to shape our life and happiness ourselves, and to work with that purpose. Secretly we all nourish the hope that a man will come and offer us happiness, so that we need not make any effort ourselves. The most womanly of us, who by happiness mean only idleness and finery, hang on to the man who can give them plenty of it. If amongst us there are a few who really have the right feelings and are longing to become good and strong, and making efforts in that direction — we still hope to meet a man on the way and to become what we want to be through his love.

"We can work for a time pretty honestly and seriously, and take a pleasure in it too, but in our hearts we are waiting for a still greater joy, which we cannot acquire by our work, but must receive as a gift. We women can never get to the point where our work is everything to us."

"Do you believe work alone is enough for a man? Never," said Gram.

"It is for Gunnar. You may depend on it that he will keep women in their right place in his life — as trifles."

Gram laughed: "How old is your friend Heggen? I hope for the man's own sake that he will change his opinion some day about the most conclusive influence in life."

"I don't," said Jenny vehemently, "but I hope I, too, shall learn some day to put this nonsense about love in its right place."

"My dear Jenny, you speak as if — as if you had no sense, I was going to say, but I know you have," said Gram, with a melancholy smile. "Shall I tell you something of what I know about love, little one? If I did not believe in it, I should not have the least particle of faith in men — or in myself. Do you believe that it is only women who think life meaningless, and find their hearts empty and frozen if they have nothing but their work to love or to depend upon? Do you believe there is a single soul living who has not moments of doubt in himself? You must have somebody in whose keeping you can give the best in you — your love and your trust.

"When I say that my own life since my marriage has been a hell, I am not using too strong words, and if I have been able to stand it in a way it is because I think the love Rebecca has for me partly exonerates her. I know that her feelings of mean pleasure at having the power to torment and humiliate me with her jealousy and rage are a caricature of betrayed love, and it is a kind of satisfaction to my sense of justice that there is a reason for my unhappiness. I betrayed her when I took her love without giving her mine — intending secretly to give her only crumbs — the small coin of love — in payment for the best of herself she offered me. If life punishes every sin against the sacredness of love so ruthlessly, it proves to me that there is nothing holier in life, and that he who is true to his ideal of love will reap his recompense in the greatest and purest bliss.

"I told you once that I learnt to know and to love a woman when it was too late. She had loved me from the time we were children without my knowing, or caring to know it. When she heard of my marriage she accepted a man who vowed that she could save and raise him if she married him. I know you would scorn any such means of saving, but you don't know, child, how you would act yourself, if you knew the being you loved with your whole soul was in the arms of another, and found your life not worth living, and if you heard an erring human being ask you to give him the life you did not value and save him thereby.

"Helene was unhappy, and so was I. Later we met, understood one another, and it came to an explanation which, however, did not result in what people call happiness. We were both bound by ties we dared not break, and I must admit that my love for her changed as the hope of making her my wife slowly died, but the memory of her is the greatest treasure of my life. She is now living in another part of the world, devoting her life to her children and trying to lessen for them the misery of having to live with a father who is a drunkard and a moral wreck. For her sake I have held on to my faith in the purity of the human soul, in its beauty and its strength — and in love, and I know, too, that the remembrance of me inspires Helene with the strength to struggle on and to suffer because she loves me today as she did in our childhood, and believes in me, in my talent, my love, and that I was worthy of a better fate. I am still something to her, don't you think?"

Jenny did not answer.

"The happiness in life is not only to be loved, Jenny; the greatest happiness is to love."
"H'm. A very poor sort of happiness, I should say, to love when your love is not returned."

He sat quiet for a while, looking down; then said almost in a whisper:

"Great or small, it is happiness to know somebody of whom one thinks only good, about whom one can say: God give her happiness, for she deserves it — give her all that I never had. She is pure and beautiful, warm-hearted and sweet, talented and kind. It means happiness to me, dear Jenny, to be able to pray like this for you. No; it is nothing to be afraid of, little one."

He had risen, and she rose too, making a movement as if she were afraid he would come nearer. Gram stopped and smiled:

"How could you help seeing it — you who are so clever. I thought you saw it before I understood it myself. It has come quite naturally. My life is running its course towards old age, inactivity, darkness, death, and I knew that I should never reach what I have longed for all my life. Then I met you. You are to me the most glorious woman I have ever known; you had the same ideals I once had, and you were on the way to attain them. How could I help crying out in my heart: God help her to succeed. Do not let her be wasted as I have been!

"You were so sweet to me; you came to see me in my den, and you told me about yourself. You listened to me, you understood, and your beautiful eyes were so full of sympathy, so soft and loving. Dearest, are you crying?" He seized both her hands and pressed them passionately to his lips:

"Don't cry, dear; you must not. Why do you cry? You are shivering — tell me why you are crying like this?"

"It is all so sad," she sobbed.

"Sit down here." He was on his knees before her — for a second he rested his forehead against her knee.

"Do not cry because of me. Do you think for a moment I wish that I had never met you? If you have loved, and you wish it had never been, you have not really loved. Believe me, it is so. No, Jenny, not for anything in the world would I miss what I feel for you!

"And you must not cry about yourself. You will be happy. I know it. Of all the men who will love you, one will lie at your feet some day, as I do now, and say that to him it is life itself to be there, and you will think so too. You will understand that to sit thus with him is the only happiness to you, even if it were a brief moment of rest after a day full of toil and hardships, and in the poorest of cottages — a far greater happiness than if you became the greatest artist that ever existed and enjoyed the highest measure of fame and praise. Is not that what you believe yourself?"

"Yes," she whispered, exhausted with weeping.

"You must not despair of winning that happiness some day. All the time you are striving to become a true artist and a good and able woman, you are longing to meet some one who thinks that all you have done to attain your aim is right and that he loves you for it — is it not so, Jenny?"

She nodded, and Gram kissed her hands reverently.

"You have already reached the goal. You are everything that is good and refined, proud and lovely. I say it, and one day a younger, better, and stronger man will say the same — and you will be happy to listen. Are you not a little pleased to hear me say that you are the best and sweetest and most wonderful little girl in the world? — look at me, Jenny. Can I not give you a little pleasure by saying that I believe you will have all possible happiness because you deserve it?"

She looked down into his face, trying to smile; then, bending her head, she passed her hands over his hair:

"Oh, Gert, I could not help it — could I ? I did not want to do you any harm."

"Do not grieve about it, little one! I love you because you are what you want to be — what I once hoped to be. You must not be sad for my sake, even if you think you have caused me pain; there are sorrows that are good, full of blessing, I assure you."

She went on crying softly. Presently he whispered:
"May I come and see you now and again? Will you not send for me when you are sad? I

144

should so like to try and be of some help to my dear little girl." "I dare not, Gert."
"Dear child, I am an old man; remember, I might be your father." "For — for your sake, I mean. It is not right."

"Oh yes, Jenny. Do you believe that I think less about you when I don't see you? I ask only to see you, talk to you, to try and do something for you. Won't you let me? Do let me come."

"I don't know — I don't know what to say, but please go now. I cannot bear any more today — it is all so terrible. Won't you go, dear?"

He rose slowly:

"I will. Good-bye! Jenny, dear child, you are quite be- side yourself." "Yes" — in a whisper.

"I will go now, but I want to see you before you go aw r ay. I shall come back when you are yourself again and not frightened of me; there is no reason for that, dear."

She was quiet for a little, then suddenly drew him close to her for a second, brushing his cheek with her lips.

"Go now, Gert."

"Thank you. God bless you, Jenny."

When he was gone she paced up and down the floor, shivering without knowing why. In her heart she felt a certain pleasure in remembering his words when he was on his knees before her.

She had always looked upon Gert as a weak man, as one who had suffered himself to be dragged down and been trodden upon as those who are down always will be. And now he had suddenly revealed himself to her as possessing a great fortitude of soul, and a being rich enough and willing to help, while she was bewildered, distracted, and sick with longing in her inmost heart behind the shield of opinions and thoughts which she had made for herself.

She had asked him to go. Why? Because she was so miserably poor herself and had complained of her need to him who, she thought, was just as poor as she herself, and he had showed her that he was rich, offering gladly to help her out of his abundance. It was no doubt because she felt humiliated that she asked him to go.

To accept anything from an affection to which she could not respond had always seemed mean to her, but then she never imagined that she would be in need of such help.

He had not been allowed to continue the work to which he was devoted; the love he had borne in his heart was never to live. Yet he did not despair. That was probably the advantage of having faith — it did not matter so much what one believed, provided there was somebody beside oneself one could trust, for it is impossible to live with only oneself to love and trust.

She was quite familiar with the thought of voluntary death. If she died now there were a few she cared for and who would be sorry, but none who could not do without her, nor any one to whom she was so necessary that she would feel it her duty to prolong her life for their sake. Provided they did not know she had done it herself, her mother and sisters would mourn her for a year and then remember her with gentle melancholy. Cesca and Gunnar would be more sorry than anybody else, because they would understand that she had been unhappy, but she was outside their life. The one who loved her most would miss her most, but as she had nothing to give him he might love her just as well dead. To love her was his happiness; he had the capacity in him to be happy, but if she had not, it was no good living. Work could not till her life to such an extent that she would not long for anything else besides. Why then go on living because they said she had talent? Nobody had more pleasure of her art than she had in exercising it, and the pleasure was not great enough to satisfy her.

Gunnar was not right in what he had once said, rather brutally, that she was a martyr to her own virtue. That could easily be remedied, but she dared not, because she was always afraid of meeting later what she had been longing for. And the least satisfactory of all would be to live close to another human being and yet in one's inmost soul be just as lonely as before. Oh no — no. She would not belong to a man and submit to all the physical and mental intimacies as the consequence of it, and then discover one day that she did not know him, and that he had never known her — that the one had never understood the language of the other.

She lived because she was waiting; she did not -want a lover, because she was expecting a master, and she did not wish to die — not now while she was waiting.

No, she was not going to throw away her life either this way or that; she could not die so poor that she had not a single beloved thing to bid farewell to. She dared not, because she wanted to believe that some day things would be different.

There was nothing else to do but to take up painting again, although it would probably not be much good now, love-sick as she was. She laughed. That was just what she was — love-sick. The object did not exist at present, but the love was there.

Jenny went to the window and looked out. In the gathering darkness the sky looked almost violet, and the tiled roofs, the chimney-pots, and the telephone wires all melted together into one grey tint in the twilight. A reddish light rose from the streets, coloring the frosty haze. The rolling of carriages and the screech of a tram on the rails sounded clearly on the frozen ground.

She did not feel inclined to go home to dinner, but, having promised her mother to come, she put the stove out and left.

The cold was raw and damp; the fog smelt of soot and gas and frozen dust. What a dull street it was where her studio lay. It led down from the centrum, with its noise and traffic, its shops with brilliant show windows and people streaming in and out, and its course ended by the lifeless grey walls of the fort. The houses on either side looked grey and deserted: the new buildings of stone and glass, where business fluttered in and out on paper, prepared by busy young people in the strong white light behind big windows, and people talked to each other by telephone — and the old ones remaining from the time the town was small were low and brown, with shiny fronts and linen blinds in the office windows. Here and there behind a small pane with curtains and flower-pots was a humble home — strangely solitary dwellings in this thoroughfare, where the houses mostly were deserted at night. The shops were not of the kind that people rush in and out of. Some of them had wallpaper, plaster ornaments for ceilings, and stoves for sale; others were furniture stores, with the windows full of empty mahogany beds and varnished oak chairs that looked as if nobody would ever sit on them.

In a gateway a child was standing — a little boy, blue in the face from cold with a big basket on his arm. He was looking at two dogs fighting in the center of the street and making the frozen dust fly about. He started when the dogs came tumbling near the place where he was standing.

"Are you afraid?" asked Jenny. As the boy did not answer, she continued: "Would you like me to see you past them?" He came to her side immediately, but did not speak.

"Which way are you going? Where do you live?" "In Voldgata."

"Did you come on an errand all the way here, such a little boy? — it was very brave of you."

"We deal with Aases in this street because father knows him," was the boy's answer. "This basket is so heavy."

Jenny looked about her; the street was nearly empty:

"Give it to me. I will carry it for you a bit of the way." The boy gave her the basket reluctantly.

"Take my hand till we have got past those dogs. How cold your hands are! Have you no gloves?"

The boy shook his head.

"Put your other hand in my muff. You won't? You think it a silly thing for a boy to carry a muff — is that it?"

She remembered Nils when he was small; she had often longed for him. He was big now and had many friends; he was at an age when it was no fun to walk about with an elder sister. He came seldom to her studio now. The year she had been abroad and the months she had spent with Helge had changed their relations; perhaps when he got older they would be friends again as before. They probably would, for they were fond of each other, but just now he was happy without her. She wished he were a small boy now, so that she could take him on her lap and tell him stories full of adventures while she washed and undressed him and kissed him — or a little bigger, as in the time when they went out together for excursions in Nordmarken, and the road to the butcher's was long and full of remarkable happenings.

"What is you name, little boy?" "Ausjen Torstein Mo."

"How old are you?" "Six."

"I suppose you don't go to school yet?" "No, but I shall in April."

"Do you think it will be nice?"

"No — the teacher is so strict. Oscar goes to school, but we shan't be together, for he is being moved into the second form."

"Is Oscar your friend?" asked Jenny. "Yes; we live in the same house."

After a short pause Jenny spoke again: "Aren't you sorry there is no snow? You have got the hill by the bay where you can toboggan. Have you got a sled?"

"No, but I have snowshoes and ski."

They had turned into another street. Jenny let go the boy's hand and looked at the basket. It was so heavy, and Ausjen was so small — so she kept it, although she did not like to be seen with a poor little urchin in a good street. She would have like to take him to the confectioner's, but thought it would be rather awkward if she met any one she knew there.

148

In the dark Voldgata she took his hand again and carried the basket to the house where he lived, giving him a coin as a parting gift.

On her way through the town she bought chocolates and a pair of red woollen gloves to send to Ausjen. It was nice to be able to give somebody an unexpected pleasure. She might try to get him for a model, but he was very small to sit so long. Poor little hand; it had got warm in hers, and it seemed as if it had been good for her to hold it. Yes, she wanted to try and paint him; he had a queer little face. She would give him milk with a little coffee in it and a nice roll and butter, and she would work and talk to Ausjen. . . .

PART THREE

I

TOWARDS evening of a clear and calm afternoon in May there was a haze over the black sites of the city; the naked walls looked reddish yellow and the factory chimneys a livery brown in the sunlight. Large and small houses, high and low roofs, stood outlined against the greyish-purple air, heavy with dust and smoke and vapors. A little tree by a red wall showed tiny greenish-yellow leaves, transparent in the sunlight.

The mould on the board walls of the workshops was bright green and the soot flakes on the factory walls jet black in some places and in others covered, as it were, with a thin, glistening silvery film.

Jenny had been walking about all the morning in the outskirts of the town, where the sky rose dark blue and hot over the olive-golden fir-tops and the amber-coloured buds of the leaf trees, but here in the city over the high houses and the net of telephone wires it was growing pale behind a thin veil of opal-white haze. This was really the prettier sight of the two though Gert could not see it. To him the city was always ugly, grey, and dirty; it was the city they had cursed, all those young men of the eighties who had been obliged to settle down there to work. He was probably standing at his window this moment, looking out in the sun, and to him the play of light in line and color was not worth noticing; it was merely a sunray outside his prison window.

She stopped a few steps from his door, looking up and down the street, as usual. There was nobody she knew, only business people on their way home. It was past six o'clock.

She ran up the stairs — those dreadful iron steps that echoed their movements when they stole down from his rooms late in the winter nights. The naked walls seemed ever to retain the cold, raw air.

She hurried along the corridor and gave the usual three knocks at his door. Gram opened it. He put his arm round her, and locked the door with his other hand as they kissed. Over his shoulder she could see the flowers on the little table, with wine and foreign fruits in a crystal bowl. There was a slight mist of cigarette smoke in the room, and she knew that he had been sitting there since four o'clock waiting for her.

"I could not come before," she whispered. "I was so sorry to let you wait." When he released her she went to the table, bending over the flowers. "I will take two and make myself nice, may I? I am getting so spoilt since I have come to you, Gert." She stretched out her hands to him.

"When must you go?" he asked, kissing her arms tenderly. Jenny bent her head: "I promised to be back for supper. Mother always waits up for me, and she is so tired now; she needs me to help her in the evening with one thing or another," she said quickly. "It is not so easy to get away from home, you see," she whispered in excuse.

He listened to her many words with bowed head. When she came towards him he took her in his arms so that her face was hidden against his shoulder.

She could not lie, poor little thing, not so well, anyhow, that he would believe it for a single merciful second. In the winter — the very short time of their love — and in the early spring she could always be away from home.

"It is tiresome, Gert, but now I am living at home it is much more difficult to manage; you know I have to be there because mother needs the money as well as the help. You agreed with me, did you not, that I had better move home?"

Gert nodded assent. They were sitting on the sofa close together, Jenny's head resting on his shoulder, so that she could not see his face.

"I was in the country this morning, walking where we used to go together. Let us go there again soon — the day after tomorrow if it is fine — will you? You are sorry because I have to go home so early today, are you not?"

"My dear, have I not said that thousands of times already?"

She could hear from his voice that he was saying this with his melancholy smile again. "I am grateful for every second of your life that you give me." "Don't speak like that, Gert," she said, pained.

"Why should I not say it when it is true? Dearest little girl, do you think I will ever forget that all you have given me is as a princely grace, and I can never understand how you came to give it to me at all?"

"When I realized last winter that you were fond of me — how much you really loved me — I said to myself it must stop. But then I understood that I could not be without you, and so I gave myself to you. Was that a grace? When I could not let you go?"

"I call it an inconceivable grace that you ever came to love me." She nestled in his arms without speaking.

"My own darling ... so young and sweet you are. . . ."

"I am not young, Gert. When you met me I was already beginning to get old without ever having been young. You seemed young to me, much younger at heart than I, because you still believed in what I called childish dreams and used to laugh at them. You have made me believe in love and tenderness and all such things."

Gert Gram smiled, and whispered: "Perhaps my heart was not older than yours — for it seemed to me that I had never yet had any youth, and deep down in my soul I still entertained the hope that some day youth would touch me, if only for once, with his wand. But my hair has turned white meanwhile."

Jenny raised her head and laid her hand caressingly on his head. "Are you tired, little one? Shall I take off your shoes?

Will you not lie down and rest?"

"No, let me stay as I am; it is nicer so."

She drew her feet up under her and nestled closer in his lap. He laid one arm about her, and with the other hand he poured out some wine, holding the glass to her lips. She drank readily. He dropped cherries into her mouth and took the stones from her lips, putting them on the plate.

"More wine?"

"Thanks. I think I will stay with you. I can send a message home to say I have met Heggen — I believe he is in town — but I must go home before the trams stop."

"I'll go and see about it now." He let her down gently on the sofa. "Lie still there and rest, little one."

When he was gone she took off her shoes, drank some more wine, and lay down on the sofa with her head deep in the cushions, pulling a rug over herself.

After all, she loved him, and was glad to be with him. Sitting as she had been a moment ago, resting in his arms, she was happy. He was the only one in the world who had taken her on his knee, warming her and hiding her and calling her his little girl. He was the only being who had stood by her really — so why should she not be close to him?

When he held her close to him and hid her so that she saw nothing, but only felt that he had his arms round her and warmed her, she was contented. She could not do without him, so why not give him the little she had to give, when he gave her what she needed most of all?

He could kiss her, do with her what he liked, provided he did not speak, for then they drew so far apart. He spoke of love, but her love was not what he believed it to be, and she could not explain it in words. It was no grace or princely gift — she clung to him with a poor, begging love ; she did not want him to thank her for it, only to be fond of her and say nothing.

When he came back she was lying with her eyes wide open, but she closed them under his discreet caresses, smiling a little; then she put her arms round his neck and pressed close to him. The faint scent of violet that he used was mild and agreeable. She nodded slightly when he lifted her up with questioning eyes. He wanted to say something, but she put her hand across his mouth and then kissed him so that he could not speak.

He saw her to the car. She remained an instant standing on the platform, looking after him as he walked down the street in the blue light of a May night. Then she went in and sat down.

Gram had left his wife that Christmas, and lived alone in the office building, where he had taken another room. Jenny understood that he was going to get a separation later on when Rebecca Gram had seen that he was not coming back to her. It was his way of doing it; he had not the strength to break with her at once.

Jenny dared not think of what his plans for the future might be. Did he think they would marry?

She could not deny to herself that she had never for a second thought of binding herself to him for good, and that was why she felt the bitter, hopeless humiliation and shame at the thought of him when she was not with him and could hide in his love. She had deceived him — all the time she had deceived him.

"That you have learnt to love me, Jenny, that is what I call an inconceivable grace" — was it her fault that he looked upon it in that way?

He could not have made her his mistress unless she had wanted it herself or made him feel that she wanted it. She understood that he was longing for her; it worried her every time they were together to know herself desired and to see his efforts to conceal it — he was too proud to let her see it, too proud to beg where he had once offered to give — and too proud to risk refusal. Knowing that she did not want to reject his love and to lose the only being who loved her, what else could she do, if she wished to be honest, but offer him what she had to give when she accepted from him something she could not do without?

But she had been faced with the necessity of saying words stronger and more passionate than her feelings, and he had believed them. And it happened again and again. When she came to him depressed, worried, tired of thinking what the end of it all would be, and saw that he understood, she used again the tender words, feigning more feeling than she had, and he was deceived at once.

He knew no other love than the love which was happiness in itself. Unhappiness in love came from outside, from some relentless fate, or from stern justice as a vengeance for old wrongs. She knew what his fear was — he dreaded that her love would die one day when she saw that he was too old to be her lover, but he never had a suspicion that her love was born a weakling and had in it the germ that would lead to death. It was no good trying to explain this to Gert; he would not understand. She could not tell him that she had sought shelter in his amis because he was the only one who had offered to shelter her when she was weary to death. When he offered her love and warmth she had not the strength to reject, although she knew she ought not to accept it — she was not worthy of it.

No, he was not old. It was the passion of a youth of twenty, a childish faith, a reverent worship, and the kindness and tenderness of a grown man — all the love that filled a man's life — that flared up on the border of old age. And it should have been given to a woman who could love him in return, who could live with him for those few years the life he had dreamt of, longed and hoped for, would last — _ live with him so that she would be bound to him by a thousand happy memories when old age came, having been in true love the wife of his youth and manhood, and ageing with him.

But she — what could she give him if she remained? She had never been able to give him anything, only taken what he gave. If she tried to stay, she would not be able to make him believe that all her longing for life was quenched for ever in the love of their youth. He would himself tell her to go. She had loved and given; she did not love any more, and would be free. That is how he would look upon it; he would never understand that she mourned because there was nothing — nothing she had been able to give.

She could not bear to hear him speak about her gifts to him. It is true that she had brought him her pure soul when she gave herself to him. He could never forget it, and he measured, as it were, the depth and strength of her love by this fact, for she had given him the purity of her youth — of twenty years.

She had kept it as a white bridal dress, unused, unstained, and in her longing and anxiety lest she should never come to wear it, in despair over her cold solitude and her inability to love, she had clung to it, crumpled it, and soiled it with her thoughts. Was not any one who had lived the life of love purer than she, who had been brooding and spying and longing until all her faculties were paralyzed by that longing?

154

She had given herself — and yet what a slight impression it had made on her. She was not altogether cold; sometimes she was carried away by his passion, but she feigned passion while she was cool, and when she was away from him she scarcely remembered it at all. Yet, to please him, she wrote of a longing which did not exist — yes, she had been feigning, feigning all the time before his honest passion.

There was a time when she had not been a hypocrite, or if she had lied to Gert she had also lied to herself. She had felt a storm in herself; it was perhaps pity for him and his fate and rebellion against her own — why should they both be harried by a longing for something impossible? — and in the growing anxiety for where it all would lead, she had rejoiced that she loved him, for she was forced to fall into the arms of this man, however mad she knew it to be. She would sit in the tram when she left him of an evening, looking at all the sleepy, placid faces of the people, and rejoicing that she came from her lover — that he and she were whirled by the tempest of their fate. They had been driven into it and did not know where they were going, and she was proud of her fate because unhappiness and darkness threatened.

And now she was sitting here only wishing for it to end, planning a journey abroad to escape from it all. She had accepted a invitation to stay at Tegneby with Cesca to prepare the break. It was better for Gert that he was alone — if she could manage to end the life between them now, she could have done him some good.

Two young women were sitting opposite her. They were probably not older than she, but stupefied by a few years of marriage. Three or four years ago they had no doubt been a couple of neat office girls, who dressed attractively and sported with their admirers in Nordmarken. She knew the face of one of them, now she thought of it; she had seen her at Hakloa one Easter. Jenny had noticed her then because she was such a good ski-runner and looked so brisk and smart in her sportsuit. In a way she was not badly dressed now either; her walking habit was fashionable enough, but did not fit. The figure had no firmness; she was well covered, and at the same time the shoulders and hips were angular. The face under a big hat with ostrich feathers was old, with bad teeth, and furrows round the mouth. She was talking, and her friend listened interestedly, sitting there heavily and painfully enceinte, with knees apart and her hands in a colossal muff. The face was originally pretty, but fat and red, and with a treble chin.

"I have to lock up the cheese in the sideboard; if it goes into the kitchen only the rind is left the next day — a big piece of Gruyére costing nearly three kroner."

"I quite believe it."

"And then there's another thing. She is very fond of eggs. The other day I went into her bedroom — she is such a pig and her room is very smelly; the bed had not been made for I don't know how long. ' Really, Solveig,' I said, lifting the blankets, and what do you think I found? Three eggs and a paper of sugar in the bed. She said she had bought it herself — and perhaps she had."

"I don't think so," said the other.

"The sugar was in a paper bag, so she may have bought it, but the eggs she had certainly taken, and I gave her a scolding. Last Saturday we were to have rice pudding. When I went into the kitchen I found the rice boiling on the gas and quite burnt, while she was sitting in her room doing needlework. I called her while I was stirring the rice, and what do you think I found in the spoon? An egg, if you please. She boils eggs for herself with the rice! I had to laugh, but did you ever hear anything so dirty? I gave her a piece of my mind.

Don't you think she deserved it?"

"Certainly. Servants are a bother. What do you think mine did the other day? . . ."

They had also been longing for love when they were young girls — their ideal of love was a smart, straight lad with a secure position, who could take them away from the monotonous work in office or shop and settle them in a little home, where the three rooms would hold all their belongings, and they could spread out all the pieces of needlework with embroidered roses and bluebells which they had made while dreaming their girlish day-dreams about love. They smiled at those dreams now with a superior air, and to those who still dreamed they had the satisfaction of stating that the reality was quite different. They were pleased to be among the initiated who knew what it really meant — and they were perhaps content.

But there was happiness all the same in not being content, in refusing to put up with things and be thankful when life offered things of little worth; far better to say: I believe in my dreams; I will call nothing happiness but that which I claim, and I believe it exists. If it is not to be mine, it is my own fault; it is because I have been one of the foolish virgins who did not watch and wait for the bridgegroom, but the wise will see him and will enter in with rejoicing.

When Jenny came home she saw there was a light in her mother's room, so she went in to tell her about the party at Ahlstrom's studio, and how Heggen was. Ingeborg and Bodil slept farther down in the room, with their black plaits across the pillows. Jenny felt no compunction at standing there telling falsehoods to her mother. She had always done it from the time she was a schoolgirl and used to tell merry tales about the children's parties, where she had in reality been sitting alone, watching the others dance — an unhappy and lonely little girl who could not dance or talk of anything that the boys cared for.

When Ingeborg and Bodil came home from a dance their mother sat up in bed listening and smiling and asking questions, young and rosy in the lamplight, and they could always tell the truth, because it was full of merriment and laughter.

There may have been a thing or two so nice that they wanted to keep it to themselves, but it did not matter, for their smiles were true.

Jenny kissed her mother good-night. Passing through the sitting-room, she happened to pull down a photograph; she picked it up, knowing in the dark that it was a brother of her own father, with his wife and little girls. He had lived in America, and she had never seen him; he was dead, and his picture stood in its place without anybody ever thinking of it. She herself dusted it every day, yet never looked at it.

She went into her own room and began to take down her hair.

She had always lied to her mother — could she ever have been truthful to her without making her suffer, and to what purpose? Mother would never have understood. She had had happiness and sorrow since she was quite young; she had been happy with Jenny's father and had bemoaned his death, but she had her child to live for, and learnt to be content. Then she met Nils Berner, who filled her life with fresh happiness and fresh sorrow — and again the children consoled her, inasmuch as they filled the emptiness of her life. The joy of motherhood is bought with too much suffering; it is too actual, when held living in one's arms, for one ever to doubt its existence. To love one's child is so natural that there is no cause for reflection. A mother never doubts that she loves her child, or that she wants it to be happy — that she does her best for it, or that it returns her love. The grace of nature is so great to mothers that children instinctively shrink from confiding their sorrows and disappointments to her; illness and money troubles are almost the only sorrows she ever gets to know. Never the irreparable, the shame, the failures in
life, and were she told of them ever so emphatically by her own children, she would never believe they were irreparable.

Her mother was not to know anything about her sorrow — nature itself had raised a wall between them. Rebecca Gram would never know a tenth part of the sufferings her children had endured for her sake. And a friend of her mother's was still mourning her handsome boy, who had been killed by an accident, and dreaming of the future that would have been his; she was the only person who did not know that he had shot himself as the only way of escape from insanity.

Love of one's children did not exclude any other love; one or two mothers among her acquaintances had lovers, and believed that the children did not know. Some were divorced, and found happiness in new ties; only if the new love brought disappointment did they ever complain or regret. Her own mother had idolized her — yet there was room for Berner in her heart too, and she had been happy with him. Gert had been fond of his children — and a father's affection is more understanding, more a matter of reflection and less instinctive than a mother's — yet he had scarcely thought of Helge all last winter.

II

JENNY had been to fetch their mail bag at the station; and gave Francesca the papers and the letters, and opened the one addressed to herself. Standing on the gravel of the station platform in the blazing sun, she looked through Gert's long effusion, reading the expressions of love at the beginning and the end and skipping the rest, which was only a mass of observations on love in general. She put it back in the envelope and placed it in her hand-bag. Ugh! those letters from Gert — she could not be bothered to read them. Even' word proved to her that they did not understand one another; she felt it when they talked together, but in writing it was more painfully distinct still. Yet there was a mental relationship between them — how was it that they did not harmonize?

Was he stronger or weaker than she? He had lost repeatedly, had resigned, stooped, and submitted in every way, and yet he went on hoping, living, and believing. Was it weakness or vitality? She could not make out.

Was it the difference in their ages after all? He was not old, but his youthfulness belonged to another period, when youth was more unsophisticated and had a healthier creed. Perhaps she was naive too — with her aims and opinions — but it was in a quite different way. Words change their meanings after twenty years — was that the reason?

The gravel glittered red and purple, and the paint on the station building was blistered by the scorching sun. As she looked up everything went dark before her eyes for a moment; it was a peculiar sensation, but probably the effect of the heat, which she seemed to feel more than usual this summer.

The haze hung trembling over fields and meadows, reaching right out to where the forest lay, a dark green line under the deep blue summer sky. The foliage of the birches had already changed its color to a darker green.

Cesca was reading a letter from her husband. Her linen dress was strikingly white against the dark gravel of the platform.

Gunnar Heggen's luggage had been put on the pony cart, and he stood stroking the horse's head and talking to it while he waited for the ladies. Cesca put her letter in her pocket, shaking her head as if trying to drive away a thought.

"Sorry to keep you so long, boy — now let us start." Jenny and Cesca took the front seat; she was taking the reins herself. "I am so pleased, Gunnar, that you could come. Won't it be nice to be together again for a few days, we three? Lennart sends his love to both of you."

"Thanks — is he all right?"

"Oh yes — first-rate, thanks. Brilliant idea of father, wasn't it, to go away with Borghild and leave the house to me and Jenny? Old Gina looks after us, and is ready to stand on her head for us. I call it perfectly lovely."

"It is delightful to see you again, you two."

He laughed and chatted with them, but Jenny imagined she noticed a touch of sadness behind his merry talk. She knew that she looked worn and tired herself, and Cesca in her cheap, ready-made costume looked like a tomboy beginning to get old without having been properly grown up. Cesca seemed to have shrunk very much in the one year they had been separated, but she chatted on as before, telling them w T hat they were going to have for dinner, that they would have coffee in the garden, and that she had bought liqueurs and whisky and soda to celebrate the occasion of their visit.

That night, when Jenny came into her bedroom, she sat down on the window-seat to cool her face in the fresh breeze made by the fluttering curtain. She was not sober; it was an extraordinary thing, but it was a fact. She could not understand how it had happened; all she had had was one glass and a half of toddy and a couple of small liqueurs after supper. True, she had not eaten much, but she had no appetite lately.

She had had strong coffee, so perhaps it was that and the cigarettes which affected her, although she smoked much less now than she used to.

Her heart beat irregularly, and hot waves were rushing over her till she felt moist all over. The landscape she was looking at from the window, the greyish fields, the soft coloured flower-beds in the garden, and the dark trees against the pale summer sky turned and twisted before her eyes, and the room seemed turning round. A taste of whisky and liqueur rose to her throat. How horrid!

She spilt the water when she poured some in the basin, and she felt unsteady on her feet. Jenny mia, this is scandalous. You will soon be done for, my girl, if you cannot stand that much. In the olden days you could have taken twice as much.

She bathed her face and her hands for a while, keeping her wrists under water; then she pulled off her clothes and squeezed the full sponge over her body. She was wondering if Cesca and Gunnar had noticed it; she had not realized it herself till she got to her room; a good thing the Colonel and Borghild had not been there.

She felt better after her wash, got into her nightdress, and went to sit by the window again. Her thoughts were wandering about confusedly, calling up fragments of conversation between Cesca and Gunnar, but all of a sudden she felt wide awake,

160

realizing with vivid surprise that she had been drunk. Never before had she had such an experience; she used scarcely to feel it at all, even if she took quite a lot of wine.

Anyhow, it had passed off now, and, feeling limp and cold and sleepy, she went to lie down in the big bed. Fancy if she were to wake up tomorrow with a "head" — that would be a new experience.

She had scarcely settled down in the bed and closed her eyes when the disagreeable heat again stole over her, plunging her whole body in a bath of perspiration. The bed seemed to rock under her like a ship in a storm, and she felt sea-sick. Lying perfectly still, she tried to overcome the nausea, telling herself: I will not, I will not, but it was no good. Her mouth filled with water, and she had scarcely time to get up before she was overcome with sickness.

Heavens! Was she really as drunk as that? It became most embarrassing, but it ought to be over now. She tidied up, drank some water, and went to bed again, hoping to sleep it away, but after a brief moment of rest, with her eyes shut, the rocking began again and with it the heat and the nausea. It was astonishing, for her head was now quite clear — yet she had to get up once more.

Stepping back into bed, a thought suddenly struck her.

Nonsense! She lay down again, pressing her neck deep into the pillows. It was impossible. She did not want to think of it, but, unable to dismiss the thought from her mind, she began a review of recent events. She had not felt quite well lately, had been tired and worn out, worried and nervous generally; that was probably why the little she had taken last night had been too much for her. She could quite understand now that people become abstemious after a few nights of the kind she had just experienced. The other matter she would not consider; if things had gone wrong she would know it in due time - — _ it was no good worrying unnecessarily. She was going to sleep; she was so tired — but she could not keep her thoughts away from that awful subject — ugh!

At the beginning of their relations the possibility of consequences had quite naturally presented itself to her mind, and once or twice she had been in the throes of anxiety, but she had been able to master it and had forced herself to look reasonably at the matter. What if it were true? The dread of having a child is really a senseless superstition; it happens every day. Why should it be worse for her than for any poor working girl, who was able to provide for herself and her child? The anxiety was a remnant from the times when an unmarried woman in similar circumstances had to go to the father or her relations and confess that she had had a good time, and that they had to pay the expenses — with the sad prospect of never afterwards having her provided for by somebody else — a quite sufficient reason for their anger.

Nobody had any right to be angry with her. Her mother would, of course, be sorry, but when a grown-up person tried to live according to his conscience the parents had nothing to say. She had tried to help her mother as much as possible, she had never worried her with her own troubles, her reputation had never been spoilt by any tales of levity, flirtation, or reveling, but where her own opinions about right and wrong differed from that of other people, she meant to follow them, even if it would be painful to her mother to hear disagreeable things said about her.

If her relations with Gert were a sin, it did not mean that she had given too much, but too little, and whatever the consequences would be, she had to bear them without complaint.

She could provide for a child just as well as many a girl who had not a tenth part of her knowledge. There was still some money left of her inheritance — enough for her to go abroad. If the profession she had chosen was a poor one, she knew that several of her fellow-artists were able to keep wife and children with it, and she had been used to helping others from the time she was almost a child. She would, of course, prefer not to have to do it; so far everything had been all right — she would not think of it.

Gert would be in despair.

If it was true, how dreadful that it should happen now. If it had happened when she loved him, or thought she did, and she could have gone away in good faith, but now, when everything that had been between them had crumbled to pieces, torn asunder by her own thinking and pondering. . . .

During these weeks at Tegneby she had made up her mind not to go on any longer. She was longing to go away to new conditions, new work. Yes, the longing for work had come back; she had had enough of this sickly desire of clinging to somebody, to be cuddled and petted and called little girl.

At the thought of breaking with him her heart winced with pain. She shrank from causing him sorrow, but she had kept it up as long as possible. Gert had been happy while it lasted, and he was free from the degrading slavery with his wife.

She was perfectly resigned to the thought that her life henceforth would be work and solitude only. She knew she could not obliterate the past months from her life; she would always remember them and the bitter lessons they had taught her.

The love that others found enough was not enough for her — it was better for her to dispense with it altogether than to be contented.

Yes, she would remember, but as years went by the memory of the short happiness mixed with so much pain and bitter repentance would perhaps be less poignant, and she would be able partly to wipe out the memory of the man to whom she had done a deadly wrong — and whose child perhaps she bore.

No; it was impossible. Why lie here brooding over it? But if it were true. . . .

When Jenny at last sank into a heavy and dreamless sleep it was almost daylight, but when she awoke again with a shock, it was not much lighter. The sky was a little more yellow above the garden trees, and the birds were chirping sleepily. She was instantly wide awake, and the same thoughts returned; she would hardly get any more sleep that night, and she resigned herself to thinking them over and over again.

III

H EGGEN had left; the Colonel and Borghild had returned and gone again to pay a visit to a married sister of Francesca's. Jenny and Cesca were alone, and they went about by themselves, deep in their own thoughts.

Jenny was convinced now of her condition, but she had not been able to realize what it all meant; if she tried to think of the future, her imagination stood still. She was, on the whole, in a better frame of mind now than in the first desperate weeks when she was waiting anxiously for her suspicions to be disproved.

She told herself that there would be a way out of it for her as for so many other women. Fortunately she had spoken of going abroad since last autumn. She had not made up her mind about telling Gert or not, but she thought she would not do it.

When she was not thinking of herself she thought of Cesca. There was something the matter — something that was not as it ought to be. She was sure Cesca was fond of Ahlin. Did he not care for her any longer?

Cesca had had a bad time of it this first year of her married life; there had been serious money troubles. Cesca looked so small and dejected. Hour after hour of an evening she would sit on Jenny's bed telling her about all her household worries Everything was so expensive in Stockholm, and cheap food was bad, especially when one had not learnt to cook. Housework was all so difficult when one was brought up in such an idiotic way as she had been, and the worst of it was that it had to be done over and over again. She had scarcely finished cleaning the house before it was in an awful state again, and the moment she had finished a meal there was the washing up — and so it went on indefinitely, cooking things, soiling plates, and washing up again. Lennart tried to help her, but he was just as clumsy and unpractical as she was. Then, too, she worried about him. The commission for the monument had been given to some one else after all; he was never appreciated, and yet he was so gifted, but far too proud, both individually and as an artist. It could not be helped — and she would not have had him different. In the spring he had had a long illness, being confined to bed for two months with scarlet fever, pneumonia, and subsequent complications — it had been a very trying time for Cesca.

But there was something else — Jenny felt it distinctly — that Cesca did not tell her, and she knew she could not be to Cesca now what she had been in the old days. She had no longer the tranquil heart and open mind, ready to receive the sorrows of others and able to give comfort; and it hurt her to feel that she could no longer help.

Cesca had gone to Moss one day to do some shopping. Jenny preferred to stay at home, and was spending the day in the garden reading, so as not to think. Then, when she found

164

that she could not pay attention to her book, she started knitting, but soon lost count of her stitches, pulled them out, and went on again, trying to be more attentive. Cesca did not come back to dinner as she had promised, and Jenny dined alone, killing the afternoon by smoking cigarettes which she did not enjoy, and knitting, though her work constantly dropped on to her lap.

At last, about ten o'clock Cesca came driving up the avenue; Jenny had gone to meet her, and the moment she sat down beside her in the cart she saw that something had happened, but neither of them said a word.

Later, when Francesca had had something to eat and they were having a cup of tea, she said quietly without looking at Jenny:

"Can you guess whom I met in town today?"

"No."

"Hans Hermann. He is on a visit at the island and living with a rich woman who seems to have taken him up."

"Is his wife with him?" asked Jenny.

"No; they are divorced. I saw in the papers that they had lost their little boy in the spring. I am sorry for her" — and Cesca began to talk of other things.

When Jenny was in bed Cesca came quietly into her room, sitting down at the foot end of the bed and pulling her nightdress well over her feet. She sat with her arms folded round her knees, her little dark head making a black shadow on the curtain.

"Jenny, I am going home tomorrow. I will send a wire to Lennart early in the morning and leave in the afternoon. You must stay here as long as you like, and don't think me very inconsiderate, but I dare not stay. I must go at once." She was breathing heavily. "I cannot understand it, Jenny. I have seen him. He kissed me, and I did not strike him. I listened to all he had to say, and I did not strike him in the face as I ought to have done. I don't care for him — I know that now — and yet he has power over me. I am afraid. I dare not stay, because I don't know what he might make me do. When I think of him now I hate him, but when he speaks to me I seem to get petrified; and I could not believe that anybody could be so cynical, so brutal, so shameless.

"It seems as if he does not understand there is such a thing as honor or shame; they do not exist for him, and he does not believe that anybody else cares for them either. His point of view is that our talking of right and wrong is only speculation, and when I hear him speak I seem to get hypnotized. I have been with him all the afternoon, listening to his talk. He said that as I was married now I need not be so careful about my virtue any longer, or something to that effect, and he alluded to his being free again, so as to give me some hope, I suppose. He kissed me in the park and I wanted to scream, but could not make a sound. Oh, I was so afraid. He said he would come here the day after tomorrow — they were going to have a party tomorrow — and all the time he smiled at me with that same smile I was always so afraid of in the old days.

"Don't you think I ought to go home when I feel like this?" "Yes; I think so."

"I am a goose, I know. I cannot rely upon myself, as you see, but you can be certain of one thing: if I had been false to Lennart, I would go straight to him and tell him, and kill myself the same instant before his eyes."

"Do you love your husband?" asked Jenny. Francesca was silent a moment.

"I don't know. If I loved him really as one ought to love, I suppose I should not be afraid of Hans Hermann. Do you think I should have let Hans behave like he did and kiss me?

"But I know, anyhow, that if I did wrong to Lennart I could not go on living. You understand, don't you? While I was Francesca Jahrman I was not very careful about my good name, but now I am Francesca Ahlin, and if I let fall the very faintest shadow of a suspicion on that name — his name — I should deserve to be shot down like a mad dog. Lennart would not do it, but I would do it myself."

She dropped her arms suddenly and crept into the bed, nestling close to Jenny.

"You believe in me, don't you? Do you think I could live if I had done anything dishonorable?"

"No, Cesca." Jenny put her arms round her and kissed her. "I don't think you could."

"I don't know what Lennart thinks; he does not understand me. When I get home I will tell him everything just as it is, and leave it to him."

"Cesca," said Jenny, but checked herself. She would not ask, after all, if she was happy. But Cesca began to tell by herself:

"I have had many difficulties since I married, I must tell you, and I have not been very happy, but then I was so foolish and ignorant in many ways.

"I married Lennart because Hans began to write to me when he was divorced, saying that he was determined to have me, and I was afraid of him and did not want to have anything

166

to do with him. I told Lennart everything; he was so kind and sympathetic and understood me, and I thought he was the most wonderful man in the world — and so he is, I know.

"But I did something awful. Lennart cannot understand it, and I know that he has not forgiven me. Perhaps I am wrong in telling you, but I must ask somebody if it is really so that a man can never forgive it, and you must answer me frankly — tell me if you think that it is impossible ever to get over it.

"We went to Rocca di Papa in the afternoon when we were married. You know how dreadfully afraid I have always been of marriage, and when Lennart took me into our room in the evening, I began to cry. Lennart was such a dear to me.

"This was on a Saturday. We did not have a particularly pleasant time — I mean Lennart did not, for I would have been delighted to be married like that, and every morning when I awoke I was so grateful to him, but I was scarcely allowed to kiss my husband.

"On the Wednesday we had gone to the top of Monte Cavo, and it was marvellously beautiful up there. It was in the end of May and the day was glorious. The chestnut wood was light green, the leaves had just come out, the broom was blossoming madly in the crevices, and along the road grew heaps of white flowers and lilies. There was a haze in the air, for it had rained earlier in the day, and the Nemi and Albano lakes were lying silvery white below, with all the little white villages round. The whole Campagna and Rome were wrapped in a thin veil of mist, and farther out the Mediterranean shone like a golden line on the horizon.

"Oh, it was such a day! And life seemed wonderfully beautiful to me — but Lennart was sad. To me he was the most perfect man in the world, and I was immensely fond of him.

All of a sudden it seemed so silly of me to make a fuss, and I put my arms round his neck and said: ' I want to be yours, for I love you.' "

Cesca was silent a second, taking a deep breath.

"Oh, Jenny — how happy he was, poor boy!" She swallowed her tears. "He was so pleased. 'Now?' said he — 'here?' and took me in his arms, but I resisted. I don't know really why I did it. It would have been beautiful in the deep forest and the sunshine.

"He rushed out and stayed away all night. I lay awake. I was anxious, wondering what he had done, where he had gone. Next day we went back to Rome and stayed at an hotel. Lennart had taken two rooms. I went to him in his room — but there was no beauty in it. We have never been quite happy since. I know that I have offended him frightfully, but tell me, Jenny, if you think it a thing a man never can forget or forgive?"

"He ought to have realized afterwards that you did not understand what it was you were doing — how it would hurt him."

"No." Cesca was shivering. "But I do now. I see that it was something pure and beautiful that I soiled, but I did not understand it then. Jenny, do you think a man's love could ever get over that?"

"It ought to. You have proved since that you want to be a good and faithful wife to him. Last winter you worked so hard and suffered without complaining, and in the spring when he was ill you nursed him week after week, watching night after night by his bedside."

"That is nothing to speak of," said Cesca eagerly. "He was so good and patient, and he helped me in the house as much as he could. When he was ill some of our friends came sometimes to help me to sit up with him in the night. That week when he was near death we had a nurse, but I sat up just the same because I wanted to — although I was not really needed."

Jenny kissed Cesca's forehead.

"There is one thing I have not told you, Jenny. You warned me, you remember, to be more careful with men, and said I had no instincts. Gunnar used to scold me, and Miss Linde said once, don't you remember, that if you make a man excited that way he goes to somebody else."

Jenny felt quite cold with fright for what was coming next. "Well, I asked him something about that on this first morning."

Jenny could not say a word. "I understand that he cannot forget it and perhaps not forgive, but I wish he would find an excuse for me, remember how very stupidly I looked at it all." She hesitated, searching for words. "Our life has been so horrid ever since. He does not really wish to kiss me — if he ever does, it is almost against his will, and he is angry afterwards with himself and with me. I have tried to explain, but it is no good. To be quite honest, I don't know what to make of it all, but I do not mind anything any longer if I could only make him happy. Anything that makes Lennert happy is good and beautiful to me. He thinks that I sacrifice myself, but it is no sacrifice — quite the contrary. Oh, I have cried for nights and days in my room because I saw that he was longing for my love, and I have tried to kiss him, but he pushes me away.

"I am very fond of him, Jenny. Tell me, can't one love a man in that way too? — can I not say that I love Lennart?"

"Yes, Cesca."

"You cannot think how desperate I have been. But I cannot help being as I am. When we are out of an evening with other artists I see that he is in a bad humor; he does not say anything, but I see he thinks I flirt with them. It is true, perhaps, for I get into good spirits when I can have a meal out and need not cook and wash up once for a change, and not be afraid of spoiling the food when Lennart has to eat it all the same because we cannot afford to throw it away. Sometimes I was glad, too, of not having to be alone with Lennart, though I am fond of him and he is of me — I know he is. If I ask him about it he says, ' You know it quite well,' and smiles in a queer way, but he does not trust me because I cannot love with my senses and yet like to flirt. Once he said I had not a notion of what love really meant and that it was his fault for not being able to awaken it in me, but there would probably be another man some day who could. O God, how I cried!

"You know we are ever so poor. Well, in the spring Gunnar managed to get my still-life picture sold — the one I had at the exhibition three years ago. We got three hundred kroner for it and we lived on it for several months, but Lennart did not like spending the money I had earned. I cannot see what difference it makes when we are fond of each other, but he talked about having brought me into misery and so on. We have got debts too, of course, so I wanted to write to father asking him for a few hundreds, but he would not let me. I thought it so ridiculous. Borghild and Helga have lived at home or abroad all these years and had everything given to them, whereas I have saved and pinched with the little I had from mother since I came of age, because I did not want to take anything from papa after what he said to me when I broke my engagement with Kaasen and there was all the talk about Hans and me. Father has since admitted that I was right. It was mean of Kaasen and of them at home to try and force me to marry him because he had beguiled me into an engagement when I was only seventeen, and did not know that marriage meant anything else but what you read in silly girl stories. When I began to understand, I knew I would rather kill myself than marry him. If they had succeeded in forcing me to it, I would have led them a life, taking all the lovers I could get just out of spite and to pay them out. Papa sees it now, and he says I can have money whenever I want it.

"Lennart was very weak after his illness, and the doctor said he must go into the country — and I myself was tired and overworked, so I said I ought to go away for a change and a rest as I was going to have a baby. I got his permission to write to papa for money. We got it and went to Wårmland, having a lovely time. Lennart was getting well and strong, and I took up my painting again. When he understood I was not expecting a child really, he asked if I had not made a mistake, and I told him I had tricked him, not wanting to lie to him. But he is angry with me for it, and I can see that he does not quite believe me. If he understood my nature, don't you think he would believe in me?"

"Yes, Cesca dear."

"You see, I had told him the same thing once before — about the baby, I mean — in the autumn, when he was so sad and we were not happy. I wanted him to be pleased and to be kind to me, and he was. It was a lovely time. I had really lied, but I began to believe it myself at last, for I thought God would make it true, so that I need not disappoint him. But God did not do it.

"I am so unhappy because I can't have one. Do you think it is true — some people say it is so," she whispered emotionally — "that a woman cannot have a child if she cannot feel — passionate?"

"No," said Jenny sharply. "I am sure it is only nonsense."

"I am sure everything would come all right then, for Lennart wishes it so very much. And I — oh, I think I should be so good — an angel for joy at having a dear little child of my own. Can you imagine anything more wonderful?"

"No," whispered Jenny, confused, "when you love each other. It would help you to get over many difficulties."

"Yes, it would. If it were not so awkward I would go and see a doctor. Don't you think I ought to? I think I will some day, but I am so stupid about it — I feel so shy. I suppose it really is my duty as I am married. I might go to a lady doctor — one who is married and has children of her own.

"Think of it! A tiny little creature all your own; Lennart would be so happy!" Jenny set her teeth in the dark. "Don't you think I ought to go home tomorrow?"

"Yes."

"I will tell Lennart everything. I don't know if he will understand me — I don't myself, but I am going to tell him the truth always. Should I not, Jenny?"

"When you think it is right you should do so. One must always do what one thinks right, and never do anything one is not absolutely sure about."

"Good-night, Jenny dear." She embraced her friend with sudden earnestness. "Thank you! It is so lovely to have you to talk to; you are so good, and you know how to take me. You and Gunnar always get me on to the right way. I don't know what I should do if it weren't for you."

Then, standing by the bed, she said: "Won't you come through Stockholm when you go abroad this autumn? Please, do! You could stay with us. I am getting a thousand kroner from father because he is going to give Borghild the same for her trip to Paris."

"Thanks, I should like to, but I don't know yet what I am going to do." "Do come if you can! Are you sleepy? Do you want me to go now?"

"I am a little tired," and, pulling Cesca's head down, she kissed her. "God bless you, darling."

"Thank you." Cesca went across the floor on her bare feet; at the door she turned, saying in a sad, childish voice: "I do wish Lennart and I could be happy!"

IV

GERT and Jenny were walking side by side down the windy path under ragged pines. He stopped to pick some little wild strawberries, ran after her, and put them in her mouth. She thanked him with a smile, and he took her hand as they walked towards the sea that showed glittering blue between the trees.

He looked bright and young in a light summer suit, the panama hiding his hair completely. Jenny sat down near the edge of the wood, Gert lying on the grass beside her in the shade of big drooping birches.

It was scorching hot and still; the grassy slope by the water was dried yellow. Over the point hung a blue metallic bar of haze with white and smoke-yellow clouds in front. The fjord was light blue, streaked with the currents, the sailing boats lay still and white, and the smoke from the steamers hung long in the air in grey strips. There was a slight swirl of water round the pebbles, and the twigs of the birches moved gently above their heads, dropping one or two leaves dried by the heat.

One of them fell on her fair curly hair — she had taken off her hat — and Gert removed it. Looking at it, he said :

"Queer how the rain keeps off this summer. You women are much better off than we are, wearing such thin dresses. It would look as if you were in half-mourning but for those pink beads. It is very becoming, though."

The dress was a dead white, with small black blossoms, gathered all over and held at the waist by a black silk belt. The straw hat in her lap was black, trimmed with black velvet roses, and the pale pink crystal beads shone against the delicate skin of her neck.

He bent forward to kiss her foot above the rounding of the shoe, and, following with his fingers the delicate bend of her instep in the thin stocking, grasped her ankle. She loosened his hand gently and he seized hers, holding it, smiling, in a firm grip. She smiled back at him and turned away her head.

"You are so quiet, Jenny. Is it the heat?" "Yes," she said, and then was silent again. At a short distance from them, where the garden of a villa reached down to the sea, some children were playing on a landing-stage; a gramophone was singing sleepily inside the house. Now and again the breeze brought the sound of music from the band at the bathing establishment.

"Gert" — Jenny took hold of his hand suddenly — "when I have been a short time with mamma and come back to town again, I shall go."

"Where?" He raised himself on his elbow. "Where do you think of going?" "To Berlin." She felt her voice tremble as she spoke.

Gert looked into her face; neither of them spoke. At last he said: "When did you make up your mind to go?"

"You know it has been my intention all along to go abroad again."

"I know. But I mean how long have you been determined — when did you decide to go so soon?"

"At Tegneby."

"I wish you had told me before," said Gram, and his voice, low and calm as it was, cut her to the heart.

She was silent for a moment.

"I did not want to write it, Gert. I would rather tell you. When I wrote you yesterday to come and see me I meant to tell you, but I could not."

His face turned livid.

"I see. My God, how you must have suffered, child!" he exclaimed. "Yes, mostly for your sake, Gert. I will not ask you to forgive me."

"I forgive you? Great heavens! Can you forgive me? I knew this day would come." "I suppose we both did."

He threw himself suddenly face downwards on the ground. She bent and laid her hand on his neck.

"Oh, my dear Jenny — my little one — what have I done to you?" "Dearest. . . ."

"Little white bird, have I touched you with my ugly unclean hands — spotted your white wings?"

"Gert" — she took both his hands, speaking impetuously — "listen to me. You have done nothing but what was good and kind; it is I who have done wrong. I was tired and you gave me rest; I was cold and you warmed me. I needed rest and I needed warmth; I needed to feel that somebody loved me. I did not wish to deceive you, Gert, but you did not understand — I could not make you see that I loved you in a different way — with a very poor love. Can you not understand?"

"No, Jenny, I don't believe that a young innocent girl gives herself to a man if she does not believe her love will last."

"That is just what I ask you to forgive — I knew you did not understand, and yet I accepted all you gave me. It became more and more unendurable, and I realized that I could not go on. I am fond of you, Gert, but I cannot go on only taking when I can give you nothing that is real."

"Is this what you wanted to tell me yesterday?" asked Gert after a pause. She nodded.

"And instead. . . ." Jenny turned scarlet.

"I had not the courage. You were so happy to come, and I saw that you had been longing and waiting."

He raised his head quickly: "You should not have done it. No, you should not have given me — alms."

Her face was turned away; she remembered the painful hours of yesterday in her hot, stuffy studio, hurriedly dusting and tidying to receive him, her heart aching with sorrow; but she did not care to tell him: "I did not quite know myself — when you came. I thought for an instant — I wanted to make sure."

"Alms." He moved his head as if in pain. "It was alms all the time, then — what you gave me."

"But, Gert, don't you understand that it is just what I have accepted from you — alms — always?"

"No," he said abruptly, lying face downwards again. After a little he lifted his head: "Jenny, is there any one else?"
"No," she replied, vexed at the thought.

"Don't think I would reproach you if there had been another — a young man — your equal; I could understand that easier." "You don't seem able to realize — I don't 'think there need be another."

"Perhaps not. It seemed to me more likely, and, remembering what you wrote about Heggen being at Tegneby and going to Berlin. . . ." Jenny blushed deeply: "How can you think that I would have — yesterday?" Gert was silent.

Then he said wearily: "I cannot quite make you out."

She was suddenly seized by a wish to hurt him.

"In a way it would not be wrong to say that there was another — a third person." He looked at her searchingly, then clutched her arm all of a sudden: "Jenny — good God! — what do you mean?"

But she regretted her words already, and said hurriedly: "Yes, my work — my art." Gert Gram had risen to his knees before her: "Jenny — is there anything- — particular — tell me the truth — don't lie to me — is there anything the matter with you?"

She tried for a second to look him straight in the eyes, then bent her head. Gert Gram fell forward with his face in her lap.

"O God! — O God! . . ."

"Gert, dear, compose yourself. You irritated me with your talk about another. I ought not to have told you. I did not mean to let you know until afterwards."

"I would never have forgiven you for not telling me," said Gram. "You must have known this some time. Do you know how . . . ?"

"Three months," she answered shortly.

"Jenny" — he seized her hands in awe — "you cannot break with me now — not in this way. We cannot part now."

"Oh yes." She stroked his face caressingly. "If this had not happened I daresay we could still have been together some time, but now I must arrange my life accordingly, and make the best of it."

He was silent a moment.

"Listen to me, little one. You know I was divorced last month. In two years' time I shall be free, and then I will come to you to give you — and it — my name. I ask nothing from you, you understand — nothing — but I claim the right to give you the redress I owe you. God knows I shall suffer because it cannot be done before. Nothing else will I claim; you shall not be tied in the least to me — an old man."

"Gert, I am glad that you are separated from her, but I will tell you once and for all that I am not going to marry you when I cannot be your wife in truth. It is not because of the

175

difference in age. If I did not feel that I have never wholly been yours, as I should have been, I would stay with you — - your wife as long as you were young, your friend when old age came — even your nurse — willingly and happily. But I know I cannot be what a wife ought to be, and I cannot promise a thing I could not keep just because of what other people might say — church or civil contract, it makes no difference."

"It is madness, Jenny, to talk like that."

"You cannot make me change on that point," she replied quietly.

"What are you going to do, child? I cannot let you go now. What will happen to you? — you must let me help you."

"Hush. You see I take it calmly. I suppose once you are in for it, it is not so bad as you imagine. Fortunately I have still some money left."

"But, Jenny, think of the people who will be unkind to you — look down on you."

"Nobody can do that. There is only one thing I am ashamed of, and it is that I allowed you to waste your love on me."

"Such foolish talk! You don't know how heartless people can be; they will treat you unkindly, insult and hurt you."

"I don't mind that very much, Gert." She smiled vaguely. "Fortunately I am an artist; people expect a little scandal now and then from us."

He shook his head. In a sudden desperate regret at having told him and given him so much pain she took him in her arms:

"My dear friend, you must not be so distressed — you see that I am not. On the contrary, I am sometimes quite happy about it. When I think that I am going to have a child — a sweet little child, my very own — I can scarcely believe it. I think it will be so great a happiness that I can hardly grasp it now. A little living being, to belong to me only, to love, to live and work for. I sometimes think that then only will my life and my work be of some purpose. Don't you think I could make a name for myself good enough for the child too? It is only because I don't know yet how to arrange it all that I am a little depressed sometimes, and also because you are so sad.

"Perhaps I am poor and dull and an egoist, but I am a woman, and as such I cannot but be happy at the prospect of being a mother."

He kissed her hands:

"My poor, brave girl! It makes it almost worse for me to see you take it that way." Jenny smiled faintly:

"Would it not be worse still if I took it in another way?"

V

TEN days later Jenny left for Copenhagen. Her mother and Bodil Berner saw her off at the station in the early morning.

"You are a lucky one, Jenny!" said Bodil, smiling all over her little soft brown face. And she yawned till the tears came into her eyes.

"Yes, some must be the lucky ones, I suppose. But I don't think you have anything to complain of either," said Jenny, smiling too; but she was several times on the point of bursting into tears when she kissed her mother farewell. Standing at the compartment window looking at her, it seemed as if she had not really seen her mother for ever so long. She took in with her eyes the slightly stooping, slender figure, the fair hair that scarcely seemed grey at all, and the strangely unaffected girlish expression of her face, despite its wrinkles. Only the years, not life, had made the furrows, in spite of all she had gone through.

How would she take it if she knew? No, she would never have the courage to tell her and see her under the blow — she who knew nothing about it all and would not have understood. If it had been impossible to go away Jenny thought she would rather have taken her life. It was not love — it was cowardice. She would have to tell her sometime, of course, but it would be easier to do that later, from abroad.

As the train began to glide out from the station she saw Gert walking slowly down the platform behind her mother and sister, who were waving their handkerchiefs. He took off his hat, looking very pale.

It was the first of September. Jenny sat by the window looking out. It was a beautiful day, the air clear and cool, the sky dark blue, and the clouds pure white. The morning dew lay heavy on the rich green meadows where late daisies were in bloom. The birches at the edge of the forest were already turning yellow from the summer heat, and the bilberry shrub was copper coloured. The clusters of the rowan were deep red; where the trees stood on richer soil the leaves were still dark green. The coloring was splendid.

On the slopes stood old silver-grey farmhouses or newer shining white or yellow ones with red-painted outhouses and crooked old apple trees with yellow or glassy green fruit showing among the foliage.

Time after time tears veiled her eyes; when she came back — if she ever did. . . .

The fjord became visible near Moss, a town built along the canal, with factory walls and the small wooden houses in gay colors surrounded by gardens. Often when passing it in the train she had thought of going there some day to paint.

The train passed the junction where a branch line turns off to Tegneby. Jenny looked out of the window at the familiar places; there was the drive leading to the house, which lay behind the little fir grove, and there was the church. Dear little Cesca liked to go to church; she felt herself safe and protected there, borne away by a sentiment of supernatural strength. Cesca believed in something — she did not quite know what, but had created some kind of a God for herself.

Jenny was pleased to think that Cesca and her husband seemed to be getting on better. She had written that he had not quite understood her, but had, nevertheless, been so kind and dear and convinced that she would never do anything wrong — on purpose. Strange little Cesca! Everything must come right with her in the end. She was honest and good.

But she herself was neither, not to any considerable degree. If only she need not see her mother's tears; she could bear to hurt her — it only meant that she was afraid of scenes.

And Gert? Her heart shrank at the thought of him. A feeling of physical sickness rose in her, a despair and loathing so profound that she felt herself played out — on the point of becoming indifferent to everything.

Those awful last days in Christiania with him. She had given in at last.

He was coming to Copenhagen, and she had to promise to stay somewhere in the country so that he could come and see her. Would she ever be able to get quite free of him?

In the end she would perhaps have to leave the child with him and run away from it all — for it was a lie, all she had told him about being happy about it and the rest. Sometimes at Tegneby she had really felt so, because she only remembered it was her child — not his at all. But if it were to be a link between him and her humiliation she would have nothing to do with it. She would hate it — she hated it already at the memory of the last days before her departure. The morbid desire to cry and sob to her heart's content was gone; she felt dry and hard as if she could never cry again.

A week later Gert Gram arrived. She was so worn out and apathetic that she could pretend to be almost in good spirits, and if he had proposed that she should move into the hotel where he was staying, she would have done so. She made him take her to the theatre, to supper at restaurants, and one day, when the weather was fine, for an excursion to Fredensborg, because she saw that it pleased him if she seemed w r ell and happy. She gave up thinking — it was no sacrifice, for as a matter of fact her brain was tired out.

Jenny had taken rooms with a teacher's widow in a country village. Gram accompanied her there and went back the same evening to Copenhagen. At last she was alone.

She had engaged the rooms without seeing them beforehand. When she had been studying in Copenhagen some years ago she had gone with her fellow-students into the country one day, lunching at an inn and bathing among the rocks, and she remembered it was pretty out there, so when a certain Mrs. Rasmussen, in answer to her advertisement, had offered to house the young lady who was expecting a child, she decided to go there.

The widow lived in a tiny yellow, sadly ugly brick cottage outside the village by the main road, which ran dusty and endless between open tilled fields, but Jenny was pleased on the whole. She liked her bedroom with the blue wall-paper, the etchings on the wall, and the white crochet-work d'oyleys all over the place, on the bed, on the back of the American rockingchair, and on the chest, where Mrs. Rasmussen had placed a bunch of roses the day she arrived.

From her two little windows she could see the main road winding past the house and the small front garden, where roses, geraniums, and fuchsias grew, heedless of the dust. On the other side of the road was a bare hill at the back of the field. Stone fences, along which the vividly coloured autumn flowers grew between bramble bushes, divided the slope into squares of stubble, greeny-brown meadow, and blue-green turnip field; spriggy wind-blown willow bushes grew along the boundaries. When the evening sun had left Jenny's window the sky was flaming red and golden above the ridge and the meager twigs of the willows.

At the back of her room was a neat doll's-house kitchen with red brick floor, opening into the back yard, where the widow's chickens were cackling and the pigeons cooing. A small passage ran through the house; on the farther side Mrs. Rasmussen had her parlor, with flower-pots in the window and crochet work everywhere, daguerreotypes and photographs on the walls, and a book-case with religious books in black paper covers, bound volumes of periodicals, and a few novels. At the back was a small room where she slept, and where the air was al- ways heavy with an indefinable odor, though everything in the room was spotlessly clean. She could not hear in there if her boarder on the other side of the passage spent a night now and again in tears.

Mrs. Rasmussen was not so bad, on the whole. Tall and lanky, she pattered about in some kind of felt slippers, always with a worried look on her long yellow face, which was rather like that of a horse and had straggling grey hair combed back from it, forming quaint little wings over the ears. She scarcely ever spoke, save for an anxious question as to whether the lady was pleased with the room or the food, and when Jenny went to sit in the parlor with her needlework they were both perfectly quiet. Jenny was specially grateful to the woman for not mentioning her condition; only once when she went out with her painting paraphernalia did Mrs. Rasmussen ask her anxiously if she did not think it unwise. She had worked hard at first, standing behind a stone fence with her field easel, which threatened to be upset every instant by the wind.

Below the stone fence the stubby rye field sloped towards a swamp where the bog bean round the bluish water pools was whitening, and velvety black peat stacks stood piled on the grass. Beyond the swamp were the chalk-white peasants' huts set in rich dark green groves and surrounded by meadows, stubbed rye fields, and turnip land as far as the wafer's edge. The beach was cut into tiny bays and points, the sand and the short dried grass making it look a whitish yellow. To the north a heather-brown hill with a windmill on top sloped down towards the bay. Light and shadow flitted alternately over the landscape as the clouds traveled across the wide, ever restless sky.

When Jenny got tired she lay down by the fence, looking up at the sky and out over the bay; she could not stand for long at a time, but it made her only more eager. Two small pictures painted from the fence were finished, and she was pleased with them; a third one she painted in the village, where the low whitewashed houses with thatched roofs almost covering the windows, and climbing roses and dahlias in the gardens, stood along a velvety green ditch, and a red brick church stretched its gabled tower above the foliage of the vicarage garden. But it made her nervous when people came to look at her, and flaxen-haired youngsters clustered round her when she was painting. When the picture was finished she moved with her easel again to the stone fence.

In October the rain came, pouring down for a week or two. Now and again the skies cleared a little, letting out a sickly yellow ray of light between the clouds over the hill with the pitiable willows, and the puddles in the road lay shining a little while before the rain troubled their surface again.

Jenny borrowed Mrs. Rasmussen's books and learnt to knit the kind of lace that bordered her curtains, but neither reading nor knitting came to much. She sat in the rocking-chair by the window all day long, not even caring to dress properly, only wearing her old faded kimono. As her condition became more and more apparent she suffered agonies.

Gert Gram had written to say he was coming to see her, and two days later he arrived, driving up in the early morning in pouring rain. He stayed a week, putting up at the railway hotel two miles from the village, but spending all his time with her. When he left he promised to come again soon — possibly in six weeks.

Jenny lay awake all night with her lamp burning. She knew she could not bear it again; it had been too awful. Everything was unbearable from the moment he arrived — his first worried, compassionate glance when he saw her — dressed in a new navy blue straight frock made by the village dressmaker. "How lovely you are," he said, and declared she was like a madonna. Madonna, indeed! His arm placed cautiously round her waist, his long, guarded kiss on her forehead, made her feel as if she could die of shame. And how he had worried her with his concern about her health and his advice about taking enough exercise. One day when the rain stopped he dragged her for a long walk, insisting that she should hang on his arm for support. One evening he had looked at her needle-work — stealthily — expecting probably that she would be hemming baby linen. He meant it all so kindly, and there was no hope of a change for the better when he would come again — more likely the reverse; she simply could not endure it.

One day she had a letter from him in which, among other things, he said she ought to see a doctor, and the same night she wrote to Gunnar Heggen telling him that she was expecting a child in February, and would he let her have the address of a quiet place where she could stay until it was over. Heggen answered by return:

"Dear Jenny,- — I have advertised in a couple of papers and will send you the answers when they come, so you can see for yourself. If you would like me to go and look at some of the places before you decide, I will do so with pleasure — you know that. I am at your disposal in every way. Let me know when you leave, what way you are coming, and if you want me to meet you, or if I can help you in any other way. I am sorry about it, of course, but I know you are comparatively well equipped to face trouble. Please write and say if there is anything else I can do for you; you know I am only too pleased to be of any service. I hear you have a good picture at the State exhibition — congratulations.

"Kind regards from your sincere friend, G. H."

A few days later came a whole bundle of letters. Jenny waded through some of the writing, printed in an awful gothic scrawl, and then wrote to a Mrs. Schlessinger in the vicinity of Warnemunde, renting a room from the fifteenth of November. She gave Mrs. Rasmussen notice, and told Gunnar by letter of her decision.

On the eve of her departure she wrote to Gram:

"Dear Friend, — I have formed a decision which I am afraid will hurt you, but you must not be angry with me. I am tired and unnerved; I know I was tiresome and disagreeable to you when you were here, and I don't want it to happen again, so have decided not to see you until all is over and I am normal again. I am leaving here tomorrow early, going abroad. I am not giving you my address at present, but you can send your letters via Mrs. Ahlin, Varberg, Sweden, and I will write you through her. Do not be anxious about me. I am quite well and everything is all right, but I beg of you, dear, not to try to get into communication with me in any other way than the one I have suggested. Do not be vexed with me, for I believe this arrangement to be the best for both of us, and please try not to worry about me more than you can help. — Yours affectionately, Jenny Winge."

So she moved from one widow to another, and into another small cottage — this time a red one with white-washed window-sills and standing in a little garden with flagged paths and shells around the flower-beds, where the dahlias and chysanthemums stood black and rotting. Twenty to thirty similar houses stood along a small street leading from the railway station to the fishing harbour, where the waves foamed against the long stone piers. On the beach, a little away from the village, stood a small hotel with the shutters up. Endless roads, with bare, straggling poplars bending in the wind, led out over interminable plains and swamps past small brick farms with a strip of garden front and a couple of haystacks at the back.

Jenny walked along the road as far as she could manage, returning home to sit in her little room, which this time was overloaded with precious knick-knacks, coloured plaster casts of castles, and merry scenes at country inns in brass frames. She had not the strength to change her wet shoes even, but Mrs. Schlessinger took off the boots and stockings, talking all the time, exhorting her to keep up her courage, telling her about all the other young ladies she had had in the house — how So-and-so had married and was well off and happy now.

When she had been there a month Mrs. Schlessinger came into her room one day, excited and beaming — a gentleman had come to see the young lady. Jenny was paralysed with fright, but managed at last to ask what he looked like. "Quite young," said Mrs. Schlessinger, with a lurking smile — "and very nice looking." It dawned upon her that it might be Gunnar, and she got up, but, suddenly changing her mind, wrapped herself up in a rug and sat down in the deepest of her armchairs.

Mrs. Schlessinger departed, pleased to announce a visitor. Showing Gunnar into the room, she remained an instant smiling by the door before closing it.

He squeezed her hand, almost hurting her, and greeted her with a beaming smile:

"I thought I had better come up here to see what kind of a place you had settled on. It is rather a dull part of the world you have chosen, but it is healthy anyway." He shook the water from his hat as he spoke.

"You must have some tea and something to eat," said Jenny, making a movement as if meaning to rise, but remained sitting, saying with a blush: "Do you mind ringing the bell?"

Heggen ate with excellent appetite, talking all the while. He was delighted with Berlin; he had lived in a -workmen's quarter — the Moabit — and spoke with equal enthusiasm about the social democrats and the military, for "there is something grand and manly about it, and the one stimulates the other." He had been over some great factories and had studied night life, having met a Norwegian engineer who was on his honey-moon and a

Norwegian couple with two lovely daughters, who were dying to see a little vice at close quarters. They had been to National, Riche, and to Amorsaale, and the ladies had enjoyed it all immensely.

"But I offended them, I'm afraid — asked Miss Paulsen to come home with me late one evening."

"Gunnar, how could you!"

"Well, I was not quite sober, you understand; it was only a joke, you know. If by any chance she had consented, I should have been in an awful fix. Might have had to marry a little girl who amuses herself sniffing at such things — no, thank you. It was great fun to see her so virtuously offended. There was no danger really — little girls of that sort don't give away their treasure without making sure of a fair return."

He blushed suddenly. It struck him that Jenny might think it tactless of him to speak like that before her — now. But she only laughed:

"What mad things you do!"

As Heggen went on talking, the unnatural, painful shyness gradually left her. Once or twice, when she did not notice it, his eyes anxiously scanned her face — heavens! how thin and hollow-eyed she was, and furrowed about the mouth. The sinews of her neck were prominent, and there were a couple of ugly lines across the throat.
The rain had stopped, and she consented to go for a walk with him. They walked in the sea-mist along the deserted road with the scraggy poplars.

"Take my arm," said Gunnar casually, and Jenny took it, feeling heavy and tired.

"It must be awfully dull for you here, Jenny — don't you think it would be much better if you went to Berlin?"

Jenny shook her head.

"You would have the museums there to go to and other things besides — and somebody to be with at times. You don't care to go to National anyway. Won't you come, just for a bit of a change? You must be deadly dull here."

"Oh no, Gunnar — I could not go now, you understand."

"You look quite nice in that ulster," said Gunnar cautiously, after a short pause. Jenny bent her head.

"Oh, I am a fool," said he suddenly. "Forgive me. You must tell me, Jenny, if I bother you."

"Oh no, you don't bother me. I am glad you came."

"I realize that it must be awful for you, Jenny." His voice had changed completely. "I quite realize it, but I am sure you are making it still worse by going about here all alone.

I do think you ought to go somewhere else — somewhere a little less hopeless than this." He was looking at the dark plain and the rows of poplars losing themselves in the distance.

"Mrs. Schlessinger is so very kind," said Jenny evasively.

"Oh yes, good soul; I am sure she is." He smiled. "I think she suspects me of being the culprit."

"Probably," said Jenny, smiling too.

They walked on in silence. After a while Gunnar asked: "How are you going to arrange matters? Have you made any plans as to the future?"

"I don't know yet. I suppose you mean about the child? I may leave it with Mrs. Schlessinger for a time; she would look after it all right, I dare say. Or I may get some one to adopt it; you know, such children are adopted sometimes. I might call myself Mrs. Winge and never mind what people think."

"You are quite decided, then, to break completely with — er — the man concerned? You wrote me to that effect."

"I am," she said firmly. "It is not the man I was engaged to," she added, after a pause. "Thank God!" he burst out, so relieved that Jenny could not help smiling a little.

"Well, you know, Jenny, he was not worth reproducing — not by you anyway. I saw in the papers recently that he has got his doctor's degree. Well, it might have been worse — I was afraid . . ."

"It is his father," she said abruptly.

Heggen came to a dead stop. She fell to crying desperately, and he put his arm round her and laid his hand to her cheek while she went on sobbing with her head on his shoulder.

Standing so, she began to tell him all about it. Once she looked up at his face; it was pale and haggard; and she started crying again. When she stopped, he lifted her head, looking at her:

"My God, Jenny — what you must have suffered! I cannot realize it." They walked back to the village in silence.
"Come with me to Berlin," he said suddenly. "I cannot bear to think of you here alone and brooding over this."

"I have almost given up thinking," she said, tired.

"Oh, it's too awful!" he burst out, with such violence that she came to a sudden stop. "Always the best of you that get let in for this kind of thing, and we have no idea of what you have to go through. It is dreadful!"

Heggen stayed three days. Jenny could not explain why, but she felt much better after his visit. The unbearable feeling of humiliation was gone; she was able to face her confinement with more composure and confidence.

Mrs. Schlessinger went about smiling slyly in spite of Jenny's declaration that the gentleman was her cousin.

He had offered to send her some of his books, and at Christmas a whole case arrived, besides flowers and chocolates. Every week he wrote her a long letter about all manner of trifles, en- closing cuttings from Norwegian papers. In January he came up for her birthday and stayed two days, leaving behind some of the latest Norwegian books. Shortly after his last visit she fell ill. She was poorly, worried, and sleepless during the remaining weeks. She had never busied her thoughts with the actual confinement or been anxious about it before, but, feeling always wretched now, she was seized by a sudden dread of what she had to go through, and when the time came she was quite worn out with insomnia and anxiety.

It was a nasty case. Jenny was more dead than alive when the doctor, who had been sent for from Wamemunde, at last held her son in his hands.

VI

JENNY'S son lived six weeks — exactly fourty-four days and a half, she said bitterly to herself, thinking again and again of the short time she had felt really happy. She did not cry for the first days after his death, but she could not leave the dead child, and sat moaning deep down in her throat and taking it in her arms to caress it:

"Darling little boy — mother's pretty little boy, you must not go — I cannot let you go. Can't you see I want you so?" The child was tiny and feeble at birth, but Jenny and Mrs. Schlessinger had both thought he was thriving and making good progress. Then one morning he fell ill, and by midday it was all over.

After the funeral she started to cry, and could not stop; for weeks afterwards she sobbed unceasingly night and day. She fell ill herself too; inflammation of the breasts developed, and Mrs. Schlessinger had to send for the doctor, who performed an operation. The despair of her soul, together with the pains of her body, gave her many a dreadful, delirious night.

Mrs. Schlessinger slept in the adjoining room, and on hearing her cries of agony, rushed in and sat down by tire bed, comforting her, stroking her thin, clammy hands with her own fat, warm ones, and coaxing and lecturing her a little. It was God's will, and was probably much better for the boy and for her too — still so young as she was. Mrs. Schlessinger had lost two children herself — little > Bertha when she was two years old, and Wilhelm at fourteen, such a dear boy too — yet they were born in wedlock and should have been the support and comfort of her old age. But this little one would only have been a chain round the feet of the Fraulein who was so young and pretty. He had been very dear and sweet, the little angel, and it was very hard. . . .

Mrs. Schlessinger had lost her husband too, and many of the young ladies who had stayed in her house had seen their little ones die; some of them had been pleased, others had put their babies out to nurse at once so as to get rid of them. It was not nice, of course, but what could one do? Some had cried and wailed as Jenny did, but they got over it in time, and married and settled down happily afterwards. But a despair like Fraulein's she had never yet witnessed.

Mrs. Schlessinger suspected in her heart that her patient's despair was caused to a great extent by the departure of the cousin first to Dresden and then to Italy just about the time the boy died. But that is exactly what they always did — the men.

The memory of those maddening, agonizing nights was ever afterwards associated with the picture of Mrs. Schlessinger sitting on the stool by her bed while the light rays from the lamp were refracted in the tears dropping from her small, kind eyes on to her round red cheeks. And her mouth, which did not stop talking for a second, her little grey plait of hair, the white night-jacket trimmed with pointed lace, and her petticoat of grey and pink stripped flannel scalloped at the bottom. And the small room with plaster medallions in brass frames.

She had written to Heggen about her great joy, and he had replied saying he would have loved to come and have a look at the boy, but the journey was long and expensive and he was on the point of starting for Italy. He sent his best wishes to her and the little prince, hoping to welcome them both in Italy soon. At the time of the child's death Heggen was in Dresden and sent her a long and sympathetic letter.

As soon as she was well enough to write she sent a few lines to Gert, giving him her address, but asking him not to come and see them until the spring, when baby would be big and pretty.

Only his mother could see now that he was lovely. She wrote him a longer letter when she was up and about again.

On the day the child was buried she wrote telling Gram in a few words of her loss, informing him of her intention to go south the same evening, and asking him not to expect to hear from her until she was more like herself again. "Do not worry about me," she wrote. "I am fairly composed now, but hopelessly miserable, of course."

Her letter crossed one from Gert, who wrote: "My Dearest Jenny, — Thank you for your last letter. I see that you reproach yourself because of your relations to me; my dear little girl, I have nothing to reproach you for, so you must not do it yourself. You have never been anything but kind and sweet and loving to your friend, and I shall never forget your tenderness and affection during the short time you loved me — your charming youth, your gentle devotion in the days of our short happiness.

"We ought to have known, both of us, that it would be short. I certainly ought to have understood, and if you had reflected you might have known too, but do two people, who are attracted by one another, ever reflect? Do you think I reproach you because one day you ceased to love me and caused me the greatest suffering in my far from happy life — a twofold suffering when I learnt simultaneously that our relations would have consequences which you would have to bear all through life?

"From your letter I see too that those consequences, which have probably been a much greater source of despair to me than to you, in spite of all you may have experienced of worry and bodily suffering, have brought a deeper joy and happiness than anything else in all your life — that the joy of being a mother gives you peace, satisfaction, and courage to live, and that with your child in your arms you think you will have strength to meet all difficulties, economic as well as social, which the future may place in the way of a young woman in your position. It gives me more pleasure than you think to read it. It is to me a fresh proof that the eternal justice, which I have never doubted, exists. To you, who made a mistake because your heart was warm and tender and thirsting for love, this very mistake, which has caused you so many agonizing hours, will in the end bring you all you have sought, in a better, finer, and purer degree than ever you dreamt of, now that your heart is filled with love for your child. And it will increase as he grows and begins to know his mother, to cling to her, and to return her love with a stronger, more profound and conscious affection as the years go by.

"And to me, who received your love, although I should have known that love between us was impossible and unnatural, to me these months have brought indescribable suffering and sorrow and — emptiness. You have no idea, Jenny, how I miss you, your youth, your beauty, the bliss of your love; and every memory of it all is embittered by repentance, an insistent questioning : How could I let her do it? How could I accept it — how believe in the possibility of happiness for myself with her? I did believe it, Jenny, however mad it may sound, because I felt young when I was with you. Remember that I forfeited my own youth when I was much younger than you; the happiness of work and the happiness of love in youth have never been mine, and it was all my own fault. And this was retribution! My dead youth came back to life when I met you; in my heart I did not feel older than you. Nothing is more terrible in life than for a man to be old while his heart is still young.

"You write that you wish me to come some day when the boy has grown a little, to see you and our child. What a preposterous thought — our child! Do you know what constantly comes into my mind? The old Joseph on the Italian altar paintings. You will remember that he is always standing in the background, or on one side, sadly and tenderly contemplating the Divine Child and its young and beautiful mother, who are absorbed in each other and do not notice his presence. Don't misunderstand me, dear Jenny; I know that the little child lying in your lap is also flesh and blood of mine, but, when I think of you as a mother, I cannot help feeling myself out in the cold like poor old Joseph.

"You must not hesitate to accept my name as my wife and the protection it would give you and the child any more than Mary hesitated to submit herself to the care of Joseph. And I do not consider it quite right towards the child to rob it of its father's name, to which it has a right, however much confidence you may have in yourself. It goes without saying that in such a marriage you would remain as free and independent as before, and that it could be legally dissolved whenever you wished. I beg of you to think it over. We might go through the ceremony abroad, and a few months afterwards steps might be taken to obtain a divorce, if that is your wish; you need not come back to Norway, nor even live under the same roof with me at all.

"There is not much to tell about myself. I have two small rooms in this part of the country, not far from the place where I was born and lived till I was ten years old. From my window I can see the tops of the two big chestnut trees standing at the entrance to the home of my childhood. They look very much the same as they did then. Up here the evenings are beginning to be long and light and spring like, and their naked brown branches stand outlined against the pale green sky, where a few solitary stars glitter in the sharp, clear air. Evening after evening I sit by my window staring in the same direction, dreaming and recalling to memory my whole life. How could I ever forget, Jenny dear, that between you and me there was a whole life almost twice as long as yours, and more than half of it spent in incessant humiliation, defeat, and sorrow?

"That you think of me without anger and bitterness is more than I dared to hope and expect, and to read your joy between every line of your letter has given me the greatest satisfaction. May God bless and help you and the child, and grant you all the happiness I wish for both of you.

"My fondest love is yours, dear Jenny — you who were once mine. — Your devoted, Gert Gram."

VII

JENNY remained with Mrs. Schlessinger; it was cheap, and she did not know what to do with herself. Spring was in the air. She walked on the pier in the evenings. Heavy clouds, bordered by the sun, with red and burning gold, chased across the immense open dome of the sky, and were reflected in the restless sea. The dark and desolate plain turned light green and the poplars reddish brown with young shoots. Along the railway line violets and small white and yellow flowers were coming up in hundreds, and at last the whole plain was luxuriously green, and a world of color sprang forth along the ditches; sulphur-tinted irises and big white lilies were reflected in the pools of the marsh. Then one day the air was permeated by a sweet scent of hay, mixing with the smell of tar from the shore.

The hotel opened, and the small houses by the pier were filled with summer visitors; children swarmed on the white beach, rolling in the sand and paddling in the water. Mothers and nurses in national costumes of the Spreewald sat on the grass with their sewing, looking after them. The bathing-huts had been transported into the sea, and young girls were shouting and laughing in the water. Sailing yachts anchored by the pier, tourists came from the town, in the evenings there was dancing in the hotel, and couples walked about in the small plantation where Jenny used to lie in the grass early in the spring listening to the wash of the waves and the rustling of the wind in the scraggy tree-tops.

One or two of the ladies looked at her with interest and compassion when she walked on the beach in her black and white dress. The summer visitors staying in the village had got to know that a young Norwegian girl had had a child and was disconsolately mourning its death, and some of them found it more touching than scandalous.

She much preferred walking out into the country, where the summer boarders never went. Once in a while she went as far as the cemetery, where her boy was buried. She sat staring at the grave, which she had not wished to have tended in any way, sometimes laying on it some wild flowers which she had picked on the way, but her mind refused to associate the little mound of grey earth with her beloved little boy.

In her room in the evenings she sat staring at the lamp — with needlework which she never touched. And her thoughts were always the same: she remembered the days when she had the boy — first the faint, peaceful joy while she was in bed, getting well, then when she was sitting up and Mrs. Schlessinger showed her how to bath and dress and handle him, and when they went to Warnemünde together to buy fine material, lace, and ribbon, and how on their return home she cut and sewed, designed and embroidered. Her boy was to have nice things, instead of the common, ready-made outfit she had ordered from Berlin. She had also bought a ridiculous garden syringe of green-painted tin, with pictures of a lion and a tiger, standing by a blue sea amid palms and looking with awe at the German dreadnoughts steaming away towards the African possessions of the Empire. She had found it so amusing that she bought it for baby-boy to play with when he should be big enough — after a very long time. He must first learn to find mother's breast, which at present he only blindly sought for, and to discover his own little fingers, which he could not separate when he had clutched them together. By and by he would be able to recognize his mother, to look at the lamp and at mother's watch when she was dangling it before his eyes. There were so many things baby-boy would have to learn. All his things were in a drawer she never opened. She knew what every little piece looked like; she could feel them in the palms of her hands, the soft linen and the fluffy woollen things and the unfinished jacket of green flannel on which she had embroidered yellow buttercups — the jacket he was to wear when she took him out.

She had begun a picture of the beach with red and blue children on the white sands. Some of the compassionate ladies came to look at it, trying to make acquaintance with her: "How nice!" But she was not pleased with the sketch, and cared neither to finish it nor to make a new one.

Then one day the hotel closed up again, the sea was stormy, and summer had gone. Gunnar wrote from Italy, advising her to go there. Cesca wanted her to go to Sweden, and her mother, who knew nothing, wrote she could not understand why she stayed so long in Germany. Jenny was thinking of going away, but she could not make up her mind, although a faint longing began to stir in her.

She became restless at going about like that without being able to do anything. She had to take a decision — even if it came only to throwing herself into the sea one night from the pier.

One evening she took out Heggen's books from their case. Among them was one with poetry — Fxori della Poesia Italiana — in an edition for tourists, bound in leather. She turned the leaves to see if she had forgotten all her Italian.

The book fell open by itself at Lorenzo di Medici's carnival song, where a folded piece of paper lay in Gunnar's handwriting:

"Dear Mother, — I may tell you now that I have arrived safely in Italy and am quite comfortable, and that" — the rest of the sheet was covered with words to learn. Beside the verbs he had written down the conjugations, and the margin all along the melodramatic poetry was tightly covered with notes: Quant's bella giovenezza, che se fugge tuttavia.

Even the commonest words were written down. Gunnar had probably tried to read the book directly he came to Italy, before he knew the language at all. On the first page was written "G. Heggen, Firenze, 1903" — that was before she knew him.

She began to read here and there. It was Leopardi's "Ode to Italy," which Gunnar was so enthusiastic about. She read it. The margin was full of notes and ink-spots.

It was as if he had sent her a message more intimate than any of his letters. Young, sound, firm, and active, he was calling her, asking her to come back to life — and work. Oh, if she could gather courage and begin work again! She wanted to try — to make her choice whether for life or death; she wanted to go out there where once she had felt herself free and strong — alone save for her work. She longed for her friends, the trusty comrades who never came too near to hurt one another, but lived side by side, each minding their own business and all sharing what they possessed in common: the belief in their ability and the joy of their work. She wanted to see again the country of mountains, with proud, severe lines and sunburnished colors.

A few days later she left for Berlin, where she stayed sometime visiting the galleries, but, feeling tired and forlorn, she went on the Munich.

In the Alte Pinakothek she stopped before Rembrandt's "Holy Family." She did not look at it from a painter's point of view; she only looked at the young peasant woman who, with her garment still drawn aside from her full bosom, sat looking at her child sleeping on her lap, and holding his foot caressingly in her hand. It was an ugly little peasant boy, but in splendid condition; he was sound asleep and such a darling all the same. Joseph was looking at him across the mother's shoulder, but it was not an old Joseph, and Mary was no immaterial, heavenly bride; they were a strong, middle-aged working man and his young wife, and the child was the joy and pride of the two.

In the evening she wrote to Gert Gram a long, sad and tender letter bidding him farewell for ever.

On the following day she took a through ticket to Florence; after a sleepless night in the train she found herself sitting at the window at daybreak. Wild torrents spurted down the forest-clad mountain-sides. It grew lighter and lighter, and the towns became more and more Italian in character: rust-brown or golden-yellow tiles, loggias to the houses, green shutters against reddish stone walls, church fronts in baroque, stone bridges across the rivers, vineyards outside the towns, and grey castle ruins on the hilltops. At the stations all the signs were written in German and Italian.

She stood in the customs office looking at the first- and second-class passengers startled out of their sleep, and she felt quite happy without being able to account for it. She was back again in Italy. The customs officer smiled at her because .she was so fair, and she smiled back; evidently he took her for the maid of one or other of the lady passengers.

The misty grey mountains ridges on either side had a bluish shade in the crevices, the ground looked rusty red, and the sun flamed white and hot.

But in Florence it was bitterly cold in the early days of November. Tired and frozen, she stayed in the city a fort-right — her heart cold to all the beauty around her, and melancholy and discouraged because it did not warm her as before. One morning she went to Rome. The ground was white with frost all the way down through Toscana; in the middle of the day the frosty mist lifted and the sun shone — and she saw again a spot she had never forgotten: the lake of Trasimene lying pale blue, surrounded by the mountains. A point of land projected into the water, with towers and pinnacles of a small stone-grey town, with a cypress avenue leading from the station.

She arrived at Rome in pouring rain. Gunnar was on the platform to meet her, and he squeezed her hands as he wished her welcome. He went on talking and laughing all the time as they drove from the station' to the quarters he had engaged for her, the rain splashing against the cab from the grey sky and from the street paving.

VIII

H EGGEN was sitting at the outer side of the marble table, taking no part in the conversation; now and then he cast a glance at Jenny, who sat pressed into the corner, with a whisky and soda before her. She was chatting very merrily with a young Swedish lady across the table, without taking the slightest notice of her neighbors, Dr. Broager and the little Danish artist Loulou Schulin, who both tried to draw her attention. Heggen saw that she had had too much to drink again. A company of Scandinavians and a couple of Germans had met in a wine shop, and were finishing the night in the inmost corner of a somewhat dingy café. They were all of them more or less affected by what they had drunk, and very much opposed to the request of the landlord that they should leave, as it was past time for locking up and he would be fined two hundred lire.

Gunnar Heggen was the only one who would have liked the symposium to come to an end; he was the only sober one, and in a bad temper.

Dr. Broager was constantly applying his black moustache to Jenny's hand; when she pulled it away he tried to kiss her bare arm. He had succeeded in placing his arm behind her and they were squeezed so tight in the corner that it was useless to try and get away from him. Her resistance was, to tell the truth, somewhat lame, and she laughed without offence at his boldness.

"Ugh!" said Loulou, shrugging her shoulders. "Plow can you stand it? Don't you think he is disgusting, Jenny?"

"Yes, I do, but don't you see that he is exactly like a blue-bottle? — it is useless trying to drive him away. Ugh! stop it, doctor!"

"Ugh!" said Loulou again. "How can you stand that man?"

"Never mind. I can wash myself with soap when I get home."

Loulou Schulin leaned against Jenny, stroking her arms. "Now I will take care of these poor, beautiful hands. Look!" She lifted one of them to be admired by the company round the table. "Isn't it lovely?" and, loosening the green motor veil from her hat, she wrapped it round Jenny's arms and hands.

"In a mosquito net, you see," she said, thrusting out a small tongue swiftly at Broager. Jenny sat an instant with her arms and hands enveloped in the green veil before undoing it and putting on her coat and gloves.

Broager leaned back with eyes half closed, and Miss Schulin raised her glass: "Your health, Mr. Heggen."

He pretended not to hear, but when she repeated her words he seized his glass: "Pardon — I did not see" — and, after taking a sip, looked away again.

One or two people in the company smiled. Heggen and Miss Winge lived next door to each other on the top floor of a house somewhere between Babuino and Corso; intimate relations between them seemed therefore to be a matter of course. As to Miss Schulin, she had been married to a Norwegian author, but after a year or so of married bliss had left him and the child, gone out into the world under her maiden name as "Miss," and calling herself an artist.

The landlord came up once more to the company, urgently soliciting their departure; the two waiters put out the gas at the farther end of the room and stood waiting by the table, so there was nothing else to be done but pay and leave the place.

Heggen was one of the last as they came out into the square.

By the light of the moon he saw Miss Schulin taking Jenny's arm, both running towards a cab, which some of the others were storming. He ran in the same direction and heard Jenny calling out: "You know, the one in Via Paneperna," just as she jumped into the already filled cab and fell into somebody's lap.

But some ladies wanted to get out and others to get in — people kept on jumping out from one door and in at another, while the driver sat motionless on his seat waiting, and the horse slept with its head drooping against the stone bridge.

Jenny was in the street again now, but Miss Schulin reached out her hand — there was plenty of room.

"I'm sorry for the horse," said Heggen curtly, and Jenny started to walk at his side behind the cab, the last among those who had not got room in the vehicle, which rolled on ahead.

"You don't mean to say you want to be with these people any longer — to walk as far as Paneperna for that?" said Heggen.

"We might meet an empty cab on the way."

"How can you be bothered with them? — they are all drunk," he added.

Jenny laughed in a languid way.

"So am I, I suppose."

Heggen did not answer. They had reached the Piazza di Spagna when she stopped: "You are not coming with us, then, Gunnar?"

"Yes, if you absolutely insist on going on — otherwise not."

"You need not come for my sake. I can get home all right, you know."

"If you go, I go — I am not going to let you walk about alone with those people in that state."

She laughed — the same limp, indifferent laugh. "You will be too tired to sit to me tomorrow."

"Oh, I shall be able to sit all right."

"You won't; and anyhow, I shan't be able to work properly if I have to walk about all night."

Jenny shrugged her shoulders, but started to walk in the direction of Babuino — the opposite way to the rest of the party.

Two policemen passed them ; otherwise there was not a living soul to be seen. The fountain was playing in front of the Strada di Spagna, lying white with moonlight and bordered by black and silver glittering evergreen shrubs.

Suddenly Jenny spoke in a hard and scornful voice:

"I know you mean it kindly, Gunnar. It is good of you to try and take care of me, but it is not worth=while."

He walked on in silence.

"No, not if you have no will of your own," he said after a while. "Will" — imitating him.

"Yes; I said will."

Her breath came quick and sharp, as if she wanted to answer, but she checked herself. She was suddenly filled with disgust — she knew that she was half drunk, but she would not accentuate it by beginning to shout, moan, and explain — perhaps cry, before Gunnar. She set her teeth.

They reached their own entrance. Heggen opened the door and struck a match to light her up the endless flight of dark stone steps. Their two small rooms were on the half-landing at the end of the stairs; a small passage outside their doors ended in a marble staircase leading to the flat roof of the house.

At her door she shook hands with him, saying in a low voice: "Good-night, Gunnar — thanks for tonight."

"Thank you. Sleep well." "Same to you."

Gunnar opened the window in his room. The moon shone on an ochre-yellow wall opposite, with closed shutters and black iron balconies. Behind it rose Pincio, with sharply out-lined dark masses of foliage against the blue moonlit sky. Below him were old moss-covered roofs, and where the dark shadow of the house ended some washing was hung out to dry on a terrace farther down. He was leaning on the windowsill, disgusted and sad. He was not very particular in general, but to see Jenny in such a state. Ugh! And it was more or less his own fault; she had been so melancholy the first months of her return — like a wounded bird — and to cheer her up a little he had persuaded her to join the party, thinking of course that he and she would amuse themselves by watching the others only, never for a moment suspecting that it would have such an effect on her. He heard her come out from her room and go on to the roof. He hesitated a moment, then followed her.

She was sitting in the only chair, behind the little corrugated iron summer-house. The pigeons cooed sleepily in the dovecot above.

"Why have you not gone to bed? You will be cold up here." He fetched her shawl from the summer-house and handed it to her, sitting down between the flower-pots on the top of the wall. They sat quietly staring at the city and the church domes that seemed floating in the moonlit mist. The outlines of distant hills were completely obliterated.

Jenny was smoking. Gunnar lit a cigarette.

"I can hardly stand anything now, it seems — in the way of drink, I mean. It affects me at once," she said apologetically.

He understood that she was quite herself again.

"I think you might leave it off altogether for a time, and not smoke — at least not so much. You know you have complained of your heart."

She did not answer.

"I know that you agree with me about those people, and I cannot think how you could condescend to associate with them

— in the way you did."

"One is sometimes in need of — well, of a narcotic," she said quietly. "And as to condescending . . ." He looked into her white face; her fair fluffy hair shone in the moonlight. "Sometimes I think it does not matter, though now — at this moment — I feel ashamed, but then I am extraordinarily sober just now, you see," she said, smiling. "I am not always, although I have not taken anything, and in those moments I feel ready for any kind of revels."

"It is dangerous, Jenny," he said, and again after a pause: "I think it was disgusting tonight — I cannot call it anything else. I have seen something of life; I know what it leads to. I would not like to see you come down and end as something like Loulou."

"You can be quite easy in your mind about me, Gunnar. I am not going to end that way. I don't really like it, and I know where to stop." He sat looking at her.

"I know what you mean," he said at last. "Other women have thought as you, but when one has been gliding downward for a time one ceases to care about where to stop, as you call it." Stepping down from the wall, he went towards her and took her hand:

"Jenny, you will stop now, will you not?" She rose, smiling:
"For the present, anyway. I think I am cured for a long time of that sort of thing." She shook his hand firmly: "Good-night; I'll sit for you in the morning," she said, going down the stairs.

"All right, thanks."

He remained on the roof for some time smoking, shivering a little, and thinking, before going down to his room.

IX

NEXT day she sat to him after lunch until it grew dark; in the rests, they exchanged some insignificant words while he went on painting the background or washed his brushes.

"There," he said, putting down the palette and tidying up his paint-box. "That will do for today."

She came to look at the picture.

"The black is good, don't you think?"

"Yes," she said. "I think it is very effective." He looked at his watch: "It is almost time to go out and get something to eat — shall we dine together?" "All right. Will you wait for me while I put on my things?"

A moment later when he knocked at her door she was ready, standing before the glass to fasten her hat.

How good looking she was, he thought, when she turned round. Slim and fair in her tight-fitting steel-grey dress, she looked very ladylike — discreet, cold, and stylish. What he had thought of her yesterday seemed quite impossible today. "Did you not promise to go to Miss Schulin this afternoon to see her paintings?"

"Yes, but I am not going." She blushed. "Honestly I don't care to encourage an acquaintance with her, and I suppose there is not much in her paintings either."

"I should not think so. I cannot understand your putting up with her advances last night. Personally, I would rather do anything — eat a plateful of live worms."

Jenny smiled, and said seriously:

"Poor thing, I daresay she is not happy at all." "Pooh! not happy. I met her in Paris in 1905. I don't think she is perverse by nature — only stupid and full of vanity. It was all put on. If it were the fashion now to be virtuous she would sit up darning children's stockings, and would have been the best of housewives. Possibly painting roses with dewdrops on as a recreation. But once she got away from her moorings she wanted to see life — free as an artist, she thought she ought to get herself a lover for the sake of her self-respect. But unfortunately she got hold of a duffer who was old-fashioned enough to want her to marry him in the old non-modern way when things had gone wrong, and expected her to look after the child and the house."

"It may be Paulsen's fault that she ran away — you never know."

"Of course it was his fault. He was of the old school, wanting happiness in his home, and he gave her probably too little love and still less cudgelling."

Jenny smiled sadly:

"I know, Gunnar, that you believe life's difficulties are easily solved." Heggen sat down astride on a chair with his arms on the back.

"There is so much of life that we don't know anything about, that what we know is easy enough to manage. Have to make your aims and dreams accordingly, and tackle the unexpected as best you can."

Jenny sat down in the sofa, resting her head in her hands: "I can no longer feel that there is anything in life I am so sure about that I could make it a foundation for my judgment or the aim of my exertions," she said placidly.

"I don't think you mean it." She only smiled.

"Not always," said Gunnar.

"I suppose there is nobody who means the same thing always."

"Yes, always when one is sober. You were right last night in saying that sometimes one isn't sober even if one hasn't been drinking."

"At present — when I am sober once in a while, I" She broke off and remained silent.

"You know what I think about life, and I know you have always thought the same. What happens to you is, on the whole, the result of your own will. As a rule, you are the maker of your own fate. Now and then there are circumstances which you cannot master, but it is a colossal exaggeration to say it happens often."

"God knows I did not will my fate, Gunnar. Yet I have willed for many years and lived accordingly, too."

Both were quiet a moment.

"One day," she said slowly, "I changed my course an instant. I found it so severe and hard to live the life I considered the most worthy — so lonely, you see. I left the road for a bit, wanting to be young and to play, and thus came into a current that carried me away, ending in something I never for a second had thought could possibly happen to me.'"

After a moment's silence Heggen said:

"Rossetti says — and you know he is a much better poet than painter:

"Was that the landmark? What — the foolish well Whose wave, low down, I did not stoop to drink But sat and flung the pebbles from its brink In sport to send its imaged skies pell-mell.

(And mine own image, had I noted well!) — Was that my point of turning? — I had thought The stations of my course should raise unsought,

As altarstone or ensigned citadel.

But lo! The path is missed, I must go back, and thirst to drink when next I reach the spring which once I stained, which since may have grown black.

Yet though no light be left nor bird now sing as here I turn, I'll thank God, hastening. That the same goal is still on the same track.'"

Jenny said nothing — and Gunnar repeated: "That the same goal is still on the same track."

"Do you think it is easy to find the track to the goal again?" asked Jenny. "No, but ought one not to try?" he said, almost in a childish way. "But what goal did I have at all?" she said, with sudden vehemence. "I wanted to live in such a way that I need never be ashamed of myself either as a woman or as an artist. Never to do a thing I did not think right myself. I wanted to be upright, firm, and good, and never to have any one else's sorrow on my conscience. And what was the origin of the wrong — the cause of it all? It was that I yearned for love without there being any particular man whose love I wanted. Was there anything strange in it, or that I wanted to believe that Helge, when he came, was the one I had been longing for — wanting it so much that at last I really believed it? That was the beginning of what led to the rest. Gunnar, I did believe that I could make them happy — and yet I did only harm."

She had risen and was pacing up and down the floor.

"Do you believe that the well you speak of will ever be pure and clear again to one who knows she has muddied it herself? Do you think it is easier for me to resign now? I longed for the same that all girls long for, and I long for it now, but I know that I have now a past which makes it impossible for me to accept the only happiness I care for.

Pure, unspoilt, and sound it should be — but none of these conditions can I ever fulfill — not now. My experiences of these two last years are what I must be satisfied to call my life — and for the rest of it I shall just have to go on longing for the impossible."

"Jenny," said Gunnar, "I am sure I am right in saying again that it depends on yourself if these memories are going to spoil your life, or if you will consider them a lesson, however hard it may be, and still believe that the aim you once set for yourself is the only right one for you."

"But can you not see it is impossible? It has sunk too deep; it has eaten into me like a corrosive acid, and I feel that what was once my inmost self is crumbling to pieces. Yet I don't want it — I don't want it. Sometimes I am inclined to — I don't know really what — to stop all the thoughts at once. Either to die — or to live a mad, awful life — drown in a misery still greater than the present one. To go down in the mud so deep and so thoroughly that nothing but the end will come of it. Or" — she spoke low, with a wild, stifled voice — "to throw myself under a train — to know in the last second that now — just now — my whole body, nerves, heart, and brain will be made into one single shivering bloodstained heap." "Jenny," he cried, white in the face, "I cannot bear to hear you speak like this!"

"I am hysterical," she said soothingly, but she went to the corner where her canvases stood and almost flung them against the wall, with the painting turned out:

"Is it worth living to go about making things like those? Smearing oil paint on canvas? You can see for yourself that it is nothing now but a mess of paint. Yet you saw how I worked the first months — like a slave. Good God! I cannot even paint anymore."

Heggen looked at the pictures. He felt he had a firm ground to stand upon again.

"I should really like to have your frank opinion on — that piggish stuff," she said provokingly.

"I must admit that they are not particularly good." He stood with his hands in his trouser pockets looking at them.

"But that happens to everyoneof us — I mean that there are certain times when you cannot produce anything, and you ought to know that it is only for a time. I don't think one can lose one's talent even if one has been ever so unhappy. You have left off painting for such a long time, besides; you will have to work it up again — to master the means of action, so to say. Take life study, for instance — I am sure it is three years since you drew a live model. One cannot neglect those things without being punished for it. I know from my own experience."

He went to a shelf and searched among Jenny's sketch-books:

"You ought to remember how much you improved in Paris — let me show you."

"No, no, not that one," said Jenny, reaching her hand for it.

Heggen stood with the book in his hand, looking amazed at her. She turned her face away:

"I don't mind if you look at it — I tried to draw the boy one day."

Heggen turned the leaves slowly. Jenny was sitting in the sofa again. He looked at the pencil sketches of the sleeping infant for a moment, then put the book carefully away.

"It was a great pity that you lost your little boy," he said gently.

"Yes. If he had lived, all the rest would not have mattered. You speak about will, but when one's will cannot keep one's child alive, what is the good of it? I don't care to try to make anything of my life now, because it seemed to me the only thing I was good for and cared about was to be a mother to my little boy. Oh, I could have loved him! I suppose I am an egoist at heart, for whenever I tried to love the others, my own self rose like a wall between us. But the boy was mine alone. I could have worked if he had been spared to me. I could have worked hard.

"I had made so many plans. On the way down here they all came back to my mind. I had decided to live in Bavaria with him in the summer, because I was afraid the sea air would be too strong for him. He was going to lie in his pram under the apple trees while I painted. There is not a place in the world I could go to where I have not been in my dreams with the boy. There is nothing good or beautiful in all the world that I did not think, while I had him, he should learn and see. I have not a thing that was not his too. I used to w r rap him up in the red rug I have. The black dress you are painting me in was made in Warnemunde when I was out of bed again, and I had it cut so that it would be easy to nurse him.

"I cannot work because I am so full of him — the longing for him paralyses me. In the night I cuddle the pillow in my arms and sob for my baby-boy. I call him and talk to him when I am alone. I should have painted him, to have a picture of him at every age. He would have been a year old now, would have had teeth and been able to take hold of things, to stand up, and perhaps to walk a little. Every month, every day I think of him — how he would have grown and what he would be like. When I see a woman with a bambino on her arm, or the children in the street, I always think of him and how he would look at their age."

She stopped talking for a moment.

"I did not think you felt it like that, Jenny," said Heggen gently. "It was sad for you, of course — I quite understood that — but I thought, on the whole, it was better he was taken. If I had known you were so distressed about it, I should have come to see you."

She did not answer, but went on in the same strain : "And he died — such a tiny, tiny little thing. It is only selfishness on my part to grudge him death before he had begun to feel and to understand. He could only look at the light and cry when he was hungry or wanted to be changed; he did not know me even — not really, anyhow. Some vague glimpses of reason had possibly begun to awaken in his little head, but, think of it, he never knew that I was his mother.

"Never a name had he, poor darling, only mother's baby-boy, and I have nothing to remember him by, except just material things."

She lifted her hands as if holding the child to her heart, then let them fall empty and lifeless on the table.

"I remember so distinctly my impression when I first touched him, felt his skin against mine. It was so soft, a little damp — the air had scarcely touched it yet, you see. People think a newborn child is not nice to feel, and perhaps it is so when it is not your own flesh and blood. And his eyes — they were no special color, only dark, but I think they would have been grey-blue. A baby's eyes are so strange — almost mysterious. And his tiny head was so pretty, when he was feeding and pressing his little nose against me. I could see the pulse beating and the thin, downy hair; he had quite a lot of it — and dark — when he was born.

"Oh, that little body of his! I can never think of anything else — I can feel it lying in my hands. He was so round and fat, and every bit of him was so pretty — my own sweet little boy!

"But he died! I was looking forward so much to all that was going to happen that it seems to me now I did not pay enough attention to things when I had him, or kissed him or looked at him enough, though I did nothing else in those weeks.

"When he was gone there was nothing left but the yearning for him. You cannot understand what I felt. My whole body ached with it. I fell ill, and the fever and the pain seemed to be my longing materialized. I missed him from my arms, between my hands, and at my cheek. Once or twice in the last week of his life he clutched my finger when I put it in his hand. Once he had somehow got hold of a little of my hair — oh, the sweet, sweet little hands. . . ."

She lay prostrate over the table, sobbing violently, her whole form shivering.

Gunnar had got up and stood hesitating, emotion rising in his throat. Then he went to her and, bending down over her head, he touched her hair lightly with a shy, gentle kiss.

She continued crying, in the same position, for a little while. At last she got up and went to the washstand to bathe her face.

"Oh, how I miss him," she repeated, and he could not find anything to say but "Jenny, if I had known that you felt it so much."

She came back to where he was and, putting her hands on his shoulders, said:

"Gunnar, you must not pay any attention to what I said a while ago. Sometimes I am not quite myself, but you will understand that, for the sake of the boy, if for no other reason, I am not going to throw myself entirely into a life of dissipation. At heart, I really want to make the best I can of my life — you know that. I mean to try and work again, even if the result is poor in the beginning. I have always the comfort of knowing that one need not live longer than one cares to."

She put on her hat again, finding a veil for her tear-stained face: "Let us go and have something to eat — you must be starving by this time — it is very late."

Gunnar Heggen blushed all over his face. Now she mentioned it, he felt awfully hungry, and was ashamed of himself for admitting it at such a moment as this. He dried the tears from his wet, hot cheeks and took his hat from the table.

X

B Y tacit agreement they passed the restaurant where they usually had their meals and where there were always a number of their countrymen, and, continuing their way in the twilight towards the Tiber, they crossed the bridge into the old Borgo quarters. In a corner by the Piazza San Pietro there was a small trattoria where they had dined after going to the Vatican, and they went there.

They ate in silence. When she had finished, Jenny lit a cigarette, and sat sipping her claret and rubbing her fingers with the fragrant tangerine peel. Heggen smoked, staring in front of him. They were almost alone in the place.

"Would you like to read a letter I got from Cesca the other day?" asked Jenny suddenly.
"Yes. I saw there was a letter for you from her — from Stockholm, is it not?"
"Yes; they are back there and going to stay the winter." Jenny took the letter out of her bag and handed it to him.

"Dear, Sweet Jenny Mine, — You must not be angry with me for not answering your last letter before. Every day I meant to write, but it never came off. I am so pleased that you are back in Rome and are working, and have Gunnar to be with.

"We are back in Stockholm living in the old place. It was quite impossible to stay in the cottage when it got cold; it was so draughty that we could only get warm in the kitchen. We would buy it if we could afford it, but it would cost too much; it wants so much done to it. The garret would have to be made into a studio for Lennart, stoves would be wanted, and lots of other things — but we have rented it for next summer, and I am so happy about it, for there is no place in the world I love more. You cannot imagine anything more beautiful than the west coast ; it is so bleak and poor and weather-worn — the grey cliffs with scraggy copse in the crevices, the woodbine, the poor little cottages, the sea, and the wonderful sky. I have made some pictures out there and people say they are good, and Lennart and I have enjoyed it so much. We are always friends now, and when he thinks I am good, he kisses me and calls me a little mermaid and all kinds of nice names, and I suppose I shall grow very fond of him in time. We are back in town again and our journey to Paris will not come off this time, but I don't mind a bit. It seems almost heartless of me to write about it to you, for you are so much better than I, and it was so dreadfully sad that you should lose your little boy — and I don't think I really deserve to be so happy and get what I have wished for more than anything — but I am going to have a baby. I have only five months to wait. I could scarcely believe it at first, but now it is certain enough. I tried to hide it from Lennart as long as possible — you see, I was so ashamed of myself for having deceived him twice, and I was afraid of being mistaken. When he began to suspect it I denied it first, but I had to confess to it later. I cannot realize that I am to have a little boy — Lennart says he would rather have another little Cesca, but I think he says it only to console me before-hand in case it is, for I am sure in his heart he wants a boy. However, if it is a girl, we shall be just as fond of her — and once we have got one child we might get some more.

"I am so happy that I don't mind where we are, and I don't long for Paris. Fancy Mrs. L. asking me if I was not angry because the baby spoilt my journey abroad — can you understand it from a mother of two of the handsomest boys in the world? But they are not taken the slightest notice of, except when they are with us, and Lennart says she would willingly make us a present of them. If I could afford it I would take them, so that baby would have two darling big brothers to play with when he comes. It will be such fun to show them their little cousin — they call me auntie, you see. I think it is nice. But I must close now. Do you know I am very pleased also, because Lennart cannot be jealous now — can he? and I don't think he ever will be any more, for he knows quite well that I have never been really fond of anybody but him.

"Do you think it unkind of me to write so much about this to you and that I am so happy? I know you don't grudge me my luck.

"Remember me kindly to all my friends — to Gunnar first and foremost. You may tell him what I have written if you like. Every good wish to yourself and welcome to us next summer. — Much love from your sincere and devoted little friend, Cesca.

"P.S. — I must add something : If it is a girl she is going to be called Jenny. I don't mind what Lennart says. He sends his regards to you, by the way."

Gunnar handed the letter back to Jenny, who put it in her pocket.

"I am so pleased," she said gently. "I am glad there are some people who are happy. That feeling is something still left of my old self — even if there is nothing else."

Instead of going back to the city, they crossed the Piazza, walking in the direction of the church.

The shadows fell coal black on to the square in the moonlight. White light and night-black darkness played about ghostlike in one of the arcades. The other lay in complete obscurity but for the row of statues on top. The front of the church was in shadow, but here and there the dome glittered like water. The two fountains sent their white jets sparkling and foaming towards the moon-blue sky. The water rose whirling in the air, splashing down again to the porphyry shelves to drop and trickle back into the basin.

Gunnar and Jenny walked slowly in the shade of the arcade towards the church.

"Jenny," he said all of a sudden, in a perfectly cool and everyday voice, "will you marry me?"

"No," she answered after a pause, in a similar tone. "I mean it."

"Yes, but surely you understand that I don't want to."

"I don't see why not. If I understood you rightly, you don't value your life very highly at present, and you entertain thoughts of suicide occasionally. As you feel so inconsolable in any case, why should you not marry me? I think you might try." Jenny shook her head: "Thank you, Gunnar — but I think it would be taxing your friendship too heavily." She spoke in earnest. "In the first place, you ought to understand that

I cannot accept it, and in the second that, if you could make me accept you as a last resource, it would not be worth your troubling to reach out one of your little fingers to save me." "It is not friendship." He hesitated a little. "The truth is that I have got fond of you. It is not to save you — although I would do anything to help you, of course — but because I realize now that if anything happened to you I don't know what I should do. I dare not think of it. There is nothing in the world I would not gladly do for you, because you are very dear to me."

"Oh, Gunnar, don't!" She stopped and looked at him almost in fear.

"I know quite well that you are not in love with me, but that need not prevent your marrying me. You say you are tired of everything, and have nothing to live for, so why not try it?" His voice grew more earnest, and he exclaimed: "For I know that one day you too will be fond of me! You could not help it, seeing how fond I am of you."

"You know that I have always been fond of you," she said seriously, "but it is not a feeling you would be satisfied with in the long run. A strong and entire devotion is more than I can give."

"Not at all. We can all give that. Was I not convinced that I should never experience anything but — little love affairs? In fact, I did not believe anything else existed." His voice sank. "You are the first woman I love."

She stood still and silent.

"I have never uttered that word to any woman before — I had a kind of reverence for it, but then I have never loved a woman before. I was always in love with something particular about them — the corners of Cesca's mouth, for instance, when she smiled; her unconscious coquetry. There was always one thing or other that took my fancy and inspired me to invent adventures about them — adventures I wanted to experience. I fell in love with one woman because the first time I saw her she wore a beautiful red silk dress, almost black in the folds, like the darkest of roses. I thought of her always in that dress. And with you that time in Viterbo — you were so sweet, so gentle and reserved, and there was a glint in your eyes when the rest of us laughed as if you would have liked to be merry with us, but dared not. That time I was in love with the idea of seeing you gay and smiling.

"But I have never loved another human being till now."

He turned his face from her, staring at the jet of water rising in the moonlight, and the new sensation in him rose too, inspiring him with new words, which burst in ecstasy from his lips:

"I love you so much, Jenny, that everything else is of no account. I am not sorry you don't love me in return, for I know you will some day; I feel that my love is strong enough to make you return it. I have time to wait; my happiness will be in loving you.

"When you spoke about being trampled upon and throwing yourself under the train, something happened to me. I could not explain what it was. I knew only that I could not listen to you saying such things. I knew I would never allow it to happen — not for my life. And when you spoke of the child, I felt infinitely sad to think that you had suffered so intensely and that I could not do anything for you. And I was sad too because I wanted you to love me. Everything you said was echoed in my soul — the boundless love and the bitter longing — and I understood that my love for you was just that. While we were in the trattoria and walking out here it has grown more and more clear to me how much you are to me, how I love you — and it seems to me that it has always been so. All I know and remember of you is part of it. I understand now why I have been so depressed since you came here. It was because I saw how you suffered. You were so quiet and sad the first weeks, and then came those fits of dissipation — and I remember that day on the road to Warnemiinde, when you were crying against my shoulder — everything that concerns you is part of my love for you.

"I know how it all happened with the other men you have known — the boy's father too. You have talked and talked with them about all you have been thinking, and there was no response to your words even when you tried to make them realize what you felt, because they could not understand your mind. But I know it — all you have been telling me today and what you said to me that day in Warnemimde you could not have told to anybody else. Only to me, because I understand — is it not so?"

She bent her head in surprised assent. It was true.

"I know that I alone understand you thoroughly. I know exactly what you are, and I love you as you are. If your mind were full of stains and bleeding wounds, I would love and kiss them until you were clean and well again. My love has no other purpose but to see you become what you always wanted to be and must be to feel happy. If you did ever so foolish a thing, I would only think you were ill or that some strange influence had poisoned your mind. If you deceived me or if I found you lying drunk in the road, you would be my own darling Jenny just the same.

"Will you not be mine — give yourself to me? Will you not come into my arms and let me hold you and make you happy and whole? I don't know now quite how to set about it, but my love will teach me, and every morning you will wake up less sad — every day will seem a little brighter and warmer than the day before, and your sorrow less great. Let us go to Viterbo or anywhere you like. Give yourself to me, and I will nurse you as if you were a sick child. When you are well again you will have learnt to love me and to know that we two cannot live without each other.

"You are ill; you cannot look after yourself. Close your eyes and give me your hands; I will love you and make you well — I know I can do it."

Jenny was leaning against a pillar. She turned her white face to him, smiling sadly: "How can you imagine I would do such a great wrong, and sin against God?"

"You mean because you don't love me? But I tell you it does not matter, because I know my love is such that you will end by returning it, when you have lived wrapped in it for a time."

He seized her in his arms, covering her face with kisses. She made no resistance, but whispered:

"Don't, Gunnar, please."

He released her reluctantly: "Why may I not?"

"Because it is you. I don't know if I should have minded if it had been anybody else for whom I did not care at all." Gunnar held her hand and they walked up and down in the moonlight.

"I understand. When you had the little boy you thought your life had some aim and purpose again after all these aimless years, because you loved him and you needed him. When he died you became indifferent to everything and considered yourself superfluous in the world."

Jenny nodded:

"There are a few people I care for enough to be sorry if I knew them in distress and glad if all was well with them. But I myself cannot add either to their sorrow or their joy — it has always been so, and one of the reasons why I was unhappy and filled with longing was just that my life was spent without making anybody happy. My sole wish and yearning was to make another being happy. I have always believed in that as the greatest blessing in life. You spoke of the joy of work — to me it never seemed enough, and it is very selfish, besides, because the greatest joy and satisfaction of it is yours alone; you cannot share it with anybody else. Unless you can share your happiness with others, you lose the greatest possible joy. When you are quite young and feel strongly you are selfish perhaps sometimes — I have felt it myself when I have reached a step nearer my goal, but as a rule it is only the abnormal beings who amass riches for any other purpose than spending. A woman's life is useless to my mind if she is not the joy of somebody else — and I have never been that — I have only caused sorrow. The little happiness I have been able to give was only what any one else could have given just as well; they have loved me only for what they imagined me to be, not for my real self.

"After my baby's death I began to realize how fortunate it was that there was nobody in the world whom I could cause a really inconsolable grief — nobody to whom I was indispensable.

"And now you tell me all this. You have always been the one person I least of all wanted to drag into my confused life; I have always been more fond of you, in a way, than of any one else I know. I enjoyed our friendship so much, because I thought that love and all it brings in its train could never come between us. You were too good for it, I thought. Oh, how I wish it had never changed!"

"To me it seems now that it has never been different," he said gently. "I love you and you need me. I know I can make you happy again, and when I have done that you will have made me happy."

Jenny shook her head:

"If I had the least bit of faith in myself left, it would be different. I might have listened to you if I had not felt so keenly that I have done with life. You say you love me, but I know that what you think you love in me is destroyed — dead. It is the same old story: you are in love with some quality you dream that I possess — that I have before or might have acquired. But one day you would see me as I really am, and I should only have made you unhappy too."

"I should never look upon it as unhappiness whatever my fate might be. You may not be aware of it yourself, but I know that in the state you are now it only needs a touch for you to fall — into something that would be madness. But I love you, and I can see all the way that has led you to it, and if you feel I would follow you to try and carry you back in my arms, because I love you in spite of all."

As they stood by their doors in the dark passage he took her hands: "Jenny, rather than be alone, would you not like me to remain with you tonight?"

She looked at him with a curious smile.

"Oh, Jenny!" He shook his head. "I may come to you, all the same. Would you be angry — or sorry?"

"I think I should be sorry — for your sake. No, do not come, Gunnar. I will not take your love when I know I could just as well give mine to anybody else."

He laughed a little, half angrily, half sadly.

"Then I ought to do it. If once you were mine you would never belong to anybody else — I know you too well for that — but as you ask me not to, I will wait:" he added, with the same curious little laugh.

XI

ALL day long the weather had been bad, with cold, pale clouds high up in the sky; towards evening some thin brass-yellow stripes appeared on the western horizon. Jenny had been up to Monte Celio to sketch in the afternoon, but it did not come to much — she had been sitting listlessly on the big stairs outside of San Gregorio, looking down into the grove where the big trees were beginning to bud and daisies shone all over the grass. She came back through the avenue below the south side of the Palatine. The ruins showed dull grey against the palms of the convent on the mountain-top; the evergreen shrubs hung on the slope, powdered with chalky dust.

Some shivering postcard-sellers loitered about outside the Constantin arch on the Piazza, where the ruins of the Colesseum, the Palatine, and the Forum lay. Very few tourists were about; a couple of skinny old ladies bargained in vile Italian with a mosaic peddler.

A small boy of barely three hung on to Jenny's cloak, offering her a small wisp of pansies. He was exquisitely black eyed and long haired, and dressed in national costume, with pointed hat, velvet jacket, and sandals over white woolen socks. He could not speak distinctly yet, but he could manage to ask for a soldo.

Jenny gave him the coin, and instantly the mother came up to his side, thanking her and taking the money herself. She, too, had tried to give her dress a national touch by lacing a red velvet bodice on top of her dirty checked blouse, and pinning on top of her hair a serviette folded into a square. She carried an infant in her arms. It was three weeks old, she said, in answer to Jenny's question. Yes, the poor dear was ill.

The infant was no bigger than Jenny's own boy had been at birth. Its skin was red and sore and peeling, it was panting as if its throat were choked by mucus, and the eyes looked wearily from under inflamed, half-closed lids.

Oh yes, she took it every day to the hospital for treatment, said the mother, but they said there that it was going to die. Best thing for it, too — the woman was looking so tired and sad, besides being ugly and toothless.

Jenny felt the tears mounting to her eyes. Poor little creature, it certainly was much better for it to die. She passed her hand caressingly over the little ugly face. She had given the woman some money, and was on the point of going when a man suddenly passed her. He took off his hat and stopped for a moment, but walked on as Jenny did not acknowledge his salute. It was Helge Gram.

She was too much taken aback to think of answering. She bent down to the little boy with the pansies, taking his hands and pulling him closer to her, and talked to him, trying to master the unreasonable shivering of her whole body.

She turned her head once in the direction he had gone and saw him standing on the stairs that led to the street from the Piazza round the Colosseum, and looking in her direction. She remained in the same position, talking to the child and the woman. When she looked up again he was gone, but she waited long after she had seen his grey coat and hat disappear round a comer.

Then she went home, almost running through side streets and passages, afraid of meeting him every time she turned a corner.

She got as far as the other side of Pincio, and went to have some food in a trattoria where she had never been before. Then after a rest and some wine, she began to feel better.

If she met Helge and he spoke to her it would be very painful; she would much prefer to escape it, but if it happened, it was nothing to be so senselessly afraid of. Everything between them was finished; what had occurred after their separation was no concern of his, and he had no right to take her to task for anything. Whatever he knew about it, and whatever he had to say, she had said it all to herself, for nobody knew better than she what she had done. She had to answer only to herself; nothing else could compare with that ordeal.

Need she fear anybody? Nobody could do her a great wrong than she had done to herself. It had been a bad day — one of those days when she did not feel sober. However, she felt better now.

Scarcely was she out in the street before the same stupid, desperate fright came over her again, and, without realizing it, she rushed on as if lashed by it, with clenched hands and muttering to herself.

Once she pulled off her gloves, because she was burning hot, and she recollected suddenly having noticed a wet spot on one of them after she had caressed the child. She flung them away in disgust.

When she reached home she stood a moment hesitating in the passage, then knocked at Gunnar's door, but he was not in. She went to look on the roof; there was no one there.

She entered her room, lit the lamp, and sat staring at the flame, her arms folded. After a while she rose and began walking restlessly up and down the floor — only to sit down again as before. She listened breathlessly to every sound on the stairs. Oh, if only Gunnar would come! And not the other one. But how could he? He did not know where she lived — he might have met somebody who knew and asked. Oh, Gunnar, Gunnar, come!

She would go straight to him, throw herself in his arms. The moment she had seen Helge Gram's light brown eyes again, her whole past, that had begun under their glance, confronted her. It all came back — the disgust, the doubt of her own ability to feel, to will and to choose, and the suspicion that in reality she wanted what she said she did not. While she was pretending to herself that she wanted to be strong, pure, and whole in her feelings, and while she said she wanted to be honest, courageous, disciplined — to work and to sacrifice herself for others — she allowed herself to be tossed between moods and desires she did not care to fight, although she knew she should have done so. She had pretended to love so as to sneak into a place in life which she could never have attained if she had been honest.

She had wanted to change her nature to fall in with the others who lived, although she knew she would always be a stranger among them because she was of a different kind. She had not been able to stand alone, a prisoner, so to say, of her own nature. And her relations to those who were strange to her innermost being — the son and the father — had been unnatural and repulsive. In consequence of it her own inner self was ruined; every fixed point in herself, to which she had held on, gave way — crumbled to nothing. She felt as if she were dissolving from within.

If Helge came, if she met him, she knew that the despair and disgust of her own life would overwhelm her. She did not know what would happen, but one thing was certain — she could not face a repetition of the old scenes.

And Gunnar. All these weeks, while he had been begging of her to be his, she had not made up her mind if she loved him or not. He wanted her such as she was, and he vowed that he could help her — build up again all that had been destroyed in her.

Sometimes she wished that he would take her by force, so that she need not choose. It did not matter what he said; she knew that if she became his, the little pride she had left told her that the responsibility was her own. She had to become what she had once been — what he believed she had been and could be again. Whether she cared or not, she had to clean herself from all that soiled her now, bury in a new life every- -thing that had happened since she gave Helge Gram the kiss by which she betrayed her faith and her whole life up to that spring day on the Campagna.

Did she want to be his? Did she love him because he was all that she had wished to be, because his whole being awoke in her all that which she had once chosen to worship and to nurse — every faculty she had thought worth developing ?

The love she had looked for on byways, driven by her morbid longing and feverish restlessness — would she find it here by surrendering to him, by shutting her eyes and giving herself to the one man she really trusted — the one who all her instincts told her was her conscience and her just judge?

She had not been able to do it — not in all these weeks. It seemed to her that she ought to try and get out by her own will from the mire into which she had descended; she wanted to feel that it was her will from the old days which had taken the lead of her shattered mind, so that she could get back ever so little of the respect and confidence in herself from before.

If she was to go on living, Gunnar was life itself to her. A few words written by him on a piece of paper, a book that brought her a message from some emotion in his soul had awakened the last smouldering longing back to life when after the death of the child she had dragged herself about like a maimed animal.

If he came now — he would win her. If he would but carry her the first bit of the way, she would try to walk the rest of it herself. And as she sat there waiting for him she decided in her shrinking soul: If he comes, I shall live. If the other one comes, I must die.

And when she heard steps on the stairs, and they were not those of Gunnar, and there was a knock at the door, she bent her head and went shivering to open it for Helge Gram, instinctively feeling that she opened the door to the fate she had challenged.

She stood looking at him while he walked into the room, putting his hat on a chair. She had not acknowledged his greeting this time either.

"I knew you were in town," said he. "I came the day before yesterday from Paris. I looked up your address at the club, and meant to come and see you some day — but then I saw you in the street this afternoon. I recognized your grey fur a long way off." He spoke swiftly — out of breath, as it were. "Will you not say good evening to me? Are you vexed because I have come to see you?"

"Good evening, Helge," she said, taking the hand he offered her. "Will you not sit down, please?"

She sat down on the sofa. She could hear that her voice sounded calm and as usual. But in her brain she had the same delirious sensation of dread as in the afternoon.

"I wanted to come and see you," said Helge, sitting down on a chair close to her. "It was good of you," replied Jenny. Both were silent.

"You live in Bergen now," she said. "I saw that you had got your degree. I congratulate you."

"Thank you."

There was another pause.

"You have been abroad a long time. I meant to write to you sometimes, but it never came off. Heggen lives in this house, I see."

"Yes; I wrote him to get a studio for me, but they are so dear and so difficult to find. This room has a good light, though."

"I see that you have some pictures drying."

He rose, went across the room, but returned immediately to his seat. Jenny bent her head, feeling that he did not take his eyes from her. They tried to keep up conversation. He asked about Francesca Ahlin and other acquaintances they had in common, but there were long intervals when he sat staring at her.

"Do you know that my parents are divorced?" he asked suddenly. She nodded.

"They stayed together for our sake as long as they could, whining and creaking against each other like two millstones until they had ground everything to powder between them. There was nothing more to grind, I suppose, so the mill stopped.

"I remember when I was a boy. They did not fight, but there was something in their voices that made you think they would like to. Mother abused him and used plain talk, always ending with tears. Father kept cool and quiet, but his voice was full of hatred and so hard and cutting. I lay in my bed listening to this performance that was forced on me. I used to think what a relief it would be to put a knitting needle right through my head, in at one ear and out at the other. The voices created a physical pain in my ears and spread to the whole of my head. Well, that was the beginning — they have done their duty as parents, and now it is all over.

"Hatred is an ugly thing; it makes everything ugly that comes in contact with it. I went to see my sister last summer. We have never been sympathetic, but I thought it disgusting to see her with that husband of hers. Sometimes I saw him kiss her — taking his pipe out of his thick wet mouth, he kissed his wife. I saw Sophy get quite white when he touched her He is a pope in his pulpit and a libertine at home.

"As to you and me — it was quite natural. I understood it afterwards — that the fine, delicate threads between us should break, that they could not stand the atmosphere at home. When I had gone from you that time I regretted it, and meant to write to you, but do you know why I did not? I had a letter from my father, telling me he had been to see you and that he thought I ought to resume my relations with you. I have a superstitious objection to any advice from that quarter, so I did not write.

"All the time since we parted I have been longing for you, Jenny, dreaming of you, and recalling again and again to my memory the time I spent here with you. Do you know which place in Rome I revisited first of all — yesterday? I went to Montagnola and I found our names on the cactus leaf."

Jenny was sitting with clenched hands, very pale. "You look exactly the same as then, and you have lived three years about which I don't know anything," said Helge seems as if all that has happened since we parted here in Rome were not true. Yet you belong perhaps to somebody else now?"

Jenny did not answer.

"Are you engaged?" he asked quietly. "No."

"Jenny" — Helge bent his head so that she could not see his face — "all these years I have been hoping — dreaming of winning you back. I have imagined that we should meet again some day and come to an understanding. You said I was the first man you had been fond of. Is my dream impossible?"

"Yes," she said. "Heggen?"

She did not answer at once.

"I have always been jealous of Heggen," said Helge gently. "I thought he was the one, especially when I saw that you both lived here. So you are in love with each other?"

Jenny still did not answer. "Do you love him?"

"Yes, but I will not marry him."

"Oh, I see," said Helge, in a hard voice.

"No." She bent her head, tired, smiling sadly: "I have done with love; I don't want to have anything more to do with it. I am tired, and I wish you would go, Helge."

But he did not move.

"I cannot realize now when I see you again that it is all over. I never would believe it. I have been thinking so much of it, I suppose it was my own fault. I was so timid, I never knew what was the right thing to do. Everything might have been quite different. I have often remembered the last evening I was with you in Rome, and it seemed always that such an occasion would present itself again, for I left you then because I thought it was right. Surely, that could not have been the cause of my losing you? I had never been near a woman then," he said, looking down. "I was warned by what I had seen at home. Dreams and fancies became a hell at times, but that fear was always paramount.

"I am twenty-nine and there has been no beautiful or happy experience in my life but that short spring spent with you. Can you not understand that I have never been able to separate you from my thoughts, that I love you as before? The only happiness I have known is that you gave me. I cannot let you go out of my life — not now."

She got up, trembling, and he rose too. Instinctively she drew back a few steps from him: "Helge, there has been another."

He stood still, looking at her.

"You say there has been another — and it could have been I. I don't care; I want you all the same. I want you now because you promised me once to be mine."

Terrified, she tried to go past him, but he seized her violently in his arms. It took a few seconds for her brain to realize that he was kissing her mouth. She thought she made a resistance, but was in fact almost passive in his arms. She wanted to tell him not to, and she wanted to say who the other had been, but she could not. She would have told him about the child, but when she remembered the boy she shrank from mentioning him; she felt she must not drag her child into the disaster she knew was coming. As this thought crossed her mind she imagined she felt the dead little one caressing her, and it gave her a sensation of joy, so that her body relaxed for a second in his arms.

"You are mine — mine only — yes, yes, Jenny!"

She tore herself away from him and, running to the door, she called aloud for Gunnar. Helge was at her side again in an instant, taking her back in his arms.

They wrestled with each other by the door without a word. It seemed to Jenny that her life depended on her opening it and escaping into Gunnar's room, but feeling Helge close to her, stronger than she, as he held her, it seemed to her that there was no escape — and at last she gave way.

In the grey morning light, he came over to her to kiss her:

"My glorious Jenny. How wonderfully beautiful you are. You are mine now, and everything will come right, will it not?

Oh, I love you so.

"Are you tired? You must sleep when I have gone, and I will come to see you again at noon. Sleep soundly, my darling Jenny. Are you so tired?"

"Yes, very tired, Helge."

She was lying with her eyes half closed, looking at the pale morning light coming through the ribs of the blind.

He kissed her when he stood fully dressed, holding his hat; then he kneeled by her bed and put an arm under her shoulder: "Thank you for tonight. Do you remember that I said those same words to you the first morning in Rome, when we were at Aventine?"

Jenny nodded on her pillow.

"One more kiss — and good-night — my lovely Jenny." At the door he stopped: "What about the front door? Is there a key, or is it one of those ordinary ones with a latch?"

"Yes, an ordinary one. You can open it all right from the inside."

She remained in bed with her eyes closed. She saw her own body as it lay under the cover, white, bare, beautiful — a thing that she had flung away as she had the gloves. It was not hers any more.

She gave a start on hearing Heggen mount the stairs slowly and open his door. He walked up and down in his room, then came out again and went up the stairs to the roof. She heard him pacing to and fro above her head. She was sure he knew, but it did not make much impression on her tired brain. She felt no pain now. It seemed to her that he would probably think what had happened as natural and unavoidable as she did. She could not decide what was the next thing to do — it must just come as the other had done, as a necessary consequence of her opening the door last night to Helge.

She put out one foot from under the cover and lay looking at it. It was pretty. She bent it, accentuating the instep. Yes, it was pretty, white with blue veins and pink heel and toes.

She was tired — it was nice to feel so utterly tired. It felt like having recovered from some keen suffering. She was tired now, and what she had to do she did mechanically.

She got up and dressed. When she had put on stockings, bodice, and a skirt she slipped her feet into a pair of bronze slippers, washed, and did her hair in front of the glass without noticing the reflection of her face in it. Then she went to the small table where she kept her painting things, looking for the box containing her implements. In the night she had been thinking of the small triangular scraper, — she had sometimes played with it, putting it against her artery.

She took it out, looked at it, testing it with her finger, but she put it back again and took out a folding knife that she had once bought in Paris. It had a corkscrew, tin-opener, and many blades; one was short, pointed, and broad. She opened it.

She went back to her bed and sat down on it. Putting her pillow on the table at the side of the bed, she steadied her left hand on it and cut through the artery.

The blood spurted out, hitting a small water-color on the wall above her bed. Noticing it, she moved her hand. She lay down on the bed and mechanically pushed off her shoes with her feet, and put her hand under the cover to prevent the blood from making a mess.

She did not think; she was not afraid; she felt only that she was surrendering to the inevitable. The pain of the cut was not great — only sharp and distinct, and concentrated on one spot.

After a while a strange, unknown sensation took hold of her, an agony that grew and grew — not a fear of anything in particular, but the feeling of an ache round her heart and sickness, as it were. She opened her eyes, but black specks flickered before her sight and she could not breathe. The room seemed to crumble down on her. She tumbled out of bed, tore the door open, rushed up the stairs to the roof, and collapsed on the last step.

Helge had met Gunnar Heggen as he came out of the front door. They had looked at each other, both touching their hats, and passed on without a word.

That meeting had sobered Helge. After the intoxication of the night his mood instantly changed to the other extreme, and what he had experienced seemed to him incredible, inconceivable, and monstrous.

He had dreamt of this meeting with her all these years. She, the queen of his dreams, had scarcely spoken to him, at first sitting quiet and cold and then suddenly throwing herself into his arms, wild, mad, without saying a word. It struck him now that she had said nothing - — nothing at all to his words of love in the night. A strange, appalling woman, his Jenny. He realized suddenly that she had never been his.

Helge walked about in the quiet streets, up and down the Corso. He tried to think of her as she had been when they were engaged, to separate the dreams from the reality, but he could not form a clear picture of her, and he realized that he had never penetrated to the bottom of her soul. There had always been something about her he could not see, though he felt it was there.

He did not really know anything about her. Heggen might be with her now — why not? There had been another — she said so herself — who ? How many more? What else that he did not know — but had always felt?…

And now — after this he could not leave her; he knew it — less than ever now. Yet he did not know her. Who was she, who had held him in a spell for three years — who had this power over him?

He turned on his way, hurrying back to her door, driven by fear and by rage. The front door stood open. He rushed up the stairs — she would have to answer him — tell him everything — he would not let her go. The door was open; he looked in and saw the empty bed with the blood-stained sheets and the blood on the floor. Turning round, he saw that she was lying huddled at the top of the stairs, and that the marble steps were red with her blood.

With a scream he ran up the stairs and lifted her up. He felt her body limp against his arm and her hands hung down cold — and he understood that the body he had held in his arms a few hours ago, hot and trembling with life, was now a dead thing, and would soon be carrion.

He sank to his knees with her on his arm, calling out wildly.

Heggen tore open the door to the terrace. His face was white and drawn. He saw Jenny. Seizing Helge, he flung him aside and bent down on his knees beside her.

"She was lying there when I came back — lying there. . . "Run for a doctor — quick!" Gunnar had pulled away her clothes, feeling her heart; he steadied her head and lifted her hands. Then he saw the wound, and, pulling out the blue silk ribbon from her bodice, he tied it hard round her wrist.

"Yes, but where shall I find …

Gunnar gave a sudden cry of rage — then said in a quiet voice: "I will go. Carry her in," but he took her in his own arms and went towards the door. At sight of the blood-stained bed his face twitched. Turning away, he pushed open the door to his room and placed her on his own untouched bed. Then he rushed down the stairs.

Helge had moved at his side the whole time, his mouth half open as if paralyzed in the act of crying out. But he stopped at Gunnar's door. When he was left alone with her he stole

223

into the room, touching her hand with his finger-tips, and he fell down beside the bed, crying wildly, hysterically, with his head against it. . . .

GUNNAR walked along the narrow road, overgrown with grass, between the high, whitewashed garden walls. On the one side lay the barracks, probably with a terrace, as high up over his head some soldiers were laughing and talking. A tuft of yellow flowers, growing in a cleft of the wall, hung swaying. On the other side of the road the huge old poplars by the Cestius pyramid and the cypress grove in the new part of the cemetery stretched their tops to- wards the blue and silver clouded sky.

Outside the grated gate a girl sat crocheting. She opened to him, curtseying to thank him for the coin he gave her.

The spring air was mild and damp; in the closed green shade of the churchyard it became wet and warm as in a hothouse, and the narcissus along the border of the path gave out a hot, sickly scent.

The old cypresses stood round the graves that lay, green and dark with creepers and violets, set in terraces from the ivy- clad wall of the town. Above the flowers rose the monuments of the dead, little marble temples, white figures of angels, and big, heavy slabs of stone. Moss grew on them and on the trunks of the cypresses. Here and there a white or red flower still clung to the camelia trees, but most of them lay brown and faded on the black earth, exhaling raw, damp fumes. He remembered something he had read: the Japanese did not like camelias because they fell off whole and fresh like heads chopped off.

Jenny Winge lay buried at the farthest end of the cemetery near the chapel on a grassy slope, covered with daisies. There were only a few graves. On the border of the slope cypresses had been planted, but they were still very small, like toy trees with their pointed green tops on straight brown trunks, reminding one of the pillars in a cloister arcade. Her grave was a little way from the others; it was only a pale grey mound of earth, the grass round it having been trodden down when it was being dug. The sun shone on it and the dark cypresses formed a wall behind it.

Covering his face with his hands, Gunnar bent on his knees until his head rested on the faded wreaths.

The weariness of spring weighted his limbs, the blood flowed aching with sorrow and regret at every beat of his heavy heart.

Jenny — Jenny — Jenny — he heard her pretty name in every trill of the birds — and she was dead.

Lying far down in the dark. He had cut off a curl from her fair hair and carried it in his pocket-book. He took it out and held it in the sunshine — those poor little filmy threads were the only part of her luxurious, glossy hair the sun could reach and warm.

She was dead and gone. There were some pictures of hers . . . there had been a short notice about her in the papers. And the mother and sisters mourned her at home, but the real Jenny they had never known, and they knew nothing about her life or her death. The others — those who had known — stared in despair after her, not understanding what they knew.

She who lay there was his Jenny; she belonged to him alone.

Helge Gram had come to him; he had asked and told, wailed and begged: "I don't understand anything. If you do, Heggen, I beg you to tell me. You know — will you not tell me what you know?"

He had not answered.

"There was another; she told me so. Who was it? Was it you?"

"No."

"Do you know who it was?"

"Yes, but I am not going to tell you. It is no good your asking, Gram." "But I shall go mad if you don't explain."

"You have no right to know Jenny's secrets."

"But why did she do it? Was it because of me — of him — or of you?" "No; she did it because of herself."
He had asked Gram to leave him and had not seen him since; he had left Rome. It was in the Borghese garden, two days after the funeral, that Gram had come across him sitting in the sunshine. He was so tired; he had had to see to everything — give satisfactory explanations at the inquest, arrange for the interment, and write to Mrs. Berner that her daughter had died suddenly from heart failure. And all the time he had a kind of satisfaction in the thought that nobody knew of his own sorrow, 'that the real cause of her death was known only by him and for ever hidden with him. The sorrow had sunk so deep into him that it would for ever be the inmost essence of his soul, and he would never speak of it to any living being.

It would govern his whole life — and be governed by it; the color and form of it would change, but it would never be effaced. Every hour of the day it was different, but it was always there, and always would be. On the morning when he had run for the doctor, leaving the other man alone with her, he had wanted to tell Helge Gram all he knew, and in such a way that his heart would turn to ashes like his own had done; but in the days that followed all he knew became a secret between him and the dead woman — the secret of their love. All that had happened had happened because of her being what she was, and as such he had loved her. Helge Gram was a casual, indifferent stranger to him and to her, and he had no more wish to avenge himself on him than he had pity for his sorrow and dread at the mystery.

And he understood that what had happened was natural because she was made as she was. Her mind swayed and bent for a gust of wind, because it had grown so upright and slender; he had thought she could grow as a tree grows, and had not understood that she was only a flower, a rich, fragile stem, springing up to be kissed by the sun and to let all the heavy, longing buds break into bloom. She had only been a little girl after all, and to his eternal sorrow he had not understood it until too late.

For she could not right herself again when once she had been bent; she was like a lily, that does not grow from the root again if the first stalk has been broken. There was nothing supple or luxuriant about her mind — but he loved her such as she was. And she was his only, for he alone knew how fair and delicate she had been — so strong in her desire to grow straight, and yet so frail and brittle, and with delicate honor, from which a spot never could be washed away because it made so deep a mark. She was dead. He had been alone with his love many nights and days, and he would be alone with it all the days and nights of his life.

He had stifled his cries of despair many a night in his pillows. She was dead, and she had never been his. He was the one she should have loved and belonged to, for she was the only one he had ever loved. He had never touched or seen her beautiful, slim, white body that enclosed her soul like a velvet sheath about a thin, feeble blade. Others had possessed it, and had not understood what a strange and rare treasure had happened to fall into their hands. It lay buried in the grave, a prey to ugly change until it was consumed and reduced to a handful of dust in the earth.

Gunnar was shaking with sobs.

Others had loved her, soiled, and destroyed her, not knowing what they did — and she had never been his.

As long as he lived there would be moments when he would feel the same agony about it as now.

Yet he was the only one who owned her at the last; in his hand only would her golden hair sparkle, and she herself was living in him now; her soul and her image were reflected in him clear and firm as in still water. She was dead; she had no more sorrow — it stayed with him instead, to go on living, not to die until he died himself, and because it was living it would grow and change. What it would be like in ten years, he did not know, but it might grow to something great and beautiful.

As long as he lived there would be moments when he would feel the same strange, deep joy that it was so, as he felt now.

He remembered dimly what he had been thinking in the early morning hour when he was walking on the terrace overhead while she was ending her life. He had been enraged with her. How could she do it? He had begged and implored to be allowed to help her, to carry her away from the abyss she was nearing, but she had pushed him away and thrown herself down before his eyes — exactly in the way a woman would — an obstinate, irresponsible, foolish way.

When he saw her lying lifeless he had been in despair and rage again, because he would not have let her go. Whatever she had done he would have exonerated her, helped her, offered her his love and trust.

As long as he lived there would be moments when he would reproach her for choosing to die — Jenny, you should not have done it. Yet there would be moments when he would understand that she did so, because it was in keeping with her character, and he would love her for it as long as he lived. And never would he wish that he had not loved her.

But he would cry desperately, as he had already done, because he had not loved her long before; he would cry for the lost years when she had lived beside him as his friend and comrade and he had not understood that she was the woman who should have been his wife. And never would the day dawn when he would wish he had not understood, even if only to see that it was too late.

Gunnar rose from his knees. He took a small box from his pocket and opened it. One of Jenny's pink crystal beads was in it. He had found it in the drawer of her dressing-table when he packed up her belongings; the string had broken and he kept one of the beads. He took some earth from the grave and put it in the box. The bead rolled about in it and was covered with grey dust, but the clear rose color showed through and the fine rents in the crystal glittered in the sun.

He had sent all her possessions to her mother, except the letters, which he had burnt. The child's clothes were in a sealed cardboard box. He sent it to Francesca, remembering that Jenny had said one day she would give them to her.

He had looked through all her sketch-books and drawings before packing them and carefully cut out the leaves with the picture of the boy, hiding them in his pocket-book. They were his — all that was hers alone was his.

On the plain grew some purple anemones; he rose mechanically to pick them. Oh, spring-time!

He remembered a spring day two years ago when he had been in Norway. He had been given a cart and a red mare' at the posting station; the owner was an old schoolfellow of his. It was a sunny day in March ; the meadows were yellow with withered grass, and the dung-heaps over the ploughed fields shone like pale brown velvet. They drove past the familiar farms with yellow, grey, and red houses and apple yards and lilac bushes. The forest all round was olive green, with a purple tint on the birch twigs, and the air was full that day with the chirping of invisible birds.

Two little fair-haired children were walking in the road, carrying a can. "Where are you going, little ones?"

They stopped, looking suspiciously at him. "Taking food to father?"

They assented hesitatingly — a little astonished that a strange gentleman should know it.

"Climb up here and I'll give you a ride." He helped them into the cart. "Where is father working?"

"At Brusted."

"That's over beyond the school, is it not?"

Thus went the conversation. A stupid, ignorant man asking and asking, as grown-up people always talk to children, and the little ones, who have such a lot of wisdom, consult each other quietly with their eyes, giving sparingly of it — as much as they think convenient.

Hand in hand they walked along beside a rushing brook when he put them down, and he turned his horse in the direction he wanted to go. There was a prayer meeting that evening at his home. His sister Ingeborg was sitting by the old corner cupboard, following with a pale, ecstatic face and shining steel-blue eyes a shoe- maker, who spoke of spiritual grace; then suddenly she rose herself to bear witness.

His pretty, smart sister who once had been so fond of dancing and merriment. She loved to read and to learn; when he had got work in town he sent her books and pamphlets and the Social Democrat twice a week. At thirty she was "saved," and now she "spoke in tongues."

She had bestowed all her love on her nephew Anders and a little girl they had with them — an illegitimate child from Christiania. With sparkling eyes she told them about Jesus, the children's Friend.

The next day it was snowing; he had promised to take the children to a cinema in the small neighboring town, and they had to walk a couple of miles in the melting snow, leaving black footprints behind. He tried to talk to the children, asking questions and receiving guarded answers.

But on the way back the children were the inquisitive ones, and, flattered, he gave frank and detailed answers, anxious to give them proper information about the films they had seen — of cowboys in Arizona and cocoanut harvest in the Philippines. And he tried his best to tell them properly and answer without ever being at a loss.

Oh, spring-time!

It was on a spring day he had gone to Viterbo with Jenny and Francesca. Dressed in black, she had been sitting by the window looking out with eyes so big and grey- — he remembered it well.

The stonny clouds sent showers over the brown plains of the Campagna, where there were no ruins for the tourists to go and see, only a crumbled wall here and there and a farm with two pines and some pointed straw-stacks near the house. The pigs herded together in the valley, where some trees grew beside a stream. The train sped between hills and oak woods where white and blue anemones and yellow primroses grew among the faded leaves. She said she wanted to get out to pick them, gather them in the falling rain among the dripping leaves under the wet branches. "This is like spring at home," she said.

It had been snowing; some of the snow was still lying grey in the ditches, and the flowers were wet and heavy, with petals stuck together.

Little rivulets rushed down the crevices, vanishing under the railway line. A shower beat against the window and drove the smoke to earth.

Then it cleared over valleys and grove, and the water streamed down the sides of the hills.

He had had some of his things in one of the girls' boxes. When he remembered it in the evening they had already begun to undress and were laughing and chatting when he knocked at their door. Jenny opened it a little, giving him what he asked for. She had on a light dressing-jacket with short sleeves, leaving the slender white arm bare. It tempted him to many kisses, but he dared only give it one single, light one. He had been in love with her then, intoxicated with the spring, the wine, the merry rain, and the sudden sunshine, with his own youth and the joy of life. He wanted to make her dance — that tall, fair girl, who smiled so guardedly as if she were trying a new art, something she had never yet done — she who had stared with grey, serious eyes at all the flowers they passed and that she wanted to pick.

Oh, how different all might have been! The dry, bitter sob shook his frame again.

The day they went to Montefiascone it rained too, so hard that the water was flung back from the stone bridge on to the girls' lifted skirts and ankles. How* they had laughed, all three of them, when they walked up the narrow street, the rain-water streaming towards them in small torrents. When they reached

Rocca, the castle cliff in the center of the old town, it cleared. They leaned over the rampart, looking at the lake, which lay black beneath the olive groves and the vineyards. The skies hung low about the hills round the lake, but across the dark water there came a silver line, which broadened, the mist rolled back into the crevices, and the mountain came into better view.

The sun pierced the clouds, which sank down to rest round the small promontories with grey stone castles. Towards the north a distant peak became visible — Cesca said it was Monte Amiata.

The last rain-clouds rolled across the blue spring sky, melting before the sun; the bad weather fled westward, darkening the Etrurian heights, which sloped desolately towards the far yellow-white strip of the Mediterranean. The sight reminded him of the mountain scenery in his own country, in spite of the olive grove and the vineyards.

He and she had stooped behind the hedge, and he had held out his coat so that she could light her cigarette. The wind was keen up there, and she shivered a little in her wet clothes. Her cheeks were red and the sun glittered in her damp, golden hair as she stroked it away from her eyes with one hand.

He would go there tomorrow to meet the spring, the cold, naked spring, full of expectation, with all the buds wet and shivering in the wind — blossoming all the same.

She and the spring were one to him, she who stood shivering and smiled in the changing weather and wanted to gather all the flowers into her lap. Little Jenny, you were not to gather the flowers, and your dreams never came true — and now I am dreaming them for you.

231

And when I have lived long enough to be so full of longing as you were, perhaps I will do as you, and say to fate: Give me a few of the flowers; I will be satisfied with much less than

I wanted in the beginning of life. But I will not die as you did, because you could not be content. I will remember you, and kiss your bead and your golden hair and think: She could not live without being the best, and claiming the best as her right; and maybe I shall say: Heaven be praised that she chose death rather than living content.

Tonight I will go to Piazza San Pietro and listen to the wild music of the fountain that never stops, and dream my dream. For you, Jenny, are my dream, and I have never had any other.

Dream — oh, dream!

If your child had lived he would not have been what you dreamt when you held him in your arms. He might have done something good and great, or something bad and disgraceful, but he would never have accomplished what you dreamt he should do. No woman has given life to the child she dreamt of when she bore it — no artist has created the work he saw before him in the moment of his inspiration. And we live summer after summer, but not one is like the one we have been longing for when we stooped to gather the wet flowers in the spring showers. And no love is what lovers dreamed when they kissed for the first time.

If you and I had lived together we might have been happy or not, we might have done good or ill to one another, but I shall never know what our love would have been if you had been mine. The only thing I know is that it would never have been what I dreamt that night when I stood with you in the moonlight while the fountain was playing.

And yet I would not have missed that dream, and I would not miss the dream I am dreaming now.

Jenny, I would give my life if you could meet me on the cliff and be as you were then, and kiss me and love me for one day, one hour. Always I am thinking of what it might have been if you had lived and been mine, and it seems to me that a boundless joy has been wasted. Oh, you are dead, and your death has made me so poor. I have only my dream of you, but if I compare my poverty with others' riches it is ever so much more glorious. Not to save my life would I cease to love you and dream of you and mourn you.

Gunnar Heggen did not know that in the great storm of his heart he had lifted his arms towards heaven and was whispering to himself. The anemones he had picked were still in his hand, but he did not know it.

The soldiers on the wall laughed at him, but he did not see. He pressed the flowers to his heart, and whispered gently to himself as he walked slowly from the grave toward the cypress grove.

THE END

Lightning Source UK Ltd.
Milton Keynes UK
UKHW021844310520
364212UK00015B/398